For Violet,
My excellent student.
Best Wishes,
Don Ellson

Running Horsemen

Brown Barn Books
Weston, Connecticut

Books by Dolph LeMoult

Rock Solid (Putnam-Jove)
Street Dance (Charter/Putnam)
Dream Street (Charter/Putnam)
Death Spiral (Onyx/Penguin)
The Killing Moon (Onyx/Penguin)
Blood Tide (Onyx/Penguin)
Messages From Enrique (Puppet Press Online)

Running Horsemen

**A Novel
by
Dolph LeMoult**

Brown Barn Books
Weston, Connecticut

Brown Barn Books,
a division of Pictures of Record, Inc.
119 Kettle Creek Road, Weston, Connecticut 06883, U.S.A.
www.brownbarnbooks.com

RUNNING HORSEMEN

Original paperback edition.

Library of Congress Control Number: 2003115629
ISBN: 0-9746-4810-8

LeMoult, Dolph.

Running Horsemen: a novel by Dolph LeMoult

Printed in the United States of America

Gerry Sandweiss

Dolph LeMoult has enjoyed a sucessful career as a novelist, advertising copy-writer and creative director, illustrator, and gallery painter. His series of police novels, co-authored with NYPD Detective Bill Kelly, has attracted an avid, loyal readership. A Book-of-the-Month Club selection, his *Rock Solid* won the acclaim of critics. He has participated in writing seminars and in television and radio talk shows. As a guest lecturer at schools and colleges, he speaks of the value and satisfaction of a writing life and entreats fledgling writers to follow their dreams.

"I had been in New York City less than twenty-four hours and I had already met my first Jew and my first artist...I'd met a Miss America who'd danced the fandango with the King of the Hottentots. Whether or not this had actually happened was still unclear...I'd met a Nobel Prize-winning author who'd been imprisoned in a gulag...

And although I did not even know her name, I'd met a red-haired usherette at the Radio City Music Hall and fallen desperately in love.

If any one of these things had ever happened to me in Eula, Texas, I would probably have spent the rest of my life setting and whittling under the wooden overhangs of Main Street, telling and retelling the story, but all of this had happened to me in less than a day in New York City."

Running Horsemen

A Brown Barn Book

x

One

When I was born it smelled like apples, not real apples, but what you smell when you're thinking about apples all dimply and wormy and rotting on the ground, which was pretty much all apples ever did in that part of west Texas where cotton and soybeans and sweet corn were the crops people generally paid a mind to. A few folks had apple trees which was about as smart as ticks having toothpicks according to my Uncle Malachai Bailey, who claimed to know about such things. Trees were generally used as wind-breaks there, and an apple tree all spindly and squat was good for about nothing at all except maybe to suck up ground water when it was sorely needed elsewhere. Apples were a dime a dozen at the general store in Eula; no point in spending time and money raising something the Good Lord provided on the cheap. I cannot now say that Uncle Mal was entirely wrong, based on what I have learned about apples. I expect the reason we had apple trees at all was because they reminded my mother of New England where she grew up. She'd allowed as how she made my daddy plant them out behind the house in '26 when he first brought her to Texas, and although she spent little time admiring them, and no time at all taking care of them, I believe she was comforted just by the fact that they were there. I believe the smell of the fruit rotting on the ground the way it did opened a passage to the past for her, just as it does now for me.

Joe Carl Purdy once told me about something called a solipsism, which as nearly as I remember is the theory that everybody's brain is a universe unto itself where time and tide and concepts get turned inside out, and everything folks see is warped by their own perceptions. Thing is, everybody sees something different, hears something different, smells something different, but because they can all agree on a given thing, they're not at each others' throats about it. I expect that has something to do with the smell of apples, and with being born. I will not take an oath that I remember being born, but when I think about it I surely smell the smell of apples, as if my mother was the tree or the orchard and I was the fruit. That I think is my solipsism, although it is an opinion I do not share with a great many people. Women smell like women and apples smell like apples, and there's surely no mistaking the two.

Uncle Mal was the older brother of my daddy, Harry Bailey, who went to war in Europe in nineteen forty-one and never came back. Truth told, he did not die in that great conflict; he just did not return. I was ten years old when the war in Europe ended, and when I asked my mother why Harry Bailey had not returned with the other soldiers who filtered back through the Texas panhandle almost daily, she would get a faraway look in her eyes and busy herself with chores. Uncle Mal guessed that my daddy had received a wound in battle, possibly lost his memory, and might have been somewhere in a military hospital receiving treatment, not knowing who he was or how to contact us. As for me, I had a suspicion that Harry Bailey had found something wonderful in Europe that made returning to a dust-bowl prairie town like Eula seem like a sorry choice at best. I do not remember being sad or bitter, or even disappointed that Harry did not come back to us. I felt sorry for my mother though. Neither wife nor widow, she seemed always to be drifting in some private ether of uncertainty, suspended like a fly in a bottle of alcohol.

A year after the war ended, the Reverend Harley Brown, Pastor of the Calvary Baptist Church and Grace Ministry in Eula, came calling on my mother. Although she was herself a faithful churchgoer, a member of the Eastern Star and the Baptist choir, my mother had never compelled me to attend Sunday services with her, so my first recollection of the Reverend Brown is of that afternoon in May when he sat in our parlor eating home-made pecan sandys and drinking cold lemonade. He was decidedly ill-at-ease, as was my mother, who seemed to be forever fidgeting with the parlor appurtenances, moving things that had been in place for years from one spot to another, pretending to find dust spots on articles of furniture that had been rubbed to a high polish only hours before. My recollection is that there was very little conversation beyond a few nervous commentaries on the unusually hot spring weather. My mother spoke of the choir, about some of the other lady members whose voices rivaled those of angels; and the Reverend replied that she might indeed include herself in that heavenly assemblage; to which she hemmed and hawed and blushed a lot. Although I had no desire to stay, I was required to sit in the parlor for the entire visit, a hedge against the Devil's snares, I now suspect, and although I cannot say I observed anything other than utter discomfort passing between them, the visit ended with an unspoken agreement that from that day forward they would be keeping company.

After that, the Reverend Harley Brown visited our farm every Sunday, and occasionally on weekdays, when his pastoral duties did not require him to be elsewhere. Nothing was ever explained; he simply trickled into our lives like the spring rains and stayed. I must admit that I resented him, both for the fact that he was not Harry Bailey, and the fact that he took more from my mother than he ever gave. I always felt that he considered his attentions to her to be a favor, and that he expected her to feel that way too. She was after all, soiled merchandise, and he was a man of the gospel; worthy of the freshest flower in God's earthly kingdom.

The worst times were Sunday afternoon meals when he read from the Scriptures at the dinner table. Whole passages had to be digested while the food grew cold on our plates: *Numbers, Eight to Nineteen; Judges, Eleven to Twenty-One.* During the meal the Reverend would cite chapter and verse when censuring my table manners: *The drunkard and the glutton shall come to poverty, and laziness shall clothe a man in rags; Proverbs, 23-21*, if I happened to be eating faster than he thought fitting. Or, *A fool's mouth is his destruction*, if he judged that I was speaking out of turn. My mother abided it all, accepting Reverend Brown's injunction that the Sabbath table was a tabernacle, and that anything uttered there that did not glorify the Lord was unworthy. The few times mother and I discussed this between us, she maintained that we were better off in the hands of a righteous man than we could ever have been with the likes of Harry Bailey. We were to get on with our lives as best we could under the circumstances.

The Reverend Harley Brown had a Nash automobile, which was the only post-war automobile I had seen up to that time. Unlike the other vehicles in Eula, which were mostly pickup trucks and battered black Model T Fords, the Nash was robin's-egg blue, with rounded curves that gave it a sleek, sporty look, like the space ships I'd seen in the Buck Rogers comic strips. The car could go sixty miles an hour, the Reverend claimed, although he would not drive it above twenty on the rutted dirt road leading from our house to town. Every few miles he would stop along the side of the road and get out to inspect the tires, which were made of wartime rubber and blew out easily when they became over-heated. If I became impatient over the delay he would tell me that an automobile was like a Christian soul; run it too hard and fast and it would become wore out. It needed time to rest and contemplate the Lord's wish-es if it was to thrive. As I recall, I did not necessarily buy into that expla-nation, but I accepted it after I changed my first tire. Eula was a place where nothing ever happened so there was no great urgency to get there.

Of course there was Moon's Roadside Cafe, but Moon's was a phan-tom; a blur alongside the highway that we passed on our trips into town. To me it was a place of infinite mystery, infinite glamour, infinite wicked-ness, where men congregated to drink, gamble, have sex with women, and conspire against the righteous. Stories about the place abounded; about private rooms behind the bandstand filled with whores; about rhythmic Negro music so sensuous that it led to wholesale orgies on the dance floor; about a Mexican girl who danced naked on tables for silver dollars. They were all just stories, none supported by the personal expe-rience of anyone I'd met, but I have to say I believed them absolutely. The fact that the Reverend's neck reddened every time we sped past Moon's in the Nash was proof enough for me that the place was a vessel of iniq-uity.

At that time, my best friend was Joe Carl Purdy, the son of Amos Purdy who owned the Feed & Grain. Although he was a year older than me, Joe Carl was several inches shorter than I was, due in part to the fact that I was naturally tall for my age, and partly because he had contracted polio at age six, so his legs had never grown as long as they were sup-posed to. When he walked, he propelled himself with a kind of reeling backward gait, like someone whose torso was always hurrying to catch up with his feet. At rest, he stood as if he was preparing to sit; knees and back bent, uncommonly out of balance for a standing person, but seeming to derive no great discomfort from it. To boot, he was chicken-breasted, and freckled to the point where he could not stand in the sun for any great length of time without wearing long trousers, wrist-length sleeves, and a broad-brimmed straw hat that shadowed his entire face. While Eula was not populated with an abundance of boys my own age, there were enough that I probably could have picked one less afflicted to have as a best friend, but it seemed that Joe Carl and I just hit it off from the first time we set eyes on one another. I expect now it was because I appreciated his caustic, self-deprecating sense of humor, but back then I was concerned with more practical matters. For all his infirmities, Joe Carl had the one thing that made him invaluable as a friend—a driver's license! Not only did he have a driver's license, he had a vehicle to drive—a 1937 White chain-drive pick-up truck, acquired by his daddy from a chicken farmer in neighboring Crystal City. The truck had no springs, tires worn through to the tubes, and despite numerous washings, it reeked of poultry, but it was a vehicle, and in that world of unremitting boredom a vehicle was liberation.

Things being what they were, the Reverend Harley Brown had ordered that I could not ride in the truck at night, being too young and inexperienced to face that dark world at high speeds, but the Reverend hadn't reckoned on the resilience and artifice of youth. Night had barely fallen on his decree when, by way of my bedroom window and a sprint of almost a mile to where Joe Carl waited with the truck, we were rattling toward the high life of Moon's Roadside Cafe, heady with the stench of chickens, the taste of freedom, and the dizzying effects of a jar of home-made corn whiskey Joe Carl had stolen from the cellar of Purdy's Feed & Grain

It would be almost impossible for me to overstate the exhilaration and awe I felt that night as we pulled into the roadhouse parking lot and approached the front door. Inside was everything that had up till then been off-limits for me; everything wanton and immoral the Reverend Harley Brown had warned would send me reeling from the path of right-eousness into the arms of the archfiend, the prince of darkness—Satan. Even now I remember the rasp of my heavy breathing in the warm night air, the exaggerated beating of my heart against my chest wall, the low, sucking noises of our feet as we clomped through the muddy parking lot, coarse and swampy, keeping instinctive time with the erotic rhythms coming from behind the closed door. Although he was older, Joe Carl let me lead the way, reasoning that I was taller and better able to handle myself if trouble reared its head which, like as not, it surely would.

"You boys got business here?" The voice belonged to a bearded man of above-average height, wearing a flowered bandanna around his head and brandishing a shotgun.

"Yessir," I replied automatically.

"And what kind of business might that be?" The question was almost lost in the din of music and laughter inside.

"Well we thought we'd come in there for a snort."

"Y'all did, did you?" His face crinkled up in leathery creases.

"No harm in a man having a snort, is there?"

"Don't see no men on this porch. See a couple of snot-nose kids though."

I kicked the floorboards angrily. "If my daddy was here he'd see to it you let me in all right."

"Who's your daddy, boy?"

"My daddy's Harry Bailey, and he's well known in this place."

Another man appeared; shorter and older, with long, straight yellow hair streaming down the back of his white linen jacket. I remember thinking that he had the palest skin I had ever seen.

"The tall one says he's Harry Bailey's boy," the other told him. "Can't be much more'n fourteen but he says he wants to come in for a snort."

"Snort of what?"

"Whiskey," I rasped.

"Y'all ever drink whiskey, Boy?"

"Lots of times." I took the moonshine from Joe Carl and brandished it before him. "Been sucking on this jar this the whole way over here."

"That's corn, ain't real whiskey."

"It's got a kick though."

"Reckon." He stepped out onto the porch and bade the other to go back inside. "You say you're Harry Bailey's boy?"

"Yessir."

He inspected me in the dim porch light. "Y'all do favor him a mite. What's your name?"

"Chance."

"Chance Bailey?"

"If Harry Bailey's my daddy I expect he would give me his name."

"And your friend there?"

"He's Joe Carl Purdy. His daddy owns the Feed & Grain."

"He looks a mite poorly."

"He had polio, and he's chicken-breasted."

"Sorry to hear it. How old are you boys?"

"We're both sixteen," I lied.

"Not likely, I remember when you was born." He motioned for us to sit in two wooden chairs along the wall and he sat opposite from us on the porch railing.

"You know my daddy?" I asked him.

"Knew him," he nodded. "Sorry to hear he didn't come back from the war."

"He ain't dead, just found something more to his liking over there in Europe," I insisted.

"You know that for a fact?"

"We never got a death certificate."

"Lots of boys just got themselves blowed up; ain't no bodies to write death certificates for."

"My daddy ain't blowed up."

He shrugged. "I reckon not."

"You Moon?"

"Nah, there ain't no Moon, never was. But I own this place."

"So howcum it's called Moon's?"

"Howcum you're called Chance? Howcum y'all ask so many questions?"

"Just naturally curious I guess."

"Curiosity is what killed the cat, you know."

I scowled. "You're sounding like the Reverend Brown."

"The Reverend Harley Brown?"

"You know him?"

"Might. Reckon it's time for you two to be on your way now."

"Can't we come in for just one snort?"

"You're lucky I don't have the sheriff run the two of you in." He stood on the stairs and eased us along with the palm of his hand.

"One snort would ward off the evening chill."

He laughed. "Finish off that jar. Y'all won't mind the chill."

"Is the Reverend Brown in there now?" I yelled back at him.

"Wouldn't tell you if he was."

After that I searched the parking lot for Reverend Harley Brown's Nash but it was nowhere in sight. Still, I was convinced he patronized the place. All the time he was eating our food and consorting with my mother and preaching to us about sin and morality and God's awful vengeance, he was out here at Moon's, drinking, whoring, stacking silver dollars for the Mexican lady who did the hootchy-kootchy on the tops of tables in her birthday suit.

Two

In my fifteenth year Eula's population stood at six hundred thirty-six people, down from a high of almost eight hundred before the war started. A number of theories abounded as to the cause of the population decline, but most recognized it was because of the veterans who'd hightailed with their families after they'd gotten a taste of life outside west Texas. It was a reality seldom discussed in my family, being that my daddy, Harry Bailey, was one of those veterans and that he had not had the decency or wherewithal or who-knows-what to take us along with him, leaving us to rot from the inside out in a town where apple trees were despised and the prairie wind that rose each evening after dinner and coated everything with a layer of choking, talc-like dust was the surest sign of animated change. Those who left were seldom missed—grinning rawhide faces cracked white from squinting at the sun, hats, boots, postures swaying in the street or slumped in tractors, shouting hidey from the backs of pickup trucks, they were indistinguishable from those who stayed.

Eula had one paved street, a bank, a post office, and a movie theater named the Strand, which, when it wasn't showing movies, served as a meeting house for the Grange and 4-H, the town council, and a variety of visiting evangelists. There was a general-purpose store that sold groceries, appliances, and dispensed pharmaceuticals, a barber shop operated by Roy Eustis Hatch who was also Eula's mayor, a police station and jail, Eula's New World Hair and Nail Salon, a cafe called Stella's, despite the fact that nobody could recall anyone named Stella ever having owned it, Levy's Footwear and Dry Goods Emporium, Purdy's Feed & Grain, and, of course, Moon's, although it was technically not a part of the town proper. The town had a newspaper, The Eula *Clarion*, which was put out every two weeks or so by Mrs. Leila Dann from her home—mostly gossip and recipes. The school was one story brick, two teachers for seven grades. Anyone wanting a high school education had to travel to Breese Falls eighty miles away. There were two Baptist Churches; ours, The Calvary Baptist Church and Grace Ministry, and the colored church, also called The Calvary Baptist Church, with the unabashed augmentation, And One True Tabernacle of Jesus God. The coloreds had captured the mood of Eula to perfection—a place so lowly in God's creation that he would deem it not at all in any grand scheme or structure, yet the town's residents bragged because bragging was the principle recreation and sole deliverance of the place. Ransomed from the baking prairie with dust-clouded eyes and sun-parched lips they bragged of things that would thoroughly disgust folks with a wider vision; moonshine and tattoos, boots cracked by the sun and caked with sheep manure, pickup trucks oxidized gray like the land with confederate flags stenciled on the sides, haircuts that reamed the skull right up the back like plowed furrows, rattlesnakes, scorpions, fire ants, horse flies, dung beetles, jaguarondi cats, stinging nettles, tumbleweed, catclaw and chaparral, and chiggers in outhouses that chewed your ass to shreds (when you were taking a shit), smells of piss and lime and bone meal and wet laundry and decaying dog carcasses hung out in the fireball sun—and apples rotting on the ground.

"That boy. Fourteen years old and not a responsible bone in his body!"

"I think I'd fancy going to high school over in Breese Falls."

"High school's going to do you about as much good as an inside pocket on your underwear, boy."

"You went to high school."

"That's different, I'm a man of the cloth. Man of the cloth needs special training in the ways of The Lord."

"I could be a scientist. Joe Carl says there's scientists poking around over in Cayanosa Draw; he says they've dug up bones they think is dinosaurs'."

"Scientists ain't got the sense they was born with."

"He says they found whole dinosaurs out there; shipped the bones back east and put them together in museums."

"Darwinists and atheists all of them; they want to deny God's creation with stories about how we all came from apes. Ain't a one of them's got a good explanation about why those dinosaurs disappeared from this earth."

"Just died out is how I hear it."

"Ever hear of the flood, boy? And God looked upon the earth and behold, it was corrupt; for all flesh had corrupted his way upon the earth. And God said to Noah, The end of all flesh is come before me, for the earth is filled with violence through them; and behold I will destroy them with the earth."

"And that's why the dinosaurs disappeared?"

"I do believe that, yes."

"Howcum old Noah didn't take two dinosaurs along with him in that ark?"

"The boy is a blasphemer as well as a sluggard."

"He is only fourteen." My mother filled the Reverend Harley's plate with chicken and homemade brown dumplings.

Audrey Lou Hawley touched my dangle on the school bus yesterday.

That boy!

Mama was nineteen years old when Harry Bailey brought her here. She followed his blue eyes like a beacon light in the harbors of New England and trusted them. *So I will be a farmer's wife*, she must have thought when she saw the wretchedness of the place, *I will get used to it*, but truth told, she never did.

He must have told her there would be land to farm, but the land was leased and mortgaged to the hilt, and what he didn't lose to the banks he lost to whores and bad poker hands and frozen dice, but there were always those blue eyes, the house out back of his father's place he'd built with his own hands that was free and clear; she could stay there as long as she lived and could pay the taxes.

He planted three apple trees in the yard for her, strung a clothesline, mended the roof with galvanized aluminum when hailstones big as softballs tore it down—up there on the roof where he could see a hundred miles and she trailed those blue eyes out across the fields, out across the packed grasses where the world bellied out in waves of damp mesquite and buffalo clover to the Pecos River and beyond. She saw it then in the tilt of his head. He rubbed his blue eyes then and searched the horizon.

What I learned about Harry Bailey I did not learn whole hog but rather winnowed out in fractions from those who had known him growing up; Uncle Mal, my mother, when she had a notion, and some of the good old boys back in Eula who had nothing better to do with their time than sit beneath the overhangs on Main Street drinking beer and working their mouths more than they had a right to. He was a wild one, they said, full of piss and vinegar. Smart as a whip he was, but he got thrown out of school more times than anyone else in memory until he finally got tired of coming back and they finally got tired of throwing him out, and they all just gave it up. After that he worked his daddy's farm for a while, and by all accounts was a pretty good farmer, but his mind wasn't really in it. When he hadn't lost all his money gambling, or wasn't sleeping off a drunk in jail, folks say he would drive more than thirty miles to the bus stop at Cross Creek and buy himself a ticket out of town; didn't matter where that ticket took him, just so long as it had a saloon, a card game, and was any-place else but Eula.

Looks-wise I favored him some, tall and lank, with those same blue eyes and high-cut cheekbones that were supposed to attest to Comanche blood somewhere in our ancestry. Maybe that was what made him kill a man—that fierce Indian blood that sparked up every now and then and ran caterwauling through his brain like a war-painted brave gone clear out of reality on Mescal and dancing and the smoke from the houses of the dead. There had been a robbery at the telegraph station in Big Spring, seventy miles to the north of Eula, and the telegraph operator had been stabbed. Truth told, nobody could say for sure that it was Harry Bailey who did the actual stabbing. Even at his trial there were no witnesses who could place the knife in his hand, nobody who could testify that they saw him plunge it into in that other man's throat. But he'd been identified as being there, being part of the robbery that led to the killing, and even though bystanders had recalled another young man with him, he'd stead-fastly refused to identify his companion. So they had sent him away; two years at the county work farm because he was still underage, and when he got out he was a man; squinty blue eyes and muscles like pig iron from chopping saw-grass with a scythe in the broiling sun, and they say he stood in the middle of Main Street and took in Eula north to south, east to west, and spat. And that was the last folks saw of him until six years later when he returned with a beautiful young bride from Boston, Massachusetts, and built her a house of hickory and pine with his own hands, and planted three apple trees, and set out to work the land his daddy had left him.

Indian pride, Indian high on Loco weed.

In fact, Audrey Lou Hawley had never touched my dangle on the school bus or anyplace else for that matter. The closest she came to it was one afternoon when we were swimming in an abandoned granite quarry named Thompson's Pond, but being that standing water was suspected of causing infantile paralysis, we had, in an act of arrant disregard and consummate bravado, tagged the place Polio Pond. There the water was languid, mineral-green, deep enough in spots that even divers with the strongest lungs could not reach the bottom. Along the edges where the water was shallower, the quarry floor was littered with discarded mining equipment, making diving hazardous. The story was told, although none could confirm it, of a boy who'd dived in and got caught head and shoulders in a metal milk can underwater and drowned before anybody missed him; so mostly everyone eased into the shallows trying not to touch the bottom and swam out to where the water was deeper.

There was a float anchored in the middle - wooden planks lashed to the top of a half-dozen empty creosote drums; and it was there that Audrey Lou Hawley and I found ourselves on a sweltering August afternoon, underneath the planks, treading water in the heat and stench generated by the creosote drums, our taut, wet bodies brushing, our lips touching, our eardrums bursting; spinning together in the unreality of the place, the absurdity of the event. Later we went to a thicket and sat together, eating wild raspberries that we picked plump from the vine, and we gaggled our red tongues and held each other with arms cut and bleeding from the thorns, and she showed me her breasts firm and webbed with small blue veins. Then I led her by the hand to where Joe Carl waited (he always waited since he could not swim due to his medical condition), and he drove us home in the truck.

In the weeks that followed I thought of almost nothing else; excitement and fear wound up in me, choked me, left me aching, immobilized, bathed in sweat. An alien force had seized me and held me in its clutches; Cyclops-like it licked its chops, fixing to grind my bones and swallow me whole. Everything about it was epic, everything drowned in uncertainty and I wondered if this was the way it would always be or whether it would wind down bloodlessly on hot afternoons with lemonade and pecan sandys and devastating silences in the parlor. Had Harry Bailey felt the way I felt when he first set his blue eyes on her? Were her breasts small and firm and webbed with blue veins and did she bare them to him and let him feel her nipples until they became hard and her eyes closed and her mouth went limp and did he get to press himself against her and did he ache with the same unfulfilled desire?

All that time he was in prison did he think he would find her at the end of the bus line and build a house for her out of pine and hickory and galvanized aluminum with his own hands? Did he read Buck Rogers? Did he drink rye whiskey in Moon's and cram silver dollars in the table slots for the Mexican lady? Did he stare into the mirror until his blue eyes became a prism of his future and he could see himself older and older still and the time came when he was laid out on a white sheet in the yard and death came for him and he said get outa here, I ain't ready for you yet, and rather than risk hanging around, death skulked off and left him there smelling sour-sweet like the apples and wondering about killing a man with a knife? Would it be like slaughtering a hog, or would it be pure and silent like the water of Polio Pond and the blood-red gaggle of tongues stained with fresh raspberries?

Why did God make Eula; why did he put me there?

I suspected that the Reverend Brown was a patron of Moon's roadhouse.

"Wouldn't surprise me none," Uncle Mal said when I told him.

"Ain't he supposed to be a man of God?"

He let loose a wad of chaw. "Only two kinds of men'll do y'all in at the end; politicians and preachers."

"He ain't going to marry ma, is he?"

"Not likely for a while at least. Far as the law allows, your daddy's got to be missing for a while more before he's declared dead."

"What if he shows up before then?"

"Well that would be a different story."

"I think he'd kick the Reverend Harley Brown's ass from here to Oklahoma."

"Well, he might just do that," Uncle Mal conceded.

"I think I seen bruises on ma's face after he's been alone with her."

"Wouldn't surprise me none."

LeMoult

Three

Joe Carl needed to know. "Will you be hanging out with her now instead of me?"

"It's different," I told him.

"You're spending all your time with her. When I come by you're never there."

"I'm here now, ain't I?"

"You're only here because I came by looking for y'all."

"That don't make any sense at all. I'm either here or I ain't here; your coming by's got nothing to do with it."

"It makes sense to me. If I didn't come by here I wouldn't of had no way of knowing y'all was here."

"So I wouldn't a been here, is that what you're saying?"

"Not to me, you wouldn't."

We were at the quarry, on a sloping rock outcrop overlooking the water where we could see the hollow margins of our world dotted with shrubs and bramble tangles, clumps of saw weed and greenbrier vines, broken farm machinery left to rust on uncultivated hillocks, rotting barns and silos shivering in the prism of hot, doughy air rising from the prairie floor. It was a Sunday afternoon. Ma was at the Calvary Baptist Church listening to Reverend Brown rant against the Devil, who to my mind had done nothing more wicked than question the state of affairs in a remote, halcyon place called Heaven where I was supposed to hope someday to be sent to escape the summertime hell of west Texas. It was a proposition that might have appealed to me if I had been able to shake the notion that God had delivered us all to this festering dust-speck, this stink-hole, this dried-out depository of dirt and scum and heat and misery sight-unseen, without any of us ever getting a chance to prove we deserved a better fate. Nothing the Devil had ever done to me came close to matching that injustice.

"You think the Devil's really wicked?" I asked Joe Carl.

"Reckon he must be the way everybody carries on," he postulated.

"I don't mean because they say he's wicked. I mean has he done anything to you personally that would make you think that?"

"He gave me polio; that wicked enough for y'all?"

"Who's to say he did that?"

"If he didn't do it, who did?"

"Maybe it just happened, maybe it was God meant for it to happen."

"Sheeeit!" Joe Carl tossed a pebble from the precipice and listened it plop in the water below, then undid the buttons on his fly and began to pee from the edge of the escarpment. I knew he wanted me to join him, to stand alongside and duel with the streams of our urine as they corkscrewed downward, blending in fine spray as their inexorable paths toward the water met in knightly combat, but my mind was elsewhere, caught up in the intricacies of reasoning.

"Maybe polio's not wicked at all," I suggested. "The Reverend Brown says we suffer our infirmities at God's hands so we can be measured fit for The Kingdom."

"I think the Reverend Brown is a douche bag."

"I think I have to agree with you there."

Joe Carl thought some. "I think there's things you just know are wicked; things inside of you that sometimes get out; they just slip out sometimes, and when you see them you know they're wicked."

"I let some pretty wicked farts slip out sometimes."

"I think it would be like a fart, something bad-smelling that was brewing up inside you without you even knowing about it. That could be the Devil working on you."

"Imagine if the whole world farted at the same time. What do y'all think would happen then?"

He screwed up his face. "Now you know that's not going to happen."

"It could. God could make it happen."

"Now that's just not sensible. Just why do you think God would want to do a stupid thing like that?"

"Reverend Harley Brown says it's not for us to understand the ways of God. He come down to earth just so's he could get himself nailed on a cross and there ain't nothing sensible about that."

Joe Carl buttoned his fly. "I'm going to have an operation," he disclosed as he sat down next to me.

"What kind of operation?"

"For scoliosis. They're going to try and fuse up my spine so I can walk straight."

"I thought you walked crooked because you had polio."

"Scoliosis too."

"Jesus, you're some mess."

"I might be in the hospital up in Lubbock for three or four months, but when I get out I'll be near as tall as y'all."

"Tall don't make no difference. It all looks the same anyway."

Joe Carl thought some more. "I think it would create a whole new atmosphere," he said finally. "People would have to learn how to breathe all over."

"What the hell are you talking about?"

"Synchronous crepitation."

"What's that?"

"If everybody in the world farted at the same time. All the oxygen in the air would be replaced by fart-gas and people wouldn't be able to breathe."

"I thought you said that couldn't happen."

"It couldn't, it's just something to think about."

"Reckon."

"The Nazis had fart-gas in the war but they didn't use it because they were afraid the wind would blow it back to Germany and kill their own people."

"I think I'm going to kill the Reverend Harley Brown."

"How're you fixing to do that?"

"Maybe I'll fart him to death. Maybe I'll stick him like a hog."

That afternoon I sat plotting the Reverend's demise at the dinner table while he prophetically read the pre-meal scriptures: "What fruit had ye then in those things whereof ye are now ashamed?" He looked up long enough to rebuke me with his eyes. "For the end of those things is death; the wages of sin is death but the gift of God is eternal life."

I do not know what he believed I was ashamed of, but he likely felt it was punishable by death which he considered just desserts for anyone who did not think or act exactly as he did. As for death, somebody had got it wrong. Either death was the wages of sin or your passport into the Kingdom; they couldn't have it both ways. My take on it was that death was like Joe Carl's solipsism; everybody saw it in their own peculiar way. When I thought about it I saw death as a mischief-maker, a clever old man who rode noiselessly on the wind throwing dust in his path to blind peoples' eyes and make them confused. Then he could take them in his own good time, just swoop down and harvest them and winnow them like ripe kernels of wheat and where they'd been a whole new crop would grow up in their place. That was how they could prove they'd been there in the first place, from those newborn shoots with Comanche cheekbones and a taste for gambling and liquor and eyes as blue as the sky.

I would kill him because he hit my mother, bold-faced I'd kill him while I was short of my sixteenth birthday and still a minor. They'd send me away to the State farm for a year or two where I would grow tall and leathery on the work gang and when I got back I would stand in the middle of Main Street and look Eula up and down like I was inspecting a turd and I'd spit and hop a bus and that would be that.

The telephone in the hall rang three times, then twice, our ring on the party line. Overjoyed at the prospect of escaping the Canaanites getting their ears and toes cut off for the thousandth time, I ran and answered it.

"That you, Chance?" The male voice was barely audible.

"It's me," I shouted into the receiver.

"Is your ma there?"

"Who wants her?"

"It's your daddy."

I almost passed out. My mother must have seen the blood drain from my face because she darted from the table and grabbed the phone from my hand. She said hello into the receiver and slumped against the wall,

"What's that about?" the Reverend asked.

When I did not reply he slammed his fist on the table, rattling the glasses and silverware. "I asked you a question, boy!"

My mother did not speak. Eyes closed and growing moist she held the receiver to her ear for almost a minute, then replaced it carefully in its cradle and returned to the table. "That was Harry," she confirmed.

"Good lord, after all this time?"

"Where is he? What happened to him?" I begged.

"He's in New York City. He says he's sending us money to come there and be with him." She stared into her lap, disbelievingly.

"Well you're certainly not thinking of going after all these years," Reverend Harley howled. "The man walked out on you; he let you think he was killed in the war!"

"Was he in a hospital like Uncle Mal thought?"

"He is an adulterer, a drunkard and a whoremonger!"

"He's my husband," she managed.

"What kind of husband would vanish without a word, leaving his wife and child to fend for themselves?"

"In the sight of God we are still married."

"Don't speak to me of God!" he bellowed. "I have devoted my life to God. I took you and the boy in after he abandoned you and no other man would have you."

"What do you mean you took us in?" I objected. "This is our house you're sitting in, our food you're eating."

"Boy, you will speak when you are spoken to or you'll feel the sting of my belt across your backside!"

"You must leave Chance alone. None of this is his doing."

It was the first time she had ever stuck up for me in front of the Reverend, and I was emboldened with the intemperance of youth. "My daddy didn't build this house so you could come in here and have your way with us."

"Your daddy's passed, boy." He glared across the table at me.

"My daddy's in New York City and we're going there to be with him."

"In the sight of God and by all that's decent that man is dead to you. He has harvested the vengeance of the Lord and the Lord's vengeance is death."

My mother stood shakily. "I think I have to go to my room."

"It is Satan who does battle for your soul right now, Addie. The time is come when you shall be judged!"

"I can't talk now, Harley."

The Reverend sprang to his feet and leaned across the dinner table. "You will stay and hear me out, woman!"

"I have to go."

My eye was on the carving knife just in front of him. If he made a move I would grab it and sink the point into his belly before he got to her. It seemed as if everything that had happened in my life up until then had been directed toward that very moment, as if at last I was fulfilling a destiny that had been charted for me since the time Harry Bailey looked out from the roof of the house he had built with his own hands and saw the edges of the earth curl up and beckon him. Blood was our heritage, his and mine.

The Reverend Harley Brown stood stone still. "I will leave and I will pray for you, for both you and the boy, that you will come to your senses. If I do not hear from you again I will pray for God to overlook your transgressions."

"I just need some time, Harley."

"Lord be merciful."

After he had gone I went upstairs to her room where she sat quietly at the pink chiffon-draped vanity that had followed her out from New England. Around her were the things she had brought with her: combs and brushes, a nail file and buffer, all overlaid with nacre and silver. The bed was neatly made, pillows nestled in a quilted spread she had sewn herself, and draperies to match hanging almost to the floor and parted only slightly in the middle where an apple-scented breeze from the open window rustled the tatted edges and mingled with the smells of her hair and skin and lotion.

"Did he say where he's been all this time," I asked.

"No, only that he missed us and wanted to be with us." Her speech was slow and slurred, her hands were spread on the glass surface of the vanity where she examined them as if she was seeing them for the first time, searching the swirls and folds of her palms, her pale, translucent nails like mirrors.

"Why didn't you ask him?"

"What difference would it have made?" She began buffing her nails, slowly at first, then harder and harder.

"Don't you wonder about it? Don't you wonder what made him call after so many years?"

"I expect it just crossed his mind."

LeMoult

Four

Two weeks later a letter bearing a New York City postmark arrived at the farm. Mother opened it, removed the letter, and carefully examined the inside of the envelope before starting to read.

"What's he say?" I fairly exploded.

"He's in New York." Her eyes darted over the neatly scripted page. "He has a job at the Radio City Music Hall."

"Doing what?"

"He doesn't say."

"He still wants us to come, right?"

She nodded and put the letter in her apron pocket. "He says he does."

"Did he send any money?"

She shook her head. "There may not be any money, Chance. You might as well get used to thinking that way."

"He said he'd send money for our trip."

"Your daddy says a lot of things. He means well but things don't always work out the way he wants them to."

"But we're going, right?"

She pretended to busy herself at the kitchen sink.

"We could get the money ourselves. We could borrow it from Uncle Mal."

"Your Uncle Mal's got no money to spare. This place barely puts food on the table as is."

"I could work. I could get a job and earn it. Joe Carl's daddy said he could put me to work."

She didn't say no, she just looked at me in a funny way and went on with her chores as if nothing had happened. That afternoon I thumbed a ride into Eula and got a job at Purdy's Feed & Grain, loading sacks for sixty cents an hour.

Joe Carl had left for the hospital in Lubbock the week before, and either his leaving had put his daddy in an irritable mood or Amos Purdy had plumb forgot that I'd been his son's best and only friend. After one day of loading hundred-pound sacks of corn, oats, sorghum, concrete and bone meal in the blistering sun, It had become clear that I would receive no special favors. To the contrary, it seemed he was determined to drive me harder than anyone else in his employ. At first I believed it was because he did not want to be accused of favoritism, but after a few days I began to think he might resent me. I was the son he could not have; straight and tall and unfreckled through no endeavor of my own, while Joe Carl languished up in Lubbock, about to go under the knife just to keep from caving in on himself.

At the end of the first week, after deductions for taxes, Social Security insurance, and advances I had taken for soda pop, chips and such, my pay envelope contained thirteen dollars and fifty-seven cents. I had estimated the cost of two one-way tickets to New York City, food for both of us along the way, plus a few dollars emergency fund in case we failed to hook up with my daddy immediately upon arrival, to be almost three hundred dollars. Arithmetic had never been my strong point in school, but it didn't take long to figure out that if my earnings were all we could count on, we would spend another year in Eula, a year when anything could happen. As for Harry Bailey, no more letters came, and as the weeks piled up my mother and I both stopped anticipating the arrival of the postman or even collecting the mail, each of us in our own way calculating that it was better to remain unenlightened than be disappointed. Unable to console one another, we drew further and further apart.

Mother continued her churchgoing, even though the Reverend Harley Brown no longer came to visit. I expect their relations were strained, especially at choir practice where they were practically forced to talk to each other, but she seemed for the most part freed of pretense and not in the least upset over their estrangement. I was of mixed feelings. On one hand I was pleased to be able to eat a Sunday meal without endlessly being subjected to the woes and triumphs of the Hebrews, while on the other I was not happy at having to field the bulk of her dinner-table conversation and answer the multitude of questions about my life the Reverend Brown's departure seemed to have provoked. Where she needed responsiveness I needed secrets. Where she needed a helpmate I needed a life of my own, and as summer wound down we faced the prospect of another west Texas winter with only us together.

By the end of August the crops had been harvested and stored, winter seed had been planted, and Amos Purdy had little work at the Feed & Grain to justify keeping me on the payroll, so I collected my final pay envelope the Friday before Labor Day and added it to the total amount I had accumulated over the Summer. It came to ninety-two dollars; I had worked like a dog for an entire summer and all I had to show for it was ninety-two dollars. Granted, it was more money than I had seen in my lifetime, but it was not nearly enough for our bus fare and essentials. It became clear to me then that I would have to find another way to get us both to New York City or we would never go. One more Eula winter would ooze into the next with both of us dreamless and huddled against a cold prairie wind that would surely cut us open, rip apart our fabric, and leave us helpless; sore and old and used in a place where nobody cared and nobody mattered.

I decided to risk everything.

Moon's Roadside Cafe loomed flat, dark and intimidating as I approached it from the road; a hint of trailing music rode the breeze, or more the beat behind the music, a kind of moody, persistent rumble beneath my feet broken by the clash of a cymbal or an owl's screech in the brush or a restless coyote out on a ridge chewing off a piece of the moon.

Indian legend had it that the coyote had once been a man. There had been a great famine on the plains and most of his tribe had starved, but when he saw the moon all round and tempting like it was he'd turned himself into a coyote so he could leap high enough to grab onto a hunk, and he'd chewed off enough to save the tribe from starvation, and that was why coyotes to this day bayed at the moon. While I did not set much store by the story, I must admit I wished I could turn myself into a coyote at that moment or anything but what I was.

Ahead of me was a burly, bearded man with a shotgun in his hand whose only job was to turn me away, and ridicule me in the bargain. I would make myself older, or bigger or stronger or charged with the certainty I saw in men who frequented the place. I would swagger past him like he wasn't even there and if he made a move to stop me I would fix him with my blue, blue eyes and spit a wad of chaw and that would be that. Inside I would sit and order a whiskey, and set my stack of bills in front of me the way I'd seen it done, and I would wedge a silver dollar in the table crack.

"That's far enough!"

I brushed past him on the stair.

"I said that's far enough, boy." He blocked me with the barrel of the shotgun. "You wanta tell me just where you think you're going?"

"I'm going inside."

"And just what're y'all fixin' to do when you get there?"

"Gamble."

His eyes squinted. "With what?"

I took all the bills from my wallet and fanned them in front of him like a poker hand. "I expect you know real money when you see it," I said cool as can be, although my stomach was turning cartwheels. "I was here last year and your boss told me to come back when I had some money to gamble," I then lied.

He stood eyeing the money, indecisive.

"Go ask him yourself if you don't believe me."

"Y'all wait here." He poked me with the butt of the shotgun and went inside.

I waited only a few seconds before he returned, accompanied by the man with the long yellow hair and pale skin. "I'm Chance Bailey," I blurted.

"I know who you are. I thought I told y'all not to come around here until you was old enough," he cut me off.

"I reckon I'm old enough to put this on the line." I held the bills aloft.

"Now just what you planning to do with that there money?"

"I'm planning to bet it at the poker table."

"Y'all ever play poker, boy?"

"Lots of times."

"You ever win?"

"I know the whys and wherefores of the game if that's what you mean."

He eyed me up and down. "Why you want to gamble all that money, Chance Bailey? I'd wager that's all the money you got in the world."

"You'd be right there, but it ain't nearly enough."

"For what?"

"Bus fare for me and my mama out to New York City."

"New York City?" He let out a hoot.

"My daddy's there. He's working at the Music Hall in Radio City."

"I thought you told me your daddy was still over in Europe."

"Well now he's in New York City at the Radio City Music Hall and he wants me and my mama to go there and be with him. I got barely enough money for one ticket, and I need to get two and have some left over to live on until we hook up with him."

"So you're going to take that there money and double it inside."

"That and a little bit more, yes sir."

"In that case y'all better come with me." He motioned for me to follow him and I did. Inside the light was dim, the air thick with the smells of beer and whiskey. Below us as we entered I could see a crowd of men milling around the bar, a few familiar but most total strangers; lounging, talking, tipping Red Stag beer from bottles. Beyond the bar a dozen or more tables surrounded a small dance floor where a single couple swayed moodily to a blues rendition played by three colored musicians tucked in the corner; a piano, sax and drum, their music strained in the cloak of dark oiled beams and strangely quieter than it sounded outside. A low wall separated the dance floor from the gaming area; three pool tables bathed in smoky blue light, each with a game in progress; two large, round poker tables and two smaller ones; hushed, intent men bent around them with their cards clutched to their chests, tossing chips, gathering chips, men refracted in cigarette smoke and red-hued chips, and blue, and white. I thought we would descend the stairs to where they were but he led me around the perimeter to an office in the rear and took me inside.

"I reckon if you're bent on losing that money y'all might as well lose it to me." He pulled a chair away from a small felt-covered table in the middle of the office and bade me to sit.

"What makes you think I'm gonna lose?"

"Because I know a sucker when I see one." He sat across from me, removed an unopened box of cards from a drawer in the table and handed it to me. "Brand new deck. Your game to call, boy."

I broke the seal on the box and removed the deck. "You ain't gonna cheat me, are you?"

"Well now, if I was fixing to cheat you would you expect me to tell y'all about it?"

"I believe I'd prefer to take my chances with those men downstairs."

"What makes you think they wouldn't cheat you?"

"I don't have no way of knowing that."

"Reckon y'all don't. Want to reconsider and take that money back home with you?"

"I come to gamble and that's what I'm gonna do."

"Then I suggest you shuffle them cards and call the game. This's the only poker you're about to play tonight, boy."

I removed the jokers from the front of the deck and shuffled the cards nervously, managing to keep the unruly stack intact despite some fits and starts. "All I know is five card draw," I told him.

He shrugged. "Cut for deal."

I cut a ten of spades and he cut a jack. "Table stakes; we play one hand for everything in your bankroll there."

"All of it?"

"Y'all want to double your money, boy, or you want to piss and moan about not having enough of it?"

I took the bills from my wallet and placed them on the table in front of me. "Go ahead and deal."

The cards flew from his hand, and my heartbeat quickened as I gathered them to my chest: a heart king, another king, this time in spades, a three of diamonds, then a third king in clubs. When my final card turned out to be the fourth king I almost fainted. "I call you," I fairly croaked.

He laughed. "That's not exactly how it works, boy. How much money you have in that stack there?"

"Ninety-two dollars."

He reached into his pocket and fumbled with his change. "Well now, I seem to have come to the table without any cash. How's about I put up something of equal or greater value than that ninety-two dollars of yours?"

"Like what?"

"How about this place?"

"Moon's?"

"Moon's Roadside Cafe. If what you got in your hand there beats what I got in mine, this place'll be yours, lock, stock and barrel."

My head was spinning. There was no way I could lose, but the magnitude of the wager terrified me. "You'll put that in writing?"

"Well now you'll just have to trust me on that, boy; same as I'll have to trust y'all to hand over that ninety-two dollars if you lose."

"Okay." I clutched the hand to my chest.

"Then it's my call."

"Four kings!" I spread my cards on the table

His eyes went wide. "Four kings? If I hadn'ta seen it I wouldn't've believed it. First hand of the night and the boy draws four kings. If that don't beat all!"

"Does that mean I own this place?"

"Well it certainly would if I hadn't drawn these four aces here." He plopped them on the table one-by-one. "Got to be one of the most amazing hands I ever sat in on."

I felt like I'd been kicked in the chest. "You cheated me!"

"Now y'all got no call to say that, boy."

"No way you could deal me four kings and four aces for yourself unless you were cheating."

He gathered my money from the center of the table bill-by-bill and stuffed it in his pocket. "Maybe I was, and maybe I wasn't, but y'all got no way of knowing that, do you boy? Now if the game was on the up-and-up, I beat you fairly and squarely, and y'all got no choice but to accept losing like a man; just like I would have no choice but to turn Moon's over to you lock-stock-and barrel if I lost. But if I was cheating, you'd have every right to call me on it before the hand was over. Now that it's all said and done, I reckon it's too late."

I sat stunned. Everything I had worked so hard for all summer long was gone. It was a sealed box—I'd shuffled the cards myself.

He eyed me long and hard, then took the deck and dealt me five more cards, facedown. "That's a full house—queens and sixes." He dealt five cards to himself and without picking them up announced he'd dealt a straight flush.

"Then you admit you were cheating!"

"Y'all didn't think I'd put this place up against ninety-two bucks unless I was sure of winning, did you?"

"I guess I never did give it much thought."

"I guess you didn't. I guess y'all didn't give it much thought when you came here in the first place. Whether you know it or not, boy, I did you a real favor here tonight."

"How, by stealing all my money?"

"Well it was either me stealing it or those good old boys downstairs stealing it, and I got to think you're a whole lot better off with me than you'd be with them."

"You saying everybody cheats?"

"I ain't saying everybody cheats and I ain't saying everybody don't. I just believe a man's got no business gambling his money if it means a lot to him." He gathered the cards on the table, shuffled them expertly and dealt me another hand. "That's four nines. Did y'all see me do anything there?"

"Nothing but deal," I admitted.

"Watch again." He dealt himself a hand, slow enough for me to see him drawing the cards from the bottom of the deck.

"If you'd'a dealt like that in the first place I would've called you on it."

"Man'd have to be some kind of fool to deal that slow off the bottom of the deck. The trick is to do it so fast nobody can tell." He handed me the cards. "Go ahead, you try it."

After a few fumbling attempts I was dealing smoothly and efficiently from the bottom of the deck. "But how can you get the right cards down there so you can deal them?" I asked him.

"It ain't my job to turn you into a riverboat hustler. I just wanted to show y'all how easy it is to cheat a body if you've got a mind to. Fact is, anybody who sits down at a poker table's got to expect the dealer'll be dealing off the bottom of the deck. He'd be a idiot not to."

"But there's got to be some way of spotting it."

He shook his head. "Man's doing it right, there's no way in hell to tell."

"Might just as well not play poker then; might as well risk my money on tiddly-winks as get into a poker game. Is that what you're trying to tell me?"

"Not necessarily. I'm just telling you to be aware of the possibility. You're less likely to be cheated if the dealer knows you're onto it."

"But you said it couldn't be spotted."

"Maybe not spotted but it can be stopped. Go ahead, deal me some from the bottom and I'll show you."

I dealt a few cards from the bottom and he let them fall on the table in front of him. Suddenly as I let another fly, his hand shot forward like a striking rattlesnake and snatched the card in mid-air. "What'd you do that for?" I asked, startled.

"Look at your dealing hand, boy."

I looked down and saw that my hand was frozen palm-up on the bottom of the deck. "Holy shit, where'd you learn how to do that?"

"Down in Mexicali where the hoochy-kootchys grow; spent some time down there before the war and I can tell y'all for a fact that that's a place where they've got bottom-dealing down to a art. I was playing high-stakes in one of them fancy cantinas they got down there with a couple of hombres y'all wouldn't want at your back in a dark alley, if you know what I mean, when one of them did what I just showed you, and caught the dealer red-handed, just like I did you. Neither of them said nothing; they both just drawed on each other and let fire and when the smoke cleared I was the only one left alive at the table."

"What'd you do then?"

"Well, there was near three thousand American in the pot, so I just scooped it up and hightailed back over the border and bought this place."

"That's some story."

"Yes it is, and it's true, every word of it." He went to an iron safe in the corner of the room, opened it with a combination, and removed a thick manila envelope from inside. "I was holding this for your daddy, but he'd gone off to the war by the time I got back from Mexico. I reckon y'all can bring it to him in New York City when you go back there to see him."

I peered inside and saw a wad of bills thick enough to choke a horse wrapped tight with a rubber band. "What's this for?" I gasped.

"There's eighteen hundred dollars there. Your daddy and I were in a business venture before the war but he left before we could share the profits."

It hit me like a ton of bricks. "You're the one who was in that robbery with him, ain't you? You're the one who really killed that telegraph clerk."

He stayed silent for a long time. Finally he opened the door and signaled for me to leave. "Boy, one thing y'all better learn in life is you stop playing the hand after you've already won the game."

Five

The day I decided there was no God I was at a creek about a quarter-mile from our house which was not really a creek at that time of year but more of a sweaty scar that seeped up out of the earth in spots and formed shallow ponds coated with algae and swarming insects. The creek got that way in late summer when the lack of rain forced the water underground, but in early spring it would rise again and run, carrying weeds and lilies and water hyacinths through the scab of sun-baked prairie like Lazarus, that old phony, risen from the dead. There were catfish there then, although I am at a loss to explain what happened to them when the water dried up, or how they re-emerged when the spring runoffs fed the seep to overflowing and the ponds became deep enough for them to swim and spawn and gorge themselves on muck they could suck up from the bottom. I expected it all had to do with the cycle of death and rebirth, and the mysteries therein, but I was not of a mind to ponder it at any great length, being that I had decided, at that particular time and place, that there was no God.

God, like Lazarus and Daniel and Amos and Nahum and Joshua and Jonah and Jeremiah and Job and Zephaniah (who I always pronounced zinnia, like the flower), and Samuel and Ruth and Nehemiah and Isaiah, who foresaw the destruction of Israel by the Assyrians, and Leb and Zeb and Bleb and anybody else with a name that sounded scriptural, was a phony. I had become so sure of it I did not even ask myself the questions people ask when they come to that conclusion; questions like, if there is no God how do we account for all the stuff on earth? or, if there is no God how are we supposed to combat the evil in our midst? I would leave things like the contemplation of good and evil to people like Joe Carl with worm-hole minds where ideas burrowed in and stayed until they'd got chewed up and digested and spit out looking nothing like they did when they crawled in, or to the Reverend Harley Brown who had a mind like a flytail net that closed shut when an idea went in and didn't open up again to let that idea out come hell or high water. My mind was like the creek. Most of the time it just lay there like the shallow, murky pools, draining ideas away; but when it started running, it ran too fast for serious thought, all my ideas cascading off rocks and silty shores, muck for whatever sucked them up and swallowed them.

If God existed he would be the cruelest joker ever; pulling a string that jerked us in and out of the hellfire and the rapture. If he existed he would be a malevolent, festering creature, farting up wickedness to please his twisted sense of humor; droughts and sand-storms and tornadoes, locusts, tarantulas, scorpions, boll weevils, rattlesnakes, all manner of sickness and disfigurement, the lame, the poor, the pious (them most of all), barns that sagged and tilted in the wind with galvanized aluminum roofs you could climb and see the misery further out, and when you saw it and choked it down you could face that phony God and ask for more. Give me a rigged poker game where I can lose every cent of my earnings, you could ask him; then jerk that string of yours and pull me back to the light with eighteen-hundred dollars of my daddy's money, (granted it was ill-gotten but that shouldn't have bothered a God whose whim was to steal everything worthwhile anyway); then when the plan is fixed and paid-for in my brain, take that poor woman's vaporous mind and fix it with wild ideas from the Reverend Harley Brown, (that Devil incarnate), and while you're at it, God, give me some scabies and creeping lesions, and beetle's eggs up my ass that hatch and breed in my entrails and eat me up from inside until I'm nothing but a shell of old dried bones crawling around on the roof, squinting into that fucking sun of yours.

I'd put the envelope inside my shirt, and all the way home I'd felt it to make sure it was still there, that it was real. Eighteen hundred dollars, more money than I had ever imagined I would see in my lifetime; one thousand, eight hundred simoleons; eighteen one-hundred dollar bills, or a hundred and eighty ten dollar bills; enough money to make us forget the look and stink and crushing monotony of west Texas and deliver us to the gleaming, cosmopolitan canyons of New York City, a place of beauty and riches beyond our imagination; a place of steel and concrete skyscrapers with air-conditioning and television in every room; a place where men wore suits of gabardine and seersucker to work and women wore nylon stockings with dark seams all the way up, and trains ran underground to take them to nightclubs where they would sip cocktails from stemmed glasses and practice talking like English people talked, all so veddy smart, you know; and none of them would have ever heard of Eula, and they wouldn't give a shit. God damn.

She'd eyed the bankroll like it was a bug crawling on my arm. "Where'd you get all that money?"

"It's ours. It belonged to Daddy and the man who was holding it for him gave it to me. It's almost eighteen hundred dollars, mama; enough to take us to New York City and live like kings when we get there."

"What have you done, Chance?"

"I done nothing, mama. I got in a card game so I could double my earnings and make enough to buy us both bus tickets to New York, and the man I was playing with was Daddy's partner before he went to Mexicali and won a bundle in a card game with two Mexicans who shot each other dead, and he was holding this money for when he got state-side but by that time Daddy'd gone off to the war. Anyway, it's our money."

"Oh, Lord-a-mercy. The apple doesn't fall far from the tree," she'd wailed.

"It was my daddy's money. I can prove it."

She'd turned away from me. "I don't care whose money it is. It's the wages of sin and I don't want any part of it."

"But mama, how do you know Daddy didn't earn this money honest? He could've earned it. The man said it was a business venture."

"The Almighty knows that if your daddy came by that money, he did not come by it honestly."

"But we haven't done anything, not you and me. Maybe the Almighty wanted us to have this here money to pay us back for all the misery daddy's leaving us caused us. Maybe he figured we'd got enough of dust and donkey shit. Maybe he figured it was time we got something good in this world."

"If we take that money we are as guilty as he is. The Lord doesn't separate the sinner from those who would benefit from his sins."

I was desperate. "Look, ninety-two dollars of this is mine. I earned it honest-as-you-please this summer at the Feed & Grain. That's enough to buy your ticket to New York, and I can buy mine out of the rest of it. That way you won't have to worry about benefiting from the bad money."

She sat at the kitchen table and heaved a sigh. "You might as well know once and for all, Chance. We won't be going to New York; not now—not ever."

"What're you talking about?"

"I've agreed to marry Harley. We'll be wed the first Saturday in October."

"You can't marry him. You don't even love him!"

"Harley Brown is a good man. He'll take care of us."

I felt the breath going out of me. "You can't marry him. You're still married to Harry Bailey."

"I've not been a wife to your daddy for a long time now. The time is come to end that marriage and get on with my life."

"But you can get on with your life in New York City; that's a whole lot better than Eula. I know you still love Harry Bailey; don't tell me you don't. I can see your eyes tear up every time I talk about him."

She was silent for a while, chewing on it. "I don't know whether I can make you understand what it was like with your daddy and me," she finally said. "I will admit he was the only man I ever loved, and that I love him to this day, but it is an affliction I must struggle against with every ounce of strength in my body. Your daddy, Harry Bailey was the sun and the moon and the stars for me. All he ever had to do was fix me with those blue eyes of his and I would have followed him anywhere, done anything he asked. But he was sick inside, and he made me sick with him. It wasn't until after he was long gone and I was over the hurt of his leaving that I realized the love I had for him was a curse. It had robbed me of my dignity and sense, it had taken my soul away from me."

"I don't see how loving somebody can be a curse," I objected.

"Maybe when you're old enough you will."

That phony God had pulled the string on her; he'd took her and dunked her in the seep and let the muddy waters cloud her eyes until bad looked good and good looked bad and all the air that occupied that small room we found ourselves in smelled of apples rotting on the ground instead of the shit and piss and laundry soap moldering in the cesspool underneath the kitchen window that it really was. (God, it always smelled like shit no matter how much sachet she spread around the place. Early on I would catch her moistening her upper lip with lilac toilet water but as the years wore on she seemed to get used to it, as I had done when I wasn't really thinking about it). "Come anyway," I entreated. "If you don't want to be with Chance Bailey you can go back to New England and be with your folks. New England's a better place than this, you've said so yourself."

"I can't go back. My family disowned me when I went off with your daddy,"she said simply.

"Then go back there and live someplace else. You hate Eula; you hate it as much as I do. If you stay here and marry the Reverend Harley Brown you'll end up a dried-out old prune all cracking at the edges like all the other ladies in this place."

I brandished the bankroll in front of her. "If that God you set so much store by is worth his salt, don't you think he wants you to be happy for once in your life? Ain't all that Bible-reading and praying and choir-singing you done worth something?"

"Those who covet earthly rewards will suffer death and damnation."

"Well SHEEEIT! You tell that old phony God of yours he can come looking for me by the creek, 'cause that's where I'll be, thinking on how I'm gonna spend this money all by myself in New York City. If he's got a mind to wreak death and damnation on me for that, there ain't a whole lot I can do about it. I reckon I'd rather be dead and in the clutches of Satan than spend another day in this hell-hole of a town anyway."

I waited most of the afternoon for him out by the creek and he didn't come. I imagined him in bib overalls, wielding a scythe the way Harry Bailey had wielded it on the work gang, his face all tanned and wrinkled from the sun and bulging from a wad of Red Man tobacco in his cheek: "Y'all coming with me, boy, or do I have to lop off that head of your'n with my scythe here?" he would say. And I would say right back, "take your best swing, you bottom-dealer, 'cause I know some tricks of my own. I can move to the left and I can move to the right, and if it comes right down to it I can even duck down and burrow into the muck like a toad. What'd you think I was going to do anyway, just sit here and let you lop my head off and ship me off to perdition without even a fight? Sheeeit, I'm Harry Bailey's boy and we go down swinging. Next time you see me I'll be living the high life in New York City; you can catch me at the Radio City Music Hall if you got the admission fee and you can lop my head off there, you old fraud, you festering old liar, you wrinkled shit-god farting up evil. I wouldn't believe in you if you parted the clouds and recited the Pledge of Allegiance, if you rumbled through the whole Old Testament of the Bible, if you drew a royal flush to my four aces and stripped me naked I wouldn't believe in you. Old fraud, old fart, ain't got the balls to come down here and give me what-for for what I'm thinking. Old phony."

I took four hundred dollars from the bankroll and hid the rest under some towels in the chiffonier where my mother would find it in a day or two. Maybe she could make herself believe it was less wicked for having been through my hands. Maybe she would remember the part of Harry Bailey she had loved before he was sick, and known that he would have wanted her to have it.

Six

I was three weeks shy of my sixteenth birthday when I arrived at the Port Authority bus depot in Manhattan. Stumbling off the bus into this slick, unfamiliar world, I knew right off I'd been spotted for what I was— a wide-eyed, slack-jawed country boy—by just about everybody in the terminal. They were New Yorkers, and I had to get around to that way of thinking. Maybe they weren't outright gawking at me, but I could sense their disapproval at the way I looked—my grass-stained blue jeans and faded cotton shirt open at the neck to show the margins of my farmer's tan, my awkward slouch.

Though I was just over six feet tall, I was naturally bent over from having spent the better part of three days curled in my seat on the bus, a posture exaggerated by the weight of the suitcase I carried, the same one Mama had brought with her from New England all those years ago. Now dried and cracked at the corners, it was held together by criss-crossed, overlapping strips of friction tape - a laughable suitcase by anybody's reckoning; but made even more so by my own awkwardness and dread. What I dreaded most was their scorn, though there was little reason to. Gruff and distracted, they wanted no more of me than to move a little faster, to get my bulky suitcase out of the way with its taped edges and its sides bulged out with socks and underwear so they could push through and bump and jostle and rub flesh with one another (not like in Eula where the spaces between flesh were vast enough that an accidental brush could be deemed a testament of undying love, but also a swaggering, unapologetic gimme-a-look-and-I'll-paste-you-in-the-face kind of flesh), and escape that cavern of steel beams and glass and concrete, and get on with being as free as people had a right to be.

They parted only when a pigeon swooped down from the overhead beams and lit right on the floor in their midst. A pigeon. I had never seen a pigeon come indoors, much less one that strutted and pecked and dropped a load unconcerned in the middle of a thousand stomping feet. Never heard the crack of a shotgun, that bird, or felt a load of birdshot whistling through its tail—as different from the pigeons back in Eula as a hound was to a coyote, as different as the razor-edged throng in the bus depot was to Texas folk blunted by space and familiarity, and choking certainty.

And I came up with them, out of the cavern and into the spare, angular light; and the first person to speak to me was a beggar.

"You got any spare change; a quarter, a dime? I ain't had a good meal in a couple of days."

He was near my own age, maybe a year or two older, shorter than me and wearing a padded bombardier's jacket with a sheepskin collar, which I considered odd since it was only September and the weather was unusually warm, even by Texas standards. His face was oily and slightly scarred, not busted up from acne like Joe Carl's face could get, but more scraped red, as if he'd taken a sheet of coarse sandpaper to it, covered it with Cloverine Brand Salve, then rubbed what was left over into his long black hair to keep it from flying away in the brisk, hot wind which when he stood between me and it carried the smell of his clothing to me, sweat-soaked wool and urine and vomit and wieners boiling and popcorn in a bag he had brought up from the terminal. I thought about ignoring him, but finally decided against it, calculating that if my first deed in New York City was a charitable one I might expect to be rewarded in kind, whether or not God was still a part of my agenda.

"Thanks." He pocketed the dime I'd given him and fell in alongside me on the sidewalk. "Want some popcorn?"

"Reckon I better not."

"You look like you could use some help with that suitcase."

"I can handle it fine, thank you."

"I'll carry it for you for a quarter."

"I can carry it myself."

"How far are you going?"

"To the Radio City Music Hall."

He shrugged. "If it was me carrying that suitcase, I'd sure appreciate some help carrying it all that way."

"How far is it?"

"Over on Sixth Avenue. Might as well be a hundred miles from here." He continued to match me step-for-step.

"I thought you said you were hungry. Why don't you go get yourself something to eat with that money I gave you?"

"With what, this dime? You got any idea what you can buy in this town with a dime?"

"I read about a place called the Automat. You put a dime in a machine and a bologna sandwich comes out of the wall, just like that. Maybe a glass of milk and a piece of pie too."

"You gotta be some kind've hick thinking you can get all that for a dime. Where do you come from anyway?"

"It don't matter. You ever eat at the Automat?"

"You gotta be kidding, I eat there all the time. I know the boss of the place so he reserves a special table for me. Got my picture on the wall next to it and everything."

"You must really think I fell off the turnip truck," I hooted.

We walked side-by-side in silence for a few seconds. "You still going to Radio City?" he asked finally.

"Reckon so, why?"

"Cause you're headed in the wrong direction."

I plopped the suitcase on the sidewalk. "Well why didn't you say something about it before we walked all this way?"

"It ain't my fault you're walking west instead of east. I offered to take you there and carry the suitcase too, all for a lousy quarter."

"Why don't you just point me there?"

"Why don't you just go fuck a duck. Why don't you just keep on going the way you're going and drown yourself in the Hudson River when you get to it for all I care." He turned and started walking away.

"You really eat at the Automat?"

"Shit, no. Only hicks eat at the Automat. Now do you want me to

43

take you to Radio City or do you want to stand here all day with your tongue hanging down to the sidewalk?"

"How do I know you'll live up to your end of the bargain? How can I be sure y'all won't hightail it out of here as soon as I give you that quarter?"

He looked at me with disgust. "Because you don't give me the quarter 'till we get there. What do you think—you pay them Chinee coolies with the rickshaws up-front? Not on your life you don't, not if you want to ride you don't. Chinky-chow's gonna rob you every chance he gets, but you ain't looking at no chink. White man ain't gonna steal your money like some Chinee."

We walked uptown to Forty-second Street, then west to a place I had imagined I would see only in magazines and newsreels; the fabled Times Square; crossroads of a million, million lives, a place where the famous rubbed shoulders twenty-four hours a day and where, it was said, if you stood long enough in any one spot you would eventually meet somebody you knew. It was hard for me to imagine meeting anyone from Eula there. I expect that if we had met, or even briefly crossed paths, we would have averted our gazes away from one another, each suspecting that the other had become irretrievably corrupted in that most infamous of fleshpots.

"I seen every one of those movies," my companion bragged as we walked past dozens of theaters with lurid themes emblazoned on their marquees. "Some of them are open all night long so it's a good place to sleep if you don't mind the perverts jerking off in the seat next to you."

"They really show everything in those movies?"

"Everything worth showing and then some, but a savvy guy don't have to go to no movie to get that shit. I can get you the real thing, live and in the flesh. I can get you anything you want for five-ten bucks tops. You just say the word and I'll have more table-grade babes coming at you than you can shake a stick at."

I must admit I was flattered that he considered me worldly enough to make the offer. Judging by his looks, he could not have been much older than I was, and yet he had cranked up a thousand lifetimes to my one. While I had been creating moods and images and experiences in my room, he had been living them in Times Square. While the sum total of my sexual past consisted of those few frenzied, groping encounters with

Audrey Lou Hawley where I'd been left aching and gasping for breath, he had plumbed the depths of depravity; broken all the commandments with whores and perverts and Chinese coolies, and (give or take the fact that he did not have a permanent residence and that he wore a leather bombardier jacket on a hot September day), come up none the worse for wear,

"You got money, I can get you anything you want in this town," he went on.

"How'd you like to wear a hundred dollar suit? How'd you like to eat snails right out of the shell? How'd you like a manicure?"

"I don't think I'd cotton much to snails."

"You got enough money you learn to like them. Everybody with money eats snails. They're called S-Cargo, on account of if you don't eat them in twenty-four hours after they're unloaded from the boat they turn on you; one swallow and your tongue swells up the size of a medicine ball and strangles you to death. That's what the S is for, strangulation."

"Why would anybody want to spend good money to get strangled?"

"People who got money don't think about things like that."

"Well I ain't gonna never have that kind of money," I huffed.

"You never know, you might already. How much you got?"

"A few hundred, but that's going to buy me a room someplace until I can hook up with my daddy."

"That sure ain't gonna buy you no S-Cargoes, not many manicures either if you want the plain facts of it. Truth is, if you don't have real dough in this city you ain't gonna make it without a scam, and from the looks of you, you wouldn't know how to go about getting one."

"I'll be okay. "

His eyes drifted to the top of a wedge-shaped building in the middle of the square. "That Mantle's gonna be a good one. What's he, seventeen - eighteen? Already he's making more'n we're gonna see in our lifetimes."

I followed his gaze upward to where the latest news bulletins were being broadcast on a revolving ribbon of electric lights: YANKEES BEAT CLEVELAND INDIANS 8 - 2..... MANTLE HITS TWO MORE

ROUND - TRIPPERS. I watched fascinated as the message wrapped itself around the corner of the building and was instantly replaced by another, then another: U.S. EXPLODES WORLD'S FIRST H-BOMB AT ENIWETOK ATOLL..... KOREAN CEASE-FIRE STABILIZED AT 38TH PARALLEL.. TRUCE TALKS BEGIN IN KAESONG...

"Ain't that a pisser, you don't even need a TV to find out what's happening in the world if you live around here. Just stick your head out the window..."

When I looked he was gone. I couldn't've had my eyes off him for more than a second or two, and he was gone; not just running away, not in the middle of the street dodging traffic, not tearing through the crowd, but gone, like the earth had opened up and swallowed him whole, along with my suitcase. My first instinct was to grab someone and ask if they had seen him run, but by that time those who might have witnessed his leaving were halfway up the block and the sidewalks had spit up a whole new batch of passers-by. I could only stand there in their midst, disillusioned and shorn of my possessions, and feeling like that old schemer God (who if he existed at all was still on my shit-list) had seen through my self-serving good deed and was having the last laugh after all.

Seven

I was alone in New York City with only the clothes in my back, which, lucky for me, contained my wallet and all that was left of my money. As for the suitcase and its contents, I realized it was not much of a loss after I'd had a few minutes to cool down and think on it; a few shirts, an old pair of dungarees, some socks darned so often that the toes were bunched up like somebody'd sewed pebbles into them, an extra pair of worn-at-the-heel clodhoppers, size twelve, and a half-a-dozen comic books, which to my way of thinking was the only real loss. The clothes were all too big for that slick, bombardier jacket-wearing robber, and he couldn't even sell them in the shape they were in. Like as not he'd toss the lot when he opened the suitcase and saw what all his trouble had got him, but it burned me knowing he might get some enjoyment from the comic books. Buck Rogers was Buck Rogers, Eula or Times Square.

There was a sidewalk stand a block east, fitted out with a steam cooker, ice cabinet and a striped blue and yellow umbrella where wieners on a roll with sauerkraut and mustard were fifteen cents apiece, two for a quarter. Being that I was particularly hungry, not having eaten since the bus had stopped somewhere in New Jersey early that morning, I ate four, drank two bottles of Nehi Orange soda, and received ten cents change from the dollar bill I had given the proprietor of the stand.

"Last time I seen somebody eat that many dogs was over in Anzio when the Red Cross truck came through after my outfit hadn't eaten in four days," he said, grinning.

"Feels near that long since I ate anything." I pocketed the dime and licked the mustard from my fingers. "Can you tell me how far I am from the Radio City Music Hall?"

"Right around the corner." He motioned with a toss of his head, "but the matinee's already over and you're about three hours away from the evening show."

"I'm not fixing to go to the show. You reckon they'd let me in the place looking like this?"

He eyed my outfit critically. "Don't see why not. I seen a lot worse than you walking in and out of that place. There's people come from all over the world to go there and you never know what they'll have on. Dressed as queer as you'd ever wanta see, some of 'em. I seen guys in towels and bathrobes going in there; seen guys with zoot-suits and guys wearing nothing but loincloths. I seen a Ubangi go in there once naked as the day he was born."

"That must've been something to see."

"You live here long enough you see everything there is to see. All you gotta do is walk three blocks from here in any direction and you'll see every manner of freak and weirdo that there ever was on this planet. New York's got 'em all. If you don't believe nothing else you can believe that."

Judging by what I'd seen so far it made sense. "Well thank you for the wieners but I best be going," I told him.

"You mind my words; three blocks in any direction..." his voice carried down the street behind me as I rounded the corner onto Sixth avenue and found myself face-to-face with a giant glass and steel monument towering above the sidewalk, inscribed with the spine-tingling designation, RADIO CITY MUSIC HALL. Beneath it, a marquee announced in large black-and-white block letters that performances of the feature presentation, THE AFRICAN QUEEN, starring Humphrey Bogart and Katherine Hepburn, would be shown Monday thru Friday at 11:35 A.M. and 6:35 P.M., as well as Selected Shorts, Newsreels, and two performances daily of the FABULOUS RADIO CITY ROCKETTES. A few dozen people stood in an orderly line under the overhang, moving slowly toward the theater entrance where a richly uniformed attendant, looking much like a palace guard, collected tickets as they passed.

"Is this for the movie?" I asked a woman at the end of the line.

"For the tour," she answered over her shoulder.

"What tour is that?"

"They take you all around the inside, tell you how the place was built and stuff like that."

"Do you think they'd mind if I just went in and looked around for somebody without buying a ticket?"

"Whatta you think?"

"How much for a ticket?"

"Two dollars if you're staying for the show."

"How about just for the tour?"

She looked me up and down. "Fifty cents unless you can prove you're under sixteen, then it's a quarter."

I bought a ticket for a half-dollar, figuring there was no way they'd believe I was a week short of my sixteenth birthday. I had no proof, no papers of any kind that said I was even alive, let alone almost sixteen. The thought crossed my mind as I stood at the end of that ever-shortening line that if I dropped dead on the spot I would be no more identifiable to the folks who found my body than a stray hound, a salamander dried and flattened by the sun. My identity was back on the west Texas plain, carved in yucca and mesquite, as alien to the scripts and tokens of the city as a body could be, yet I was as close to my roots as I had been since before I could remember. Harry Bailey would attest to my birth and existence, he would vow that I was near sixteen years old, and that I'd grown like a weed since the last time he'd seen me. I would recognize him in a minute, even though he was an ever-changing portrait in my mind. He would look like me, but older; with black, black hair that might be touched with gray by now. He would have Comanche cheekbones and serious, deep-set blue eyes the color of a robin's egg (my mother had always pictured them to me), and an easy mouth that curled up in a drawl when he spoke; and on his forearm a tattoo of a spider he'd got put on in prison. (She'd said it was attractive to her at first but later on she'd come to see it as an abomination.) Like as not he would have shucked off country ways by now, being that he had been in Europe and New York City and must have picked up the best of what they both had to offer. Tall and lanky and prairie-raised with that stealthy Indian glide of his, (she'd said he could sneak up on a nervous jackrabbit and catch it by the ears with a sweep of his hand), he might look a mite out of place in hundred dollar suits and manicures, but he surely had a scam by now, and he surely must have known how to use it.

Inside the lobby, those who had gone before me were standing in a semicircle around the tour guide, a young girl who wore a starched white shirt and pants just like a man that ran straight down to the shiniest pair of black shoes I had ever seen. The uniform hat she wore was tilted back on her head, revealing a profusion of orange hair curling underneath the gold-ornamented visor and wide, freckled cheeks that puckered into dimples when she smiled. "Welcome to Radio City Music Hall, the world's largest indoor theater," she began. "If you'll all just follow me and stay in line we'll begin the tour."

Like the others, I trotted behind her, less interested, I must admit, in her effervescent descriptions of the huge Lalique glass chandeliers hanging in the mirrored grand foyer, the majestic grand staircase, or huge curved mural overhanging the mirrored lounge, than I was in watching her. Inside the theater the enormous stage lit her face in opaque flashes of light and shadow, changing its soft, mysterious contours in the semidarkness as she explained the technical and architectural marvels of the music hall: the great arched proscenium, the largest pipe organ ever made, a stage half the size of a football field with room to spare, six-thousand seats in its orchestra and three balconies. It was plain that the crowd was impressed. As for me, I spent most of the tour trying not to appear like too much of a hayseed. (Mama pointed out I could become bug-eyed and slack-jawed when I was overwhelmed, and I surely was that.) I hung back in the line as we exited the orchestra and walked through the grand foyer to the front, surrounded by silver, glass and richly ornamented carpet (a leap of centuries sweeping me along) reflected in the mirrored walls, (my gait erect but hesitant), and chalked in her laughing eyes.

She smiled a genuine-looking smile as she ushered everyone out the massive front door. "I hope you've all enjoyed this tour of Radio City's Music Hall. It's been my pleasure to be your guide today and I hope I'll see many of you again at this evening's showing of 'The African Queen,' starring Humphrey Bogart and Katherine Hepburn."

I had worked myself to the back of the line. "This is sure some place," I said when I got to where she was standing. "You must really love it, working in a place like this."

She seemed surprised at my remark. "It's a good job," she conceded.

"I'm Chance Bailey and I'm looking for my daddy, Harry Bailey."

"Well I hope you find him." She nudged me toward the door.

"I expect I'll find him here. He works here too."

"In the Music Hall?"

"That's right. Harry Bailey. He probably looks like me only older."

"I'm sorry, I don't know anyone here by that name."

"Got a tattoo of a spider on his arm, hard to miss."

She shook her head. "I've only been here a little more than a week. What kind of work does he do?"

"I can't say for sure. He does a lot of things."

"Is he part of the show?"

"Maybe if I could stay for a bit and just look around."

"I'm sorry, I'm not allowed to let people walk around unescorted."

"Well then maybe you could come with me."

She glanced at her wristwatch. "I'd like to help you, but I have less than an hour to eat and be back here for the evening show."

"You do another tour then?"

"No, I'm an usherette at night." She urged me toward the door with her eyes. "I don't mean to be rude, but I'm sure you have someplace to go too."

"Not really. I just got into town and this was the first place I came. I'll have to hook up with Harry Bailey before I have someplace to go."

"Well if you come back for the evening show you might find him then." Deftly she turned me out onto the sidewalk and slammed the door shut behind us.

"Will they let me go behind the stage to look for him?"

"You can try, but if I were you I'd wait at the stage door around the corner and ask anyone going in or out."

I followed her down the sidewalk. "Where are you going to eat?"

"What's that to you?"

"I could do with a bite. Maybe we could eat together."

"How old are you?"

"That's for me to know and you to find out."

She burst out laughing. "Well for your information I'm eating at the Automat, and I'll be meeting some friends there."

"Well good for you. Only hicks eat at the Automat anyway."

"I guess that makes me a hick. Good luck finding your daddy." She hurried off down the street.

I watched her disappear in the press of moving bodies, then went around the corner and knocked on the stage door several times but got no response.

"Won't be nobody there for a while," a voice behind me yelled over the noise of traffic. "They're all out to dinner."

He was standing in an open spot at the curb, leaning on a contraption that looked like a garbage pail on wheels; a colored man whose hair had gone stark white and wreathed his head like a sheep's-wool cap. "You know what time they'll get back?" I asked him.

"That's hard to say. They're show folks, you know."

"You don't know if one of them is named Harry Bailey, do you?"

He thought on it. "Can't say I do. What you want him for?"

"I've got my reasons." What I knew for sure was that it was not a good idea to divulge too much to a colored man. "I guess I'll just have to wait here until somebody gets back."

"Suit yourself." He took a wooden broom from the can and pushed it along the gutter unenthusiastically. I sat on a brass standpipe near the door and rested my back against the building, watching him push the broom along a few inches at a time before he scooped the soot and residue he had collected in a dustpan and deposited it in the can, seemingly indifferent to the crush of bumper-to-bumper automobiles only a few inches behind him, screeching brakes, honking horns, filling the air with exhaust so thick and noxious it caused my eyes to tear.

The smell was near as bad as the ground-up mandrake root and spearmint Mama sewed inside an assa-fidity bag that we could wear around our necks at night to mask the smells of the cesspool and the outhouse, but the stink of the herbs was near as bad as the stink of the outhouse, and it didn't let up when the wind died down. On hot nights when it got so bad I couldn't breathe, I'd go out back and sit against the split-rail fence, under the apple trees which (even though there was no sun) seemed to afford me a measure of relief from the heat. There in the darkness I would gather rotten apples from the ground and squeeze them in my hands like a cider press until their juice ran through my fingers down over my lap and legs where they joined with my dripping sweat and seeped into the dry earth. Then I took the pulp and rubbed it on my face and neck and down my chest to between my legs and rub it there too, and like as not, I would drop off in restless apple-scented sleep then.

LeMoult

Eight

"Wanta tell me what you're doing here?"

I felt his nightstick on my shoulder and rubbed my eyes looking for the day but all I saw was dark and pinpoint lights moving; red-green-yellow.

"You planning on setting up housekeeping here?"

"I must've fell asleep."

"Well you just better fall asleep someplace else or I'll run you in."

I pulled myself to my feet and stretched above him, catching the new city in all directions with a flicker of my eyeballs, putting it together. "I was waiting here for my daddy, Harry Bailey, and I must've dropped off."

"You got someplace to go now?"

"Well I reckon I should wait here until I find him. I'll be going home with him when he shows up."

"How long you been here?"

"I dunno, since sometime this afternoon. I took the tour at the Radio City Music Hall and the guide told me to come around here and wait for him, so I did, and then a colored man told me they were all gone but they were coming back for the evening show so I sat down to wait and I must've fell asleep and missed them."

He glanced at his wristwatch. "The last show ended two hours ago. If your old man was here he's long gone now. You got a place to go?"

"Reckon not."

"Well you can't stay here. We got laws against vagrancy in this city. You got enough for a flop?"

"A flop?"

"If you got no place to flop I'm gonna have to run you in."

"Where do I find one?"

"The closest I know is over on Ninth Avenue and Forty-fifth. It'll cost you fifty cents for a bed though."

"I've got fifty cents. I've got near two hundred dollars," I told him.

"Well in that case you can afford better. If I was you I'd walk over to the Soldiers and Sailors, straight over three blocks on Third Avenue and down three more, under the El."

"I ain't no soldier or sailor."

"You don't need to be. That's what they call it on a account of so many soldiers and sailors stayed there during the war. What it is, is just the YMCA. You can get a room there by the week or the month if you've got enough."

"I won't need one for that long. I'll probably hook up with Harry Bailey sometime tomorrow."

"Not if you're expecting to find him here, you won't. Tomorrow's Labor Day, the Music Hall's closed."

"You reckon they'll give me one for just a night or two?"

"You'll have to find that out for yourself, and you'd better do it quick. I see you when I come by here again and you'll be spending your night in the holding pen. You clear about that?"

"Yessir—three blocks over, the Soldiers and Sailors."

"And three blocks down, under the El."

Supported by a giant web of steel pillars and beams, the elevated train rumbled above me as I made my way downtown on Third Avenue, its roar throbbing in my ears like thunder on the roof long after it had passed overhead. Far away, it filled the sky with lightning and sucked out all the air, and I held my breath waiting for the thunder until my lungs about burst; they about burst, but there was no air to breathe there. Up till that time I had hardly even seen a train outside of pictures, much less one screaming across the sky like all the mustangs in west Texas gone wild on henbane. (I had once driven up to Lubbock with my Uncle Mal to pick up a tractor axle at the railroad depot, but the trains were idle in the freight yard and not a one of them moved during the time we were there, so I cannot count that as having really seen a train.)

The Soldiers and Sailors was a red cement building of four stories that hung back under the pillars between a saloon and a locksmith, the windowpanes in its double front doors covered with cardboard so nobody could see through. The doors opened to a large vestibule containing several sofas and chairs which while worn seemed comfortable and inviting. Like the street, the air inside was hot and dusty, metallic smelling with a hint of cooking, moved around some by a table fan wheezing on the front desk. Behind the desk a man was sprawled in a chair, sound asleep and snoring up a storm. I stood for a moment watching him, hoping he might wake on his own without my having to rouse him, but he continued snoring, his unsupported upper lip vibrating with every noisy breath, his veined, spongy nose and shaggy eyebrows twitching in a dream.

"Excuse me."

He shuddered, brushed an imaginary fly from his face, and went back to sleep.

"*Excuse me!*"

He woke with a jolt. "What the hell do you want?"

"I was fixing to get a flop."

"A flop?"

"Just for a night or two."

His eyes turned cruel. "Good God, what are you saying to me?"

"I reckon I'm saying I need a flop. You do work here, don't you?"

He stood with effort and glared at me across the desk. "If it would not be too much trouble, would you mind stating your needs in a simple declarative sentence, limiting yourself to as little of that annoying regional patois as you possibly can."

It took me back. "I guess I'm saying I need a bed for tonight, maybe tomorrow too."

"Excellent. The boy can make himself understood in something that approaches the English language." He opened a large leather-bound volume on the desk and studied it intently. "Yes, it seems we have a vacancy, but rooms are rented only by the week or month."

"I expect I'll be hooking up with my daddy day after tomorrow so I'll only need it for a night or two."

"Your daddy..." He shook his head hopelessly. "Am I to assume that this self-same daddy will be footing the bill for your stay in this establishment?"

"I got money if that's what you mean." I took my wallet from my pocket and opened it so he could see the bills inside. "Near two hundred dollars."

I saw his Adam's-apple jiggle. "In that case I suppose we can make an exception. Rooms are fifteen dollars for a week so I can let you have one for three dollars a night, as long as you wish to stay."

I ran the numbers in my head. "That would come out to twenty-one dollars a week, not fifteen."

He slammed the book shut. "I won't argue the point with you, young man. If you want to rent on a daily basis the cost will be three dollars a night, payment in advance. Take it or leave it."

"I reckon I've got no choice but to take it. Do you serve food here?"

"God no, this is the YMCA; and there'll be no cooking in your room either."

"I thought I smelled food when I came in here."

His nose twitched slightly. "That nauseating odor seeps through the walls from the bar next door—greasy hamburgers and French fries mostly, although they do occasionally cook a fairly palatable chicken."

"Sounds good to me. I ain't eaten nothing for hours."

He eyed his wristwatch. "Unfortunately they closed the kitchen a half-hour ago."

"Anyplace else around here I could get a bite before I turn in?"

"There's the Automat but that's quite a distance from here."

"Only hicks eat there," I said haughtily.

He laughed. "Well there may just be hope for you yet. There's a Salvation Army mission just down the street."

"What's a salvation army mission?"

"Well it's not exactly gourmet fare, and you do have to put up with some dreadful pontificating but they do have coffee and doughnuts and best of all it's free."

"Howcum they give away free food?"

"It's to entice you to stay and pick up the banner. They can be very persuasive, especially to the young and uninitiated as you seem to be. One day you're living your life, minding your own business, and the next day you're dressed up like a fusilier, beating a tambourine for Jesus on some street corner."

"Reckon I'll just turn in for the night then. I'm not exactly what you'd call on good terms with Jesus."

He smiled. "I had a feeling there was more to you than meets the eye. Go through that door in back and take the stairs to the fourth floor. You'll find there's more of a breeze up there."

"Do I get a key, a room number?"

"Take any room you want, they're all vacant and unlocked. The bathroom's at the end of the hall. Don't try to flush, the plumbing's been on the fritz for a week."

"I'm the only one here?"

"Jesus must be smiling on you despite your contempt. Just make sure to put that wallet under your mattress when you go to bed."

I went upstairs to the fourth floor and examined all the rooms along the hallway, settling on one in the front that seemed a little less dingy than the rest, although I would have been hard put to explain why, and as far away as I could get from the clogged toilet. The room was square and small and stuffy, with a single bed covered only with a yellow-stained sheet, a wooden chest of drawers with a circular mirror set on top, a canvas shoe bag hanging from the wall, and a shut-tight window smeared with soot and grease that faced out onto the elevated train. Heat and moisture had sealed the window shut tight, and it was only after a considerable amount of tugging that I was able to jar it open, allowing a hot, pungent breeze to drift in from the outside. Then I got undressed, down to my bare skin glistening with sweat and smelling like I needed a bath, which I plainly did.

I will find someplace to take a bath, maybe buy some new clothes so I'll look less like a country bumpkin when I see him. Naturally we'll shake hands instead of kiss, although what I miss most is the smell of shaving soap on his face when he holds me close to him.

I removed the wallet from my pants pocket and placed it under the mattress, and bolted the door from the inside, testing it several times with all my strength before I turned off the light and plopped onto the bed. Lying there, I could hear those steel pillars creaking and groaning outside my window, readying their old bones for another assault from the elevated train rumbling in the distance. When it passed it pushed the air in front of it hot through my open window, its wheels clattering on the tracks like Chinese firecrackers jumping on the ground—*take-it-to-me, take-it-to-me*, they clattered loud as hell, smelling like iron ingots rusting and the toilet clogged and my own body sweating the dark.

Sitting reverently on the toilet by his side I watch him sharpen his razor, stroking the blade deliberately back and forth until the hard edge glistens and the steel whistles on the leather strop. Then he works the soap up into a foam with a beaver-hair brush and puts it on his face, starting up at his temple and down to his neck, rubbing it in with the brush as he goes along, making it lather out in swirls and puckers like cold whipped cream, and he skews his face sideways and takes away a little lather from his sideburn with his finger and smears it on my nose.

Nine

"It's Shimmelman - three Ms, one N," the man who'd checked me in stressed when I went downstairs the following morning. "It's German Jewish. I don't suppose you have any Jews where you come from."

"Can't say that we do and I can't say that we don't either. Folks stay pretty much to themselves."

"Have you ever met a Jew before?"

"If I did he didn't own up to being one."

Shimmelman had volunteered to take me out to breakfast, or rather take me to the restaurant where I would pay for both of us. The place was called the Exchange Buffet, or the E and B, he'd told me; which should have stood for Eat 'em and Beat 'em, because they operated on the honor system and you could get away with ordering an entire five course meal and paying the price for a bowl of Corn Flakes, or the like.

"Howcum they let you work in a YMCA if you're a Jew?" I asked him as we slid our trays along a tubular metal shelf, ladling eggs, melon, pancakes, sausages, and anything else we could pile on our plates from steaming metal skillets set side-by-side under a glass canopy.

"The job requirements call for someone who is incredibly poor but who is also not incredibly stupid; a difficult admixture to find in a city where the streets are paved with gold and even the most simpleminded fool can end up rich as Croesus."

He led me to an unoccupied table and sat across from me.

"So if you're so smart how'd you get so poor?"

"Getting poor is no great accomplishment for an artist. Sadly, the lot of the artist is to live as a vagabond."

"You're an artist?"

"A very bad one, yes."

"If you're so bad why don't you try something else?" I asked him through a mouthful of scrambled eggs.

"I did, I tried teaching, but I was only able to teach bad art, and if there is one thing the world does not need it's more bad artists." He dug a morsel of sausage from his molar with a pinkie nail.

"Look around you, boy; everyone in this place has distinguished themselves by being bad at something. They're bad poets, bad philosophers, bad scientists, basically they're bad at living. They wouldn't be reduced to cadging cheap meals at the E and B if they weren't abject failures."

I looked around at the scattered crowd; older folks mostly, quietly eating alone. I realized for the first time that despite the size of the cafeteria and the number of customers at its tables, there was hardly any sound above the tinkle of flatware and glasses, the scrape of shoes moving along the food line. "Why isn't anybody talking?" I asked.

"Because they're afraid of what they might hear. Conversation is a mirror. Too much of it exposes us for what we are, and what we wish we could have been. They're best left with their silence. Silence is their truest companion."

There had been times when I'd wanted to get away by myself; when all that made sense was the sound of the wind, and the feel of raindrops trickling down my cheeks; but they were not silent times. I would lie in the tall grass and listen to the prairie noises, sometimes even mimicking the songs of grasshoppers, the beating of grouse wings, the rustle of grasses. I would even talk to her and tell her that she deserved better than to be a cook and housekeeper, better than to be a willing vessel for that pinched, self-righteous old phony, better than chamber pots and chipped fingernails and the sharp organic farm smells that crept into her clothing and stayed no matter how many sachet pellets she put between them in the drawers. But I was talking to myself, and the wind teeming with life (unlike the wind in the E and B which was leaden with food smells and the knell of silverware).

Clusters of small violets were scraped away on the washboard and left their faded imprint on her dresses, and she washed herself less in

*places where people could not see, and she put her hair up in the back
with a nacre and silver-edge comb. And the stretch went out of her life.*

She could be here, hunched over a table by herself wearing a dark
wool dress buttoned up in front to a lace collar stained at the edges, the
hair pulled up in disarray without a comb (possibly sold for food); and the
nails she buffed so diligently yellow and dirty.

"You lookin' at something, kid?"

I averted my stare.

"You heard me, snot-nose; you lookin' at something?"

Shimmelman winced. "Now you've done it. We'll never be rid of her
now."

"You know her?"

"She's Aida, Queen of the Atlantic City Boardwalk."

"But she's an old lady," I whispered.

"Don't tell her that." He put a forefinger to his temple and rotated it.

"I see you talking about me, Shimmelman!"

"Finish your pitiful meal, harridan!"

"What are you doing now, you old fart; training a whole new generation of assholes?"

Shimmelman bent over his plate and continued eating. "Pretend you
don't hear her," he said between mouthfuls. "The next thing you know
she'll be over here telling us how she came within a hair's breadth of
becoming Miss America."

"Is it true?"

"Does it matter?"

"Sure it matters."

He wiped the egg yolk from his plate with an edge of toast and
plopped it in his mouth. "Why?"

"Because it's the truth."

"It's her truth. Would it matter to you if it were a lie?"

I thought some. "That's a hard question."

"Life is made up of hard questions. Life is made up of lies. It's a bed of pain, a vale of tears, and it's too fucking short."

"So you're saying she was never almost Miss America."

"I'm not saying that at all. What I'm trying to get through that melon you call a head is that it doesn't matter. It doesn't matter whether Aida was ever Miss America, it doesn't matter whether she played volleyball with Albert Einstein or danced the fandango with the king of the Hottentots or poisoned an entire tribe of stone age aborigines. That is her truth, so it's all that matters."

"Is she crazy?"

"I expect the psychoanalysts would say so, but psychoanalysts are the scourge of the twentieth century, as malignant a bunch as sucking lice. They're so myopically intent on categorizing people that they miss the point entirely. We are what we pretend to be, no more no less. Reality is the hobgoblin of dolts and incompetents. The only sane response to it is to flee."

Aida had returned to her meal, apparently no longer interested in what we had to say.

"I have a friend back home who thinks that everybody sees the world different, only they call it the same thing. He calls it a solipsism."

"A solipsism. Your friend sounds a cut above the average country bumpkin."

"Joe Carl thinks a lot. He's got polio and scoliosis and he's chicken-breasted and freckles so bad he can't stand the sun for more than a few minutes."

Shimmelman nodded. "Infirmity often prompts great thought and achievement. Beethoven was stone deaf when he created some of the world's most stirring music. Toulouse-Lautrec was a cripple and a dwarf when he painted his greatest masterpieces."

"You think that's why you're a bad artist, because you don't have enough things wrong with you?"

The question seemed to surprise him. "I have a great many things wrong with me. Infirmity is not exclusively the province of the deaf and halt. I'm a bad artist simply because my ambitions outstrip my abilities. I paint alone, in anonymity and obscurity, searching for self-knowledge and my celestial underpinnings, so to speak, but I admit I am pitifully under-equipped for the task. I search for the beginnings of life, why we are the kind of beings we are, why everything happens the way it does."

"That's a pretty tall order."

"It is of course arrogance in extremis, which is why I shall remain forever unfulfilled, forever miserable. The kindest thing that could happen to me would be to be blown to smithereens in a worldwide atomic holocaust."

"You don't really mean that, do you?"

"Of course I mean it. I pray every day that the Russians will develop enough lift capacity to end our spiritual agony forever."

"You're not a Commie, are you?"

His eyes narrowed. "What if I was?"

"You're a Commie?"

"I didn't say that, did I?" His voice had assumed an exasperated tone. "I simply asked what difference it would make."

"I don't know. I never met a Commie before."

"Well rest assured you're not meeting one now. Frankly, I'd be rooting for anyone who could flatten this sorry planet once and for all. Can you point to one thing that wouldn't be improved in a glorious incineration?" He wiped the last of the egg from his plate and chewed the toast lustily. "Will you be finishing those pancakes, boy?"

"I don't think so. You want them?"

Shimmelman took a crumpled paper bag from his shirt and slid it across the table. "Put them in here, and anything else you're not going to finish."

"You going to eat them later?"

He shoveled the pancakes from my plate into the bag, along with a partially eaten slice of melon and a blob of applesauce. "They're not for me, you dolt; they're for Balenkin."

"Who's Balenkin?"

"He's the only one worthy of surviving the holocaust. If only one human being were to rise from the ashes and start civilization anew, I would want it to be Balenkin."

LeMoult

Ten

Outside of himself, Isaiah Balenkin was the only other permanent resident of the Soldiers and Sailors, Shimmelman told me on our way back from the E and B. He was a Nobel Laureate in literature, having been awarded the prize while he was a prisoner in the Siberian gulag where he had been sent by Stalin before the war for writing anti-Soviet propaganda. The propaganda he'd been imprisoned for writing was his great masterpiece, *Womb*, the story of a simple-minded blacksmith's apprentice who was impressed into the Czarist army during the First World War. It was not anti-socialist or anti-czarist, or anti-anything but war, according to Shimmelman. What it was, was a brilliant account of man's indomitable resilience and will to survive in the face of events too horrible to contemplate. Balenkin's hatred for war, not anti-socialism, was the real reason Stalin plunked him away to die in the frozen wastes of Siberia, Shimmelman maintained. If war was as stupid and senseless as Balenkin portrayed it, twenty million Russians would have been slaughtered for nothing on Stalin's watch.

I confess that I did not understand most of what Shimmelman told me. I had never heard of Isaiah Balenkin, I knew little to nothing of the First World War, and (I am now ashamed to admit) I had not up 'till that time read a book of any kind, much less a Nobel Prize winner. There was not a single library or bookstore back in Eula, and the few books that were available belonged to the school where they were read in classrooms and doled out to a small number of students at a time for book reports and such. I had on occasion been given copies of *Treasure Island*, by Robert Louis Stevenson, and *Huckleberry Finn*, by Mark Twain, which I did not read. (Both were available in Classics Illustrated comic books which, while not as gripping as Buck Rogers, had lively pictures and could be read in about fifteen minutes). But outside of school, reading was not high on the totem pole of activities back in Eula. The Reverend Harley Brown had even gone so far as to say that reading books only muddied up the waters; that the only book worth reading was the scriptures, and I must say I did not take issue with that.

Balenkin had escaped the gulag and walked near a thousand miles on foot, Shimmelman recounted. Traveling only at night in sub-zero temperatures he had braved snow and ice and freezing wind until he stumbled into a camp of Finnish loggers; a free man, a Nobel Prize winner, with nary the wits of a sparrow left about him.

Everything he had ever written, everything that had happened to him in the gulag and on his solitary flight to freedom, everything that Shimmelman said was the last, best hope for mankind was locked up inside his Nobel Laureate's brain, or scattered like snowflakes in the chill Siberian sky. Now he lived on handouts and the sufferance of individuals who were not worthy to shine his shoes (Shimmelman readily included himself in that category). Scraps of leftover food and spare coins were to be the final dividend of a man who had etched the human condition as nobody before or after.

"What have you brought me?" the bony old man in the bed asked.

Shimmelman tore the paper bag open and placed it on the author's lap. "We have some pancakes, a little applesauce..."

"Blini!" Balenkin cackled with delight. "I don't suppose you have any caviar to go with it?"

"They weren't serving caviar at the E and B today. There's some melon there."

"My mother served them that way on Shabbat, you know. Sometimes she would put the melon balls on top of them." He dipped a bony finger into the applesauce and put it to his lips. "Of course we were very poor then, but she would always wear her best dress, a bit tattered but always clean, and she would rub her skin with the peels of lemons."

Shimmelman took a hard roll from his pocket. "I'm sorry, but the butter was too melted in the heat to take with me."

Isaiah Balenkin stared at the roll, then at me. "Is that you, Sergei?"

"I'm Chance Bailey, sir."

"Yes you are. I should have remembered you from Vilyuisk."

"I'm from Eula, Texas, sir."

"Yes, a charming village; the crowded streets, the merchants, the fishmongers, the bloated bourgeoisie in their black silk caftans and broad-brimmed beaver hats, their plump wives strutting in astrakhan coats..." He smeared applesauce on one of the pancakes and rolled it in a tube. "You've come a long way, all the way from Vilyuisk. Do the housewives still put vases of pussy willows on the stoop on *erev* Shabbat?"

"I don't think they do that in Eula where I come from, no sir."

"I remember them so well, and the antimacassars draped over the backs of all the chairs, stained brown from the pomade my Grandfather used in his hair. He was a good man but a vain man nonetheless, but then you'd know that better than anyone, wouldn't you, Sergei? Do you remember the time he had real pearl buttons sewed on his tunic by Krik the tailor? Everyone in the shtetl thought he'd found the pot of gold at the end of the rainbow."

I shot a nervous sidelong glance at Shimmelman. "I think you might have me mixed up with somebody else, sir."

"Hah, denying who you are, eh?" He inserted the pancake tube between a ridge of pale pink gums and began chewing. "There's no point in that now, not after she caught you red-handed looking at the pictures of nymphs and satyrs she keeps locked up in her trunk. What she's doing with pictures of naked men and women is beyond me, such a pious person; but that's the way things are these days, eh? Everyone's got secrets and there's always somebody willing to inform for a few kopecks or a blind eye from the authorities. Damn old man, calling attention to us all with those pearl buttons of his. The village will probably be swarming with Cossacks before sundown." His Adam's apple convulsed as he swallowed the mouthful, almost jumping through the brittle, transparent skin of his throat.

"Oh what a life we're forced to live here!"

Shimmelman led me out of the old man's room and down the hall. "Some days he's as lucid as you or me. He can't remember anything but stories from his childhood, but he knows where he is and can still carry on a fairly stimulating conversation."

"Does he have to stay in that bed?"

"It's better that he does. When he gets like this he tends to roam. That's where I first found him a year ago, wandering aimlessly through Bryant Park in the dead of winter, asking strangers for a few pennies for bread. Ironic, don't you think? There he was only a few feet from the New York Public Library where his greatest works are enshrined, and he was staggering around in the snow, begging for food."

"I'd think a Nobel Prize winner would deserve better than that."

"You would think so, wouldn't you? I made some inquiries at the highest levels but the official government line was that they'd never heard of Isaiah Balenkin." He raised an eyebrow. "Can you imagine? The greatest writer of the twentieth century and they'd never heard of him! If you want my take on it, I think they got wind that he'd escaped from the gulag and spirited him over here to embarrass Stalin, but when they got him here they realized he could only embarrass them, so they simply put him out on the streets like a common hobo."

He stopped and unlocked a door at the end of the hall. "This is my room. You're welcome to come in for a short libation. It's not Buckingham Palace but I call it home."

Shimmelman flicked a light switch on the wall and the room lit up with a soft, yellow glow, spare but comfortable. Inside was a bed, neatly made, a sofa, stuffed and bursting at the seams from overuse, a desk and typewriter, and at the far end the wall was covered with a painting of what appeared to be the heavens; stars, planets, galaxies recreated in slashes and swirls of fiery color. "Please sit." He indicated a straight-back wooden chair near the bed. "You don't by any chance play chess?"

"Sorry. I play a decent game of checkers though."

"Pity. There are times when Balenkin plays a brilliant game, then there are others when it just seems to upset him." He took a bottle and two glasses from a cabinet on the wall, wiped the glasses with his handkerchief and placed them on the nightstand. "This is Metaxa, a very potent Greek concoction I developed a taste for during the war." He sat on the bed and poured a little from the bottle into each glass.

"Did you fight in the war?"

"God no, I can assure you that if I'd been a soldier I would have been very bad at that too." He raised his glass and took a swig of the amber liquid inside. I did the same and it about took my head off.

"What'd you say this stuff was?" I choked.

"Metaxa. It grows on you." He drained his glass and poured himself another.

"Did you paint that on the wall?"

"Certainly I painted it, or I should say I am painting it. It's a work in progress. I imagine it will go on as long as I have the strength to hold a brush."

"It's the universe, isn't it?"

"Indeed, everything we know about it and a little bit more I've figured out for myself. I add some whenever I come across anything new but it looks like I'll run out of wall before it's done." Shimmelman stood and eyed the mural moodily. "The answers are all out there, you know. Everything we ever need to know is out there in the stars. We're nothing more than microbes crawling around on this speck in space, searching for solutions in our own anguished ignorance."

"Is it a good painting?"

"It's a wretched painting. I can hardly bear to look at it without breaking into tears."

"So why do you do it?"

"How can I not do it? It's my life's work."

"But if it makes you sad..."

Shimmelman opened a drawer in the nightstand and removed a thick, well-worn volume. "This is *Womb*," he said reverently. "There is not a page of it that is not stained with my tears, and yet a day does not go by without my reading portions of it. It devastates me, drives me to the depths of despair. I cannot read even a short passage without realizing anew the futility of life and the corruption of the human condition."

I sipped the Metaxa carefully. "Wouldn't you be happier if you just didn't read it at all—if you didn't paint at all?"

"We are driven to fulfill our destinies," he said somberly. "You may not realize it but even out there in the wilderness where you come from there are men living out the roles that have been planned for them since the beginning of time. They are as powerless to deny them as I am to deny my misery." He handed me the book. "Read this. If nothing else it will teach you that."

"I couldn't take your book," I objected, feeling that the last thing I needed at that time was a good dose of misery. "It means too much to you."

"Hopefully it will come to mean as much to you. Hopefully it will make you realize that the answers are inside of you, hidden in the depths of your untutored mind."

"But I thought you said the answers were in the stars. How can they be in my mind and in the stars at the same time?"

Shimmelman nodded. A faint smile appeared at the corners of his mouth. "You're beginning to understand already. The more you learn about both of them, the more they begin to look like the same thing."

I carried *Womb* back to my room and put it carefully in a drawer, gripped with Shimmelman's sense of reverence but not quite knowing why. I would read it someday, I vowed; after I'd found my daddy and settled down to something like a normal life. Up till now, it had been anything but normal, at least for me. I had been in New York City less than twenty-four hours and I had already met my first Jew and my first artist (bad or not). I'd met a Miss America who'd danced the fandango with the King of the Hottentots. Whether or not this had actually happened was still unclear but even thinking about it was a cosmic leap from anyplace I'd been before. I'd met a Nobel Prize-winning author who'd been imprisoned in a gulag (I made a note to check whether he'd got a spider tattooed on his forearm like Harry Bailey). And although I did not even know her name, I'd met a red-haired usherette at the Radio City Music Hall and fallen desperately in love. If any one of these things had ever happened to me in Eula I would probably have spent the rest of my life setting and whittling under the wooden overhangs of Main Street, telling and re-telling the story; but all of this had happened to me in less than a day in New York City. I could only imagine the stories Harry Bailey had to tell, having lived here all these years.

The elevated train roared by, and the rattle of tracks became the beat of drums, the muted but unmistakable sound of horns coming from the street below. I worked the window open to where I could lean outside and saw that a crowd had gathered in the shadow of the pillars, cheering and applauding a ragged file of marchers in the middle of the avenue. LOCAL

941, I.L.G.W.U., their banner read, and behind them others carrying similar banners: STEAMFITTERS LOCAL 8, BROOKLYN N.Y., and BROTHERHOOD OF TEAMSTERS, reveled among prancing baton-twirlers and brightly uniformed musicians marching in precision. It was about all I could do to keep from falling out of the window. I found myself cheering along with the crowd as the marchers passed below, flabbergasted that a parade had picked my window to pass beneath, on top of everything else that had happened to me on that strange, wonderful day.

LeMoult

Eleven

The next day I called Eula from a pay phone in the lobby. Getting through took some time due to an overload on the party line but when the operator called me back Mama was waiting on the other end:

"Is that you, Chance?"

"It's me, Mama. I'm in New York City."

"Well you come home right this minute, hear?"

"I can't do that, Mama. I'm gonna stay with Harry Bailey."

There was a long silence. "Where did you find him?" She asked finally.

"We ain't exactly hooked up yet but I know where he is. I'm going over there as soon as I get off this phone."

"Where are you now?"

"At the Soldiers and Sailors. I met a lot of nice folks here, Mama. You'd really like them. You'd like everything about New York. There's artists and writers and parades right under your window in the morning; not like Eula where nothing ever happens. There's a restaurant called Eat 'em and Beat 'em where you eat anything you want and they'll take your word for it if you tell them all you had was a jellyroll. It's a whole lot better than that Automat everybody talks about. Only hicks eat at the Automat."

"I hope you're not keeping company with artists and writers," she cautioned.

"Only a bad artist, and Balenkin can't remember what he wrote anyway."

"Oh Lord amighty!"

"Did you find the money I left for you, Mama?"

"I did, and I am donating it to the church."

"What are you talking about, donating it to the church? That money was for you. Buy yourself some new dresses or dangly earrings or some fancy French perfume. If you're not going to use it yourself, give it to Uncle Mal to help pay off his note to the bank."

"You know I can't do that, Chance. That money was not come by rightfully and the only way to make it right is to dedicate it to God's service."

"You mean the Reverend Harley Brown's service, don't you? You donate that money to the church and you might just as well be putting it in his pocket. Besides, you got no way of knowing that money wasn't come by rightfully. You've just let that phony old preacher turn your head about it."

"I will not discuss the matter any more. If you need it I'll send you enough to take a bus back home where you belong. You've got no business in New York City with the likes of artists and writers. They'll turn you into one of those godless bohemians, and there's no place in the Kingdom for the likes of those."

"They're not the kind of people you think, Mama, and I'm not coming back to Eula."

"Well I'm sending the bus fare just the same. Maybe you'll have come to your senses by then. What's your address there?"

"It's the Soldiers and Sailors on Third Avenue."

"Is it a hotel?"

"It's a YMCA."

"Well at least you should be able to find some Christian folk there, if there are any in New York City."

"You want me to say hey to Harry Bailey when I see him?"

"I'll put the money in the post tomorrow. Take care of yourself in the meantime." She hung up.

Although I did not want the money she would send me, I did not want Harley Brown to have it even more. Walking across town to Radio City I decided I would tell Harry Bailey about the injustice of it all. The fact that he had phoned and asked that we both come to New York led me to believe that he still cared for her, and knowing what I did about his hair-trigger temper, I envisioned that he might just travel back there to Eula and give that sanctimonious son of a bitch what-all for his swindling. He would swagger into town just as the clock on the bank struck high noon, look that sorry street up and down and head directly for the Calvary Baptist Church and Grace Ministry where the Reverend would be hiding, quaking in his boots; and he would throw those wooden doors aside and face down Harley Brown right there in the tabernacle. He would not say a word (being the strong, silent type) but he would draw a long-barreled pistol on that whining phony and he would spin the chamber.

"You again? You just don't give up, do you?" It was that same colored street-sweeper, leaning on his broom in the gutter outside the Radio City stage door.

"What's it to you?"

"Ain't nothing to me, boy. You want to get yourself arrested it's no business of mine. Only you're too late to catch anybody going in there today. They're already inside and the stage door's locked."

"You out here every day?"

"Reckon so." He began pushing the broom lethargically.

"In this same spot?"

"Pretty much, yep."

"Ain't there any other gutter in New York that ever gets dirty?"

"Well I do expect that there is, but they're not no concern of mine, nossir. I gets paid by the Rockefellers, not the city. I been working for the Rockefeller family since the end of the war."

"You know the Rockefellers? "

"Know the whole family. Right fine folks too. Never had a minute's trouble with any of them."

"I reckon you would if they knew all you was doing was sweeping that same spot over and over every day."

"You gonna tell them, boy?"

"Ain't no business of mine," I shrugged.

"Reckon it ain't."

I watched him deposit a small quantity of soot and debris into the can. "Harry Bailey's got himself a tattoo of a spider on his forearm," I said.

"Now what makes you think I'd be interested in some man got hisself a tattoo?"

"Because that's how you can tell him; that and his blue eyes and Comanche cheekbones. He'd be better'n six foot tall too."

"What in the name of sweet Jesus are you talking about, boy?"

"Harry Bailey. I asked you yesterday if you seen him but I never told you what he looked like."

"Well now you told me and I still ain't seen him."

"There's a red-haired girl works inside as a usherette—you seen her?"

"Maybe I have and maybe I haven't. What you want her for?"

"Just want to talk is all."

He eyed me judiciously. "Well if she's here at all she's probably in the auditorium watching them rehearse. That's where she is every day when she ain't working."

I entered the Music Hall without incident, and after a moment to adjust my eyes to the dark I spotted her, sitting alone near the front of the vast, empty auditorium, staring intently up at the stage where dozens of dancers were being put through their paces by a lanky blond man dressed in a tight black outfit that clung to his body like a coat of paint.

"Come on girls. *Move it*! Five-six-seven-eight, turn-turn-kick-turn, kick-kick-kick-kick. Lift those flabby thighs! What is this anyway, a fucking hoedown? *Stop*!"

He stood looking at the panting chorines with utter disgust. "Take five, and maybe when you come back we could try doing it together!" He stormed off the stage.

I walked down the aisle and sat behind her. "Why's he being so mean to them?"

She turned and squinted at me in the darkness. "Oh, it's you. How did you get in here?"

"Walked in, same as yesterday."

"Well you're not supposed to be here."

"Who's gonna kick me out?"

She smiled. "Did you ever find your daddy?"

"Not yet, but I'll probably find him someplace here today. So how come those girls take all that guff from him?"

"Bertie's not really being mean to them. That's just his way of making them dance better."

"They looked pretty good to me. They'd probably dance a lot better if he just left them alone."

"He can't do that. He's the choreographer." She stood and headed for the aisle.

"Are they all finished?"

"They're taking five and so am I. I need a smoke."

I followed her up the aisle. "Can't you smoke in the theater?"

"You can, but I wouldn't want Bertie to see me smoking. He doesn't like his dancers to smoke. He says it cuts their wind."

We exited out into the smoking lounge where she lit a store-roll cigarette. "All the girls smoke, but not in front of Bertie. He knows they smoke, they know he knows, but everybody goes on with the deception."

"So why are you worried about it? You're an usherette, not a dancer."

"Who are you to say I'm not a dancer? Who are you to say anything at all to me? I don't even know who you are."

"I'm Chance Bailey, and I didn't mean nothing by it. It's just that you told me you were an usherette; you didn't say about being a dancer."

She took a deep drag on the cigarette and exhaled the smoke in an angry blue cloud. "Well for your information I am a dancer; a professional dancer if you must know. The other thing is just temporary until there's an opening on the Rockettes, then I'll be up there on the stage with the others."

I shrugged. "It don't look like anything I'd want to be doing if I was you, but to each his own, I reckon."

"Not want to be doing it?" She stared wide-eyed at me. "There isn't a dancer in New York who wouldn't positively kill for the chance to become a Rockette. Don't you read the papers? The Rockettes are the most famous dance troupe in the world. People come from all over to see them. Being a Rockette is the best job in show business."

"What's your name?" I asked her.

"You ask an awful lot of questions for someone I just met."

"Well I just got to New York City and I see how fast everything works here, so I reckon I better ask my questions early or I won't get a second chance."

"You sound like a country boy."

"Eula Texas -- nothing there but heat and lizards and a lot of folks wishing they wasn't."

"Are you old enough to be this far away from home on your own?"

"I'm nineteen," I lied.

She got a faraway look in her eyes. "I was nineteen when I first got here. That was almost six years ago. What dream brought you here?"

"I don't know that I have one. I'm here to meet up with my daddy, Harry Bailey, and we'll figure things out after that."

"Everybody has a dream. Sometimes they just don't know what it is."

"So what's yours?"

"To be Mona Chalfonte, the world-renowned *danseuse*."

"Mona, that's a pretty name."

"It's a *nom de theatre*. It's really Molly, Molly Cooney, but nothing very glamorous ever happened to anyone named Molly."

"I like Molly too."

She ground her cigarette out in a large metal container filled with sand. "I really have to get back inside. I memorize all the routines just in case somebody twists an ankle or something and they want me to fill in."

"Is Bertie your boyfriend?" I asked her as we walked back toward the auditorium.

"Don't be ridiculous. Bertie's gay. All the boy dancers are gay."

"I expect they would be, being that they've got the best job in show business and all."

She stood in the partially open doorway. "You really just said that, didn't you?"

"Reckon I did."

She smiled a smile that was all teeth and shook her head in a way that made her hair bounce on her shoulders, and turned so I could see her breasts taut against her sweater, and I knew she was laughing at me and I didn't care.

LeMoult

Twelve

It took a whole week for Mama's letter to get to the Soldier's and Sailors; a week that seemed to propel me from thrills to disappointments with hardly a space to breathe in-between. My disappointment came from the fact that I had not yet located Harry Bailey, and I was running out of places to look for him. What I'd learned was that he had worked briefly at the Music Hall the previous spring (three weeks to two months depending on who was doing the recalling); that he had been a stage carpenter and a good one, and that he'd disappeared after an unpleasant incident backstage. Some said he'd started a fight and cold-conked the stage manager, others said he'd been caught using loaded dice in a crap game, and still others maintained he had simply been let go when it was discovered he was not a member of the carpenter's union. Whatever the real reason for his departure, he had left no forwarding address, nor hints among the other stagehands where he might be going. He could have been anywhere in New York by then, working in any one of a thousand places or just holed up in one of a million or so apartments or stretched out on a roof somewhere scanning the sky, plotting his next moves.

It was Harry Bailey's way. Back home, he would walk all day until he came upon a spot where the land sloped just right and the grasses smelled just right and the hawthorn grew thick and plentiful, and then he would just set with the sun at his back; an hour, two, however long it took until white-tail buck showed noiselessly through the brambles like a cautious wind turning them upward to catch the departing light, and he would level his rifle without even bothering to check the windage because he knew that particular buck would be in that particular spot at that particular time.

I could not find him. Although I had that Indian blood of his I could not set out of a morning and smell the air and scan the sky and wait on a corner in Manhattan where they told me he would pass.

The good part was that I'd gotten to know Molly (or Mona, depending on her mood) pretty well. Although she'd made it clear to me that I was much too young for her to consider as a boyfriend, she seemed to enjoy my company and it got so I could look forward to spending time with her each day between shifts at the tour or usheretting at the evening show (she did the matinee on weekends as well), or the hours she spent sitting in the darkened auditorium, watching the rehearsals intently, dreaming of the day she would be up there on the line, high-stepping with the rest of the Rockettes, all rouge and mascara and lacquered hair and a smile fixed like a stereopticon slide: turn, turn, turn, kick, turn... kick, kick, kick, kick... I was learning the jargon.

Gay, I discovered, did not mean the same thing in New York City as it did back in Eula. Bertie, the Rockettes' choreographer, was a homosexual, as were the rest of the boy dancers in the troupe. I will not say that I was entirely ignorant about homosexuals, having heard the jokes and stories told about them by my classmates where they were always called homos or sometimes faggots. I can honestly say that up until that time I had never met a homosexual on my own—at least nobody who'd owned up to being one. I could not for the life of me understand what they were up to, or why they were so gay when everybody seemed bent on beating the tar out of them, but Molly (sometimes Mona) explained to me that this was New York City and if I wanted to make it here I would have to open up to all kinds of new people and new ideas. New York was like a stewpot, she told me. Maybe I wouldn't like all the stuff that got thrown in but I'd better learn to stomach the mix because it was what it was, and it was all there was. The city could be an awful place for people who didn't understand that.

Best of all, I learned that she did not have a boyfriend. New York was filled with guys who wanted only one thing, she confided to me one day over coffee. They would wine and dine you, and tell you anything they thought you wanted to hear for the chance to get you in the sack. She'd been involved with a few men she thought she could really go for but they'd all disappointed her, she said. It was better to keep your distance now, and learn about a body before you jumped right in to a love affair. Knowing her, I could not fathom how any man in his right mind could risk losing her for any reason. I considered our hours together an unwarranted gift; the carefree way she tossed her head and touched me accidentally when I least expected it, the smell of her shampoo, the soft white curve of her neck, the way she spoke to me as if she knew I would not betray her; and although I suspected that she might be using me as a shield against disappointing men, I was grateful nonetheless. Like she had told me, it was what it was, and for now it was all there was, and it was better than anything I had ever known before.

A postal money order for three hundred dollars accompanied Mama's letter:

"Dear Chance, Please use this to buy a bus ticket home. I hope the time you spend with your father is enjoyable for you both, but I also hope you will see that your future cannot be built on hopeless dreams and schemes. That is something your father was never able to learn, and as I see so much of him in you, I fear you might be headed down the same path he took many years ago. I hope you will see this for yourself and use the money to come back quickly. My prayers are with you and I look forward to your safe return. Love, Mama."

There was a P.S. penned at the bottom of the page and up the margin to avoid using another sheet of writing paper.

"I'm sorry to be the bearer of bad news, but I must also tell you that God took Joe Carl Purdy during surgery in a hospital up in Lubbock. There was a beautiful service for him here at the church. The choir sang *Nearer My God To Thee*, and several from the congregation took to the pulpit and spoke highly of him. Had you been here I am certain you would have done the same. We know that he now rests with the angels, looking down on us from the very special place the Lord has prepared for him in Heaven."

It took my breath away. Even though Joe Carl had always been sickly, it had never occurred to me that he would die; especially not during an operation that was supposed to make him better. It was the first time in my life someone close to me had passed, and I did not understand what it was I was supposed to be feeling. I expected to feel sad, and I did, but I had not expected to feel guilty, which I surely did. I was guilty because I knew that deep inside I'd wanted his surgery to fail. He was my very best friend in the world and yet I'd felt a tug of resentment when he told me the operation would leave him near as tall as I was. Now I'd got my wish and the operation had failed, and took his life in the bargain; and I felt like I had held a knife and plunged it into his heart there on the operating table in Lubbock.

Shimmelman saw me sitting dejectedly in the lobby with the letter on my lap. "Bad news?" he asked.

"Couldn't be much worse. My best friend up and died on me."

"That is bad news. How old was he?"

"Just a year older than me. He was having an operation to make his spine straighter and something happened and he never came out of it. I expect part of it was my fault since I didn't want the operation to work anyway."

"Why is that?"

"Because it would have made him tall as me -- almost. We'd always been about me being the tall, healthy one, and Joe Carl tagging along, knowing I'd stick up for him if things got tough. I never figured anything would ever happen to change that. Now he's dead and Mama says he's in the heavenly kingdom, and I reckon he won't be looking down kindly on me, knowing what I'd wished and all."

"Is that all that's bothering you, that some celestial quack will put a hex on you for your shortcomings?" He raised an eyebrow. "I would have expected more from you."

"I guess I don't really believe that. Being that I don't believe in God I can't hardly believe in angels, but I do know that I wished Joe Carl poorly and I do know that he died, and it's hard not to think that one thing had something to do with the other."

Shimmelman shook his head thoughtfully. "I've found that the best way to deal with guilt is to smother it with a good meal, especially one you can get on the arm, so to speak."

"You mean at the E and B?"

"Even better."

He closed the gate to the front desk and headed for the door, urging me along with his eyes. We walked south a few hundred feet to a squat red brick building that bore the legend Salvation Army Rescue Shelter painted on its grime-streaked picture window. Inside, a rag-tag assortment of drifters and panhandlers were spread thinly throughout a large, windowless room, stretching, dozing, listening halfheartedly to a speaker at the front who was dressed in the uniform of a captain and who exhorted them with all the forcefulness of a west Texas preacher. In a kitchen to the rear, a half-dozen more uniformed men and women stirred pots of hot, steaming soup, and wrapped sandwiches in waxed paper.

"We must endure the didactic discourse in order to partake of the repast," Shimmelman whispered to me as we took seats in the back. "While it's true that there is no free lunch, this is about as close to it as you're going to come."

The speaker read from the scriptures; a passage that I recognized from the many Sunday recitations I'd had to endure at the hands of the Reverend Harley Brown: "Lift up your hearts and rejoice for the Lord is at hand. He will take from you the wages of sin and lift from you your burden, and you shall be as children in the house of the Almighty." He paused for an Amen and when he got none, closed the book. "If any of you here are troubled, if you seek to have the burden of drink lifted from you, speak now and He will answer." His eyes raked the room. "As is our custom here, we will not feed the multitudes until someone testifies to the power and the glory."

Shimmelman was on his feet in an instant. "I am put in mind of something I learned as a child," he said, assuming a reverent tone. "It goes like this:

> Cross patch, draw the latch
> pick up your needles and spin.
> Take a cup and drink it up
> and call the neighbors in."

Everyone broke for food, bewildered but satisfied that, at least for that day, the covenant had been fulfilled.

LeMoult

Thirteen

My birthday arrived and although I had made up my mind to let it pass without fanfare I awoke feeling more lonely than I had ever felt. For the first time in memory, sixteen did not seem to be the magical bull's-eye toward which I had pointed my entire life. I did not feel suddenly wise, or mature, or even glad that I had reached that milestone age. Alone as I was in a vast metropolis I had not even begun to understand, I realized how much I missed the rites and tokens that birthdays always brought. (Cards would be hidden throughout the house with a small surprise in each; a dollar or a movie ticket or perhaps a paper strip of cinnamon buttons, and although as I got older I did not hunt for them with the eagerness of a child, I kept my eyes peeled.)

Mama would prepare a special meal of all the things I liked best: Baked ham and yams, lima beans swimming in butter, homemade biscuits and honey. There would be an icebox cake; chocolate wafers, sliced bananas and whipped cream, and at the table she would recall my birth as if it had happened just the day before; Aunt Cassie the midwife, who was at that time married to my Uncle Mal but who died of TB before I was old enough to know her, fretting when she saw me coming out feet-first, but Mama never worried for a damn minute that we would both be tough enough to come through it. It was the only time I ever heard her use the word damn, and when she said it there was always a tear brimming in the corner of her eye. It did not matter to me that New Yorkers were too worldly to let such things stir them up. At that moment I was not even close to being a New Yorker. At that moment all I wanted was to be in our parlor in Eula, scanning the corners and lintels for a hidden card, smelling the smells of cooking, and Mama humming in the kitchen, remembering.

"It's your birthday? Why didn't you say something?" Molly/Mona wanted to know. I had made up my mind not to tell her, being that I had added four years to my age anyway, but it had just slipped out over coffee that afternoon.

I shrugged. "It's no big deal."

"Of course it's a big deal. Birthdays are always a big deal. It's the only time we get to feel special. There were times when I was growing up that it seemed birthdays were the only thing that mattered. I'd go from year to year with nothing happening in my life, dreaming about the next birthday party; what dress I'd be wearing, what presents I'd get."

"Do you go back home on your birthday?"

"Not any more. I did for a few years but after a while all it did was make me depressed. Nothing's ever like we remember it."

"Eula's like I remember it. It'll always be like I remember it."

"You haven't been away from it that long. Wait 'til a few years have passed, then go back. Everything you thought was big and wonderful turns out to be small and seedy.

"Then I won't have to worry 'cause I already know Eula's small and seedy. That's why I left in the first place. Why'd you ever leave home if you thought it was so wonderful?"

"Because it wasn't enough; because it was a two-bedroom house on a street full of two bedroom houses filled with people who couldn't see beyond their front yards. There was a canal and a drugstore and the Adirondack Mountains, and if there was a dream there I could never find it."

"Sounds a little like Eula, only we don't have any mountains, and the closest thing to a canal is the creek. I know that's why Harry Bailey left there and never came back. He had his sights set on bigger and better."

"Everybody in New York wants bigger and better. That's why they're here."

"Did you always want to be a dancer?"

"I always wanted to be something, or somebody. I remember sitting on my front porch watching the shadows move across the mountains and dreaming that I'd wake up one day and everything would have changed. I'd be living in a castle on the Rhone River with dozens of servants and horses and carriages all covered with gold leaf and Japan paint, and running footmen in floppy black hats and red velvet knickers speeding alongside, ready to plop down a carpet for me to walk on in case I wanted to get out and mingle with the commoners. But then I'd snap to, and I'd be back in Whitehall again, back in the real world..." Her voice trailed off.

"I guess stuff like that never interested me; castles and servants and running horsemen and all, but I did wonder a lot if Eula was all there was to life. All I would've had to look forward to if I'da stayed there was hardscrabble farming or working in the Feed & Grain or just plain loafing. When you come right down to it, that's the major occupation of most of the folks there; setting and whittling and telling lies."

"It's footmen," she corrected me. "Running footmen."

"I'm a cowboy and we call it horsemen. Anybody fool enough to run alongside a speeding carriage damn well better have some horse in him or he's gonna swallow a lot of dust."

"Running horsemen then," she laughed. "So how do you plan to celebrate your birthday?"

"I reckon this'll be it."

Her eyes lit up. "I have a better idea. There's a party at Bertie's tonight. I wasn't going to go but now we can go together and make believe it's in honor of your birthday."

"I can't go where I wasn't invited."

"Don't be silly. Most of the people there won't be invited. It's one of those Village things where people just wander from place to place. Sometimes they can be fun; you can meet a lot of artsy-fartsy types."

"Like bohemians?"

"I guess you could call them that, or beats. Most of them are a real bore; they're all either writing a book or a play or a movie but they never seem to finish any of them. The painters are the worst of all. They won't even talk to you unless you've lived on the Left Bank."

"So why bother with them?"

"Every now and then you meet somebody worth remembering. I met Bertie at one of those parties and that's how I got the job at Radio City."

"What were you doing before that?"

"Lots of things..." She scribbled an address on a piece of paper and gave it to me. "Meet me there tonight after dinner; ten or ten-thirty. We'll make believe the whole shindig is in your honor."

Mama would've busted a gut. Here I was sixteen years old and already I was associating with bohemians, the likes of which that windbag Harley Brown railed against in his sermons Sunday after Sunday. They were the spawn of Satan, the embodiment of the anti-Christ set down here on this earth to poison the minds of the righteous with their pagan rites and culture; and while I did not set much store by the Reverend's view of things, I must admit I felt more than a little uneasy about the whole thing. God was a phony but he'd sure-as-shooting tore up Sodom and Gomorra, and I didn't want to be around if he took it into his head to do the same to New York City.

My first mistake was buying new clothes. Since everything I'd owned had been stolen by that bombardier-jacket-wearing swindler, I'd had to purchase a few things to get by, but to my mind none of it was fit for party-going, so I'd found a men's store not far from the Soldiers and Sailors and bought a whole new getup: a gray and black checked jacket, chino slacks with a belt in the back, new loafers, and a wide brown tie with the head and neck of an eight-pronged buck painted on the front (I expect now it was because the deer reminded me of Harry Bailey, although I was taken at the time with the colors.) Thus attired, I arrived at Bertie's Greenwich Village loft at ten sharp, and entered an open doorway off the freight elevator where I found myself in the middle of a noisy throng, none of whom were dressed in anything more elegant than dungarees and undershirts.

The loft was a vast hollow space, more like the inside of a barn than a place for folks to live. What light there was came from filtered spotlights set into the ceiling; ribbons of red, green and yellow showing cracked wooden beams and skylights cranked open to the outside, and stars circling in the blackest places like Shimmelman's mural splashed across the ceiling. Penetrating the haze a few candles flickered on tables, illuminating objects and faces in the black, all teeth and eyes grinning; nobody I knew, nobody I could ever know. If Molly was there I could not see her, but I spotted Bertie elbowing through the crowd, dressed only in a pair of tight leather shorts and rope sandals, his smooth chest glistening with sweat.

"Love the ensemble, darling," he said as he brushed by me, "Haven't we met somewhere?"

"You might've seen me at the music hall. I'm a friend of Molly's."

"Mona Chalfonte!" He clapped his hands. "My biggest fan."

"She loves your dancing. I like it too. "

"Dancing?" His eyelids fluttered. "That's not dancing, darling, it's close-order drill! If any of those cows had to do a real dance they'd collapse on the floor and fart themselves into oblivion. Lord knows what Mona sees in all that crap. She has some talent. She could do a lot better for herself than being a goddamn Rockette."

"Then why do you do it if you think it's so bad?"

"Because it's a job, you sweet young thing. Have you ever heard of eating?"

"Yeah, I heard of eating. You ever heard about being polite? "

"Touchy, touchy." He shrugged his shoulders extravagantly. "If you can't take the heat, darling, I'd suggest you do like Harry Truman and get the fuck out of the kitchen."

"I would but I'm supposed to meet Molly here; you remember her, your biggest fan. She thinks you're the greatest dancer since Fred Astaire, that being a Rockette is about the finest thing that could ever happen to a lady; and here you are running everybody down behind their backs."

"I'd say it to her face," he huffed.

"Well she ain't here that I can see, but I expect I'll find her any minute. When I do I'll bring her around so you can tell her how crappy her dream is."

"Suit yourself. I hope she's not bringing that dreadful Nick creature with her this time."

"Who's he?"

"God knows; some Neanderthal she picked up along the way." He sniffed the air and scanned the crowd. "Now why don't you get yourself a drink or a bone or something stimulating while you're waiting for her, darling. You're beginning to wear."

I made my way to a well-stocked bar in the rear where I opened a can of Rheingold's beer and adjusted my eyes to the crowd. They were not at all what I'd pictured when I'd thought about bohemians. Granted, the Reverend Harley Brown had a way of making anything he disagreed with sound a lot worse than it really was, but even knowing they'd be something less than the fire-breathing dragons he'd made them out to be, I'd expected that at the very least bohemians would be sinister. It was hard to see how they could have caused such an all-fire fuss if they weren't, but I'd seen a lot more sinister a band when the cattle drive came through Eula on the way from Nogales to El Paso. (The Mexican vaqueros carried bolo knives big as cavalry swords and they rode with bullwhips clenched between their teeth, and ran the cattle at full speed through the town, knowing that to tarry would be to invite the wrath of men without faces, men watching from behind windows and storefronts, whispering nervous assurances to their wives and daughters, and the smells of dust and hot breath and dung hung in the air long after they had galloped out of Eula and the good old boys had put away their rifles.)

"Happy Birthday!" Molly sneaked up on me from the side. "How are you enjoying your party?"

"It's okay. Who's Nick?"

"Who told you about Nick?"

"Bertie. He says he's a Neanderthal."

"Bertie says a lot of things."

"So who is he?"

"Well I don't see as how it's any of your business, but since it's your birthday, he's a friend."

"A boyfriend?"

"I have lots of friends." She poured a small amount of green liqueur into a glass and sipped it slowly. "Now are you going to enjoy your party or are you going to spoil the whole evening worrying about things that don't concern you?"

"I just don't want to see you hurt."

"I'm a big girl. I can take care of myself."

The crowd stirred and fell silent as a scruffy young man with a shock of unruly black hair made his way to the front and sat on a stool, fingering a stack of papers in his lap. "The road comes up to meet me," he began to read in a slow, steady voice. " Spears of white tracer-like assail, and spreading out to earthbound kine, a blur to me now..."

"What's he talking about?" I rasped.

"It's a reading. That's Frank Lupo," she whispered back.

"Who's Frank Lupo?"

"Not now." She held her forefinger to her lips and strained to hear his words, muffled in the press of bodies and the air thick with cigarette smoke.

"O say can you see
mud-caked empty huts
the mistral's come and gone
Brought the grime along
and took the folk away
from that place
where artists limned their simple ways
in simple strokes..."

They all knew him, knew who he was and what he said, and she knew too, and suddenly I felt like I'd been stripped naked in front of them, exposed for the shallow Texas hick I was. Mocking my gray checked jacket and my tie with a picture of a deer, they huddled for cover in the middle of his words, condemning me, laughing at me with lipstick-smeared mouths and eyes unblinking, nodding silent amens as they brushed away the heat with silk-ribbed fans and the music swelled from the choir-loft and they measured out the grace.

"Rain, rain, go away
I want my umbrella for a cane
a battered tin cup
and a well-fed German Shepherd
So I can stand in Wenceslas Square
and hear the sounds of pastry being et
and smell the flowery kids
working on their memories."

She believed that she could take care of herself but she was like a firefly at dusk; too dim to explode in all her brilliance, shining bright enough to attract the predators that waited in the shadows to devour her.

95

LeMoult

He would take her and tell her he would protect her, and she would love him when icy winds took the crops and hailstones took the roof and the dice went cold and a Mexican whore showed up on the doorstep and said she was carrying his child, she would love him. And when he hit her she would love him. She would tell herself that the bruises were an accident, that all he needed was a break from that old schemer, God. And when he left her forever, she would love him then.

"Ready or not here I come
bowed but unbloody
tight-assed as a drum
The road comes up to meet me
unyielding with potholes
orange leaves do an obscene dance
obstructing my traction
and my vision
And nobody's moving fast enough
for me to look around."

Fourteen

He was called the Cajun, a gnarled, bald man (what hair he had ran in gray-black clumps down the back of his head and sprouted above his sleeveless undershirt like a poorly seeded lawn) with a milky glass orb where one eye should have been and a game left leg that caused him to lurch sideways when he walked more than a foot or two. He had a notice-able accent, not altogether foreign but not American either; and finding him had been a stroke of luck, although Shimmelman insisted he had just the night before painted a star that without a doubt enhanced my chances.

Hoping that Harry Bailey had landed another stage carpenter's job, I'd spent weeks going from theater to theater, asking anyone who was willing to talk whether they had known him, but my inquiries had been ineffective and frustrating, so I was near the end of my rope the day Shimmelman showed up at the Soldiers and Sailors with the Cajun who, he explained, had testified that afternoon at the Salvation Army mission to having stabbed a telegraph operator to death before the war, a man with a tattoo of a spider on his forearm. The story was, he admitted, garbled and disconnected, but too close to what I had told him about Harry Bailey to ignore.

The Cajun was in Shimmelman's room, drinking Metaxa from a paper cup when I got there. "I hear you tell a story about killing a tele-graph operator with a spider tattooed on his arm," I said without even introducing myself.

He eyed me suspiciously. "Something wrong with that?"

"Nothing wrong with it, except that a good part of that story belongs to somebody else."

"Who else?" His eyes were slits, the good one narrower than the glass one.

"Well that would be my daddy, only the man he killed didn't have no tattoo of a spider. That's Harry Bailey's tattoo that he got in prison."

He drained the paper cup. "So what difference does it make? What concern is it to you whose story I use? One story is as good as another."

"Not when it's my daddy's story it ain't."

"Look kid, I don't know who your daddy is and I don't want to know. You hang around those places long enough and you hear all kinds of stories."

"Why not just tell your own story?"

"They don't remember faces in the missions but they remember the stories. You go back there often enough telling the same story without being saved and you don't get to eat, it's that simple. They're not looking for truth, they're looking for converts."

"So you must've heard Harry Bailey tell that story someplace."

"You think I can remember every hobo I run into at the Salvation Army?"

"Harry Bailey ain't no hobo. He's tall like me with blue, blue eyes and a tattoo of a spider on his forearm. You must've seen him to know that."

He shook his head and stared at the mural. "You do that?" he asked Shimmelman. "I seen a picture just like it in the Ninth Street Armory."

Shimmelman rose up indignantly. "Not like that, you didn't."

"Just like that. All the colors in the same places and everything."

"Harry Bailey's got prominent Indian-type cheekbones and he likely talks with a west Texas drawl," I elaborated.

"Maybe if I had another drink."

Shimmelman stood in front of the mural with his arms spread protecting it from further assault. "For your information this is the birth of stars, the grand eruption of all life as we know it."

"It was a WPA painting; not a speck of difference from what you got there. I bet there's dozens just like it got painted during the Depression by guys on the dole who couldn't draw a lick."

I took the only picture I had of Harry Bailey from my wallet, a yellowing snapshot almost ten years old of him standing in front of the house in Eula with a black felt bowler perched jauntily to one side of his head. "He'd be a mite older now, and of course a lot closer up than what he is there."

The Cajun peered at the photograph. "Hard to tell. You know if he ever shoveled seagull shit for the army?"

"I couldn't say for sure, but he was in the war."

"There are only two copies of this mural; one rests in the vastness of the cosmos and one in the inner reaches of my consciousness," Shimmelman moaned. "To say otherwise is to deny the divinity of the creative process, to deny the very essence of creation itself!"

"It could have been him," The Cajun speculated. "He looks like the sort of rough-and-ready character they picked for that duty."

"What duty was that?"

He swept the room with his good eye. "We mined seagull shit on a remote island off the coast of Louisiana for the war effort; three hundred military-trained specialists standing hip-deep in bird guano ten hours a day."

"…Every brushstroke parallels the evolution of stars, the marriage of swirling gasses to form a nuclear reaction, the celestial coupling of hydrogen nuclei and deuterons to produce their offspring, helium…"

"The seagull guano was natural phosphate, used to make batteries and bombs, the Cajun explained, "as important to the war effort as the Manhattan Project only not nearly so glamorous. They couldn't supply us by ship and risk exposing our location to Nazi submarines so we had to live off the land, sleeping in caves like Neolithic savages."

"…The birth pangs of the star begin, she contracts, her temperature rises and she squeezes out her lithium offspring which is consumed in its own fires. Again and again the birth is renewed and destroyed until exhausted, she heaves in cosmic surrender and collapses…"

"There were bats the size of B-29s in the caves and we mined their guano too, but mostly it was used to fertilize our gardens. We grew peas, tomatoes, even pumpkins, and a hybrid strain of mushrooms as big as bowling balls."

"I don't recall hearing that Harry Bailey was involved in anything like that," I remarked.

"You wouldn't have. We were sworn to secrecy. Even after the war ended our work was never acknowledged by the government. Others who had contributed far less were treated as heroes, given medals and banquets and parades, but we were forced to slink back like common criminals. Most of the Third Reich lay in smoldering ruins as a direct effect of our efforts, but our destiny was to forever remain disaffected and unappreciated. It's no wonder that so many of us took to the streets."

Shimmelman stood with his shoulders slumped, heaving with exhaustion. "...And then she dies, sinking deeper and deeper into the envelope of space until she is consumed by its blackness, never again to be seen by man. She exists only then in the imagery of my mind and I must re-create her in swirls and daubs and fiery splashes of color so she will never ever be forgotten. And if you think some booze-sodden WPA hack could do all that, you got another think coming!"

The Cajun's story was probably a bald-faced lie that he had pieced together from a hundred other stories he'd heard at a hundred other missions, the way he'd woven Harry Bailey's life into his own; or it was the impregnable truth, his truth as he had winnowed it out of the reality life had given him. Shimmelman had said reality was the hobgoblin of dolts and incompetents, that the only sane response to it was to flee, and I'm not sure I believed that at the time; but the longer I stayed in New York City the more I realized that a person could get buried in a hurry if they faced things square-on every day.

In Eula, telling bald-faced lies had been an art form, whereas here it was plain coping. Even I had found myself creating a reality that was far from the way things really were. I was barely sixteen years old with no job and no future, and I was hopelessly in love with Molly who was almost ten years older than I was. Even knowing I stood a snowball's chance in hell of ever possessing her, I could take her to my room at night and hold her next to me and feel her soft white skin pressing against mine and whisper to her under the clatter of the elevated train, and tell her what was really on my mind. I could tell her about the birth of stars; how to catch a jackrabbit with a swipe of your hand and build a cricket cage out of twigs or a raft with popsicle sticks. I could teach her all the things I knew, all the things I thought I knew; and she would be impressed by me and amused by me, and maybe even a little afraid of me (blood was my heritage after all), and most of all she would love me the way I loved her.

Shimmelman had said that we were what we pretended to be, and if that was the case there must have been a part of me that was brave and strong and worldly, but that part came in fits and starts and for the most part it was plain that all she saw in me was an awkward, tongue-tied boy shooting at being a man. Truth told, I had not lived enough life to be cynical about it like Frank Lupo or disillusioned by it like Shimmelman or embittered by it like the Cajun, who'd all got it burned into their hides like a brand. About all I could manage under the circumstances was to keep my mind on why I'd come here in the first place, try not to get too dazzled by the folks who crossed my path, and hope that things would be made clearer along the way. Maybe something good or bad might happen to me then, maybe it was happening now without my knowing it. Maybe the stars that would chart my future were already glimmering in the works of beat poets and bad artists and WPA hacks (in the twisted reality of derelicts, the unraveling minds of madmen).

LeMoult

Fifteen

The Cajun turned out to be a master handyman, willing to work for free lodging, and that was good news for the Soldiers and Sailors, which was not short on things that needed fixing, largely in the plumbing area. Most of the toilets did not flush (having had little experience with indoor toilets I did not know they needed only simple adjustments, and Shimmelman of course would never have stooped to look inside the tank), the showers barely trickled (the Cajun explained that mineral deposits clogged the shower- heads and the rubber bladders in the taps had wore out), and most important to me, the swimming pool had been bone-dry since the day I arrived. Fixing it would be a more difficult task, he allowed, but with the right parts he could have it working in a week or two. Knowing him to be a bald-faced liar, I did not expect to be swimming in that pool any time soon, but watching him work I had to admit he knew his way around pipes.

In the meantime, toilets were flushing and showerheads were squirting and I was feeling more miserable than I had in a long, long time. I thought about how all the females in my life had let me down. Part of it had to do with Mama's upcoming marriage to the Reverend Harley Brown. She had written me a second letter, begging me to be there for the nuptials on the first Saturday in October (she'd cited the thirty-four hours she'd spent in labor having me as reason enough for me to attend), but the idea of setting in the congregation of the Calvary Baptist Church and Grace Ministry while she plighted her troth to that Bible-spouting hypocrite of a parson who would up and leave her of a night and go to Moon's Roadside Cafe and consort with whores and come home drunk and mean as a rattlesnake was more than I could endure. I had made up my mind that as long as I lived, whether or not I ever found Harry Bailey (it was a possibility that was becoming more and more remote as the weeks rolled by), and whether or not she ever forgave me for the thirty-four hours of labor, I would never acknowledge that union. I would never call him Daddy, or even mention him in passing when I talked to her, and if she chose to speak of him I would act as if I did not hear her because he was an actuality I'd decided to erase from my life forever. I felt that strong about it, and so I did not responded to her letter, reasoning that nothing I could say would be more hurtful to her than my silence.

The rest of it had to do with Molly. Hanging around the Radio City Music Hall the way I had, I'd met a lot of the folks who worked back-stage, which led me to a paying job of sorts. I'd become a gofer, some-body who went out for their sandwiches or picked up their mail from the post office or their laundry from the dry cleaner or did just about anything they were too busy or too lazy to do themselves. What that job taught me was that show business people were friendly when they got to know you, generous with their tips, and that they ran off at the mouth some when they'd had too many beers. Well one of the things they ran off at the mouth about was somebody named Nick Corsi, and though I'd been taught that a man's business was his own, I couldn't help listening when Molly's name got to be part of the story.

Nick Corsi was the man behind the man who broke your legs if you didn't pay your bookie, they said. A big-time labor boss who ran the stagehand's union, he owned clubs all over Manhattan that featured exotic dancers. (I might've been a hick but you didn't have to hit me between the eyes with a tire iron for me to get what that meant.) Worst of all they let it slip that Molly had worked in one of those clubs as an exotic dancer when she first came to New York, and that he'd taken a special interest in her. Some even said that she was his girl.

A hunk of my dream had exploded right there; the thought of Molly writhing near-naked in front of a bunch of slack-jawed, hog-bellied, hooting and hollering drunk-as-a-skunk ignoramuses was just about more than I could bear,

I was angry at Molly for deceiving me, and angrier at myself for ever having thought she'd meant to. She'd spent six years making her way in New York City while I was still sniffing cow-pies out in the boondocks, and it shouldn't have surprised me that she'd had to scratch around a bit before she got a real job and settled down. It shouldn't have, but it did. Somehow I'd let myself endow her with everything that was good and pure and holy. I'd raised her so far above the commonplace that any little misstep was bound to topple her.

Alone in my room, I gloomily leafed through Isaiah Balenkin's Nobel Prize-winning novel, *Womb*, the tale of Kuryokin, a simple-minded blacksmith's apprentice from the Ukrainian village of Plenska, who was impressed into the Czarist army to fight Germans during the First World War. Given a rusting single-shot rifle, four bullets and a stale crust of bread, he was taken to the outskirts of his village and told to stand fast against the Huns when they came. Kuryokin had never seen a German, and he lacked the intelligence to understand the reasons for the conflict. More important, he had never seen a tank, and his first view of one rumbling across the open hayfields of Plenska scared him shitless. He threw down his rifle and bullets and fled into the surrounding birch forest, carrying only the crust of bread with him.

Kuryokin cowered in the forest while German soldiers swarmed about him. He hid behind a fallen tree, gnawing on the crust of bread and pieces of rotted bark as they trudged past him, so close he could hear them talking to each other in a language he could not understand. They were young like him, but fearsome-looking in their steel-spiked helmets and mud-caked leather boots. Surely a country that could afford to send its soldiers into the field with real leather boots could not be defeated, he thought.

Suddenly the forest blew up. Ear-splitting artillery bursts exploded all around him, uprooting entire trees and tearing the rank of German soldiers apart. Kuryokin huddled in horror as limbs torn from trees and from German soldiers flew past him. The ground shuddered beneath his feet and the fallen tree trunk that had been his refuge disintegrated before him, exposing the body of a German infantryman who had been hiding on the other side, the hollow of his neck pumping blood where once his head had been. Kuryokin then fouled himself and fainted.

Drifting away from Kuryokin's troubles, I thought about Molly, and how she'd tried to convince me that Nick was like a father to her—that his only interest was in seeing she got a leg up in show business.

"And what business of yours would it be if I was Nick Corsi's girl?" she'd objected when I screwed up enough courage to ask her about him.

"My life is my life. Who put you in charge of it?" she'd bristled.

"I'm not in charge. It's just that they say he's a gangster."

"Who says he's a gangster?"

"Everybody backstage says it. They say he's got guys who break your legs and I don't want you to get hurt."

"Well that's the dumbest thing I ever heard; and I told you before I'm a big girl. I don't need you to be my guardian."

"Maybe if you'd had a guardian in the beginning you wouldn't've done all that exotic dancing you did for him."

Molly had been silent for a time. "I don't expect you to understand, but for some reason I want you to," she'd said finally. "The war had just ended when I got to New York. People were dancing in the streets, falling in love; strangers would walk up to you and plant a big wet kiss on your lips and you'd kiss them back and it was okay because the war was over and the world was free and nothing anybody did could be wrong. It was like every rule that had ever been invented came crashing down and I was there in the middle of it; a nineteen year-old girl with a high school education and eighty-one dollars and change in my pocketbook and a dream of becoming another Ginger Rogers, and when Nick Corsi asked me to dance in his club I thought I'd died and gone to heaven. Maybe it wasn't exactly what I'd dreamed about back on my front porch in Whitehall, but it was dancing, and I was damn good at it, and I never did anything there to be ashamed of, and I've never looked back. If you can't accept that I guess you're not the kind of friend I thought you were."

There it was. Where Mama had made me feel ungrateful, Molly had made me feel unworthy, and there was a lot of guilt in both. I was starting to see the power of women; that awesome, irrational ability they had to turn their own transgressions into weapons that shame men.

Feeling more powerless than ever, I returned to *Womb*, where poor Kuryokin seemed in even worse shape than I was. Having come to after the artillery barrage had subsided, he'd shaken his head clear, dug himself out from under the forest debris that covered him, and stood unsteadily, surveying the horror all around him. His first thought was that he had been magically transported into another world of smoking craters and bodies stacked like cordwood. The smells of cordite and rotting flesh penetrated his nostrils as he walked among the dead German infantrymen, his simple mind robbed of any visual checkpoints he could recognize. He realized for the first time that he had been struck in the head by something. Blood trickled over the ridge of his forehead into his eyes.

Shimmelman knocked to say there was a telephone call for me in the downstairs lobby:

"It's me, Molly," her voice crackled over the receiver. "What are you doing right now?"

"Laying around, reading some. Why?"

"Because Nick asked me out to his house in New Rochelle for the weekend and I asked him if I could bring you and he said sure."

"Why would you want to bring me there?"

"Because it's a beautiful part of the world, and it'll do you good to see something in New York besides the Soldiers and Sailors and the Music Hall. The house is right on Long Island Sound and if the weather holds we can take his boat out for a picnic."

"I thought I was a big disappointment to you."

I could hear her sigh. "I never said that but you're in danger of becoming one."

"Well I'm just not sure I want to go on any picnics with you and Nick Corsi. You know what they say, two's company."

"What are you afraid of, that you'll find out he's really harmless and you won't have to protect me from him after all?"

"No, that's not what I'm afraid of. I just don't want to butt in where I'm not wanted."

"You'll like Nick; you'll hate yourself for it but you'll like him. Everybody does.

She was doing it again; using me as a shield against serious men, but it was better than having her ignore me altogether. Besides, I had never seen the ocean, and although I knew the Long Island Sound was only a branch of the ocean it was more water than I'd ever thought I would see in one place in my lifetime. Molly arrived at the Soldiers and Sailors an hour later in a chauffeured automobile that Nick had sent for her, and before long we were driving through the wooded hills of Westchester County, inhaling fresh air that held a promise of autumn (I hadn't realized how accustomed I'd become to the soot and smoke of the city, but the scent of trees made my heart soar), chatting to each other like a bad word had never passed between us, close together in the spacious back seat, our bodies brushing accidentally, too often to be accidental. She stretched across me to point things out along the way and her shirt was unbuttoned and her bra got pulled across her chest and I could see clear down to the beginnings of her nipple, and she smelled like apples at night time.

And we were almost to New Rochelle before it crossed my mind that Mama must have been Mrs. Harley Brown by then.

Sixteen

The house was on a private peninsula, framed against the panorama of Long Island Sound. At the end of the tree-lined driveway, a uniformed guard at a stone gatehouse checked our credentials before we were allowed to enter and continue on to the sprawling estate. Although I had pretty much made up my mind that it was all come by dishonestly (I could not see how somebody who operated clubs where girls danced naked could have done it any other way), I must admit I was properly impressed. The place was bigger than the Soldiers and Sailors, bigger than most of downtown Eula if the truth were told. Surrounded by an acre or two of clipped-close grass that sloped down to its own private beach and marina, it was grander by far than anything I'd seen outside of books and magazines, grander even than almost anything I'd seen in movies. (Orson Welles had a place to rival it, but he was Citizen Kane, a newspaper publisher, and you expected that sort of thing from newspaper publishers, not from people who broke other people's legs.)

Nick Corsi was a surprise too. I don't know exactly what I had expected, but it was certainly not the short, balding man in his mid-forties who greeted us at the door. Dressed in shorts and a close-fitting white T-shirt that emphasized a lean, compact body; disarming me with a ready grin and a strong, honest handshake, he seemed a whole lot less intimidating than the proprietor of that mansion should have been. In fact he could have been a cowboy if his walk and talk were just a little looser, his deep tan a mite less perfect, crinkling up white at the corners of his eyes and chapping his lips; a little less after shave splashed on the places where a cowboy would smell of horses, whiskey and cigarettes; and of course a sombrero to protect that shining bald head of his from the west Texas sun. But all in all I would have to say he set me right at ease. If I'd walked in wanting to hate him it was plain I'd have to dig a little deeper.

"Glad you could make it," he welcomed me in a voice that did not sound the way gangsters were supposed to sound; nasal and snarling like James Cagney or gravely and chilling like George Raft. "Chance, isn't it?"

"Chance Bailey, sir." I returned his handshake guardedly.

"Forget that sir stuff. It's Nick." He kissed Molly lightly on the cheek (a fatherly kiss) and ushered us both inside where another couple, a man and woman around his age, waited on a glass-enclosed porch overlooking the water. "This's Congressman Tom Creedy and his wife Betsy," he introduced us. "Mona Chalfonte and Chance Bailey."

It was a good thing all I had to do was shake hands because the idea that I was standing in the same room as a U.S. Congressman, even shaking his hand, left me tongue-tied. If Molly was as flabbergasted as I was, she did not show it, smiling through the introductions as if she met a Congressman every day. I was beginning to think I'd been caught in a solipsism; one of those private worlds that Joe Carl talked about where everything I was seeing was warped by my own perceptions. It wasn't possible that after only a little more than a month in New York City, a sixteen-year-old country shit-kicker like me could be standing in a mansion on the Long Island Sound with a girl who'd danced naked in front of men, a gangster, and a United States Congressman, all beaming and chatting about inconsequential things like the weather and the view from the porch and the traffic they'd encountered driving up, things ordinary folks talked about while they were burying what was really on their minds. They might just as well have been in Eula, where dullness disguised wishes and dreams, and every new day was a weary echo of the last.

Nick took Molly and me on a tour of the grounds while Congressman Tom Creedy and his wife waited back at the house, down to the marina where a sleek Chris-Craft motorboat was tied up at the end of the pier. "We'll take a trip up to the Thimble Islands tomorrow if the water's calm enough," he told us as he knelt and tenderly rubbed his palm along the polished mahogany sides of the boat. "We'll bring along some sandwiches and beer and make a day of it; maybe drop a line over the side and see if anything's biting. You like to fish?"

"I'm afraid I've never done any," I had to admit. "Back where I come from the only water for fifty miles is a gravel pit and a creek, and there ain't nothing worth catching in either."

Nick dangled his hand over the side of the pier and touched the surface of the water where gasoline from the boat spread out in swirls of vivid color. "Where I grew up in Brooklyn all you could catch off the piers was a kind of eel that lives off garbage. That's why I like it here so much; everything's fresh and clean. You can swim in the water, breathe the air, know what I mean?"

"Well I'm an expert fisherman," Molly bragged. "Just about the only thing Whitehall had plenty of when I was growing up was lakes and streams filled with fish, and I learned how to catch them before I learned how to walk."

"I caught a marlin off the coast of Cuba a couple of years ago, but I let it go." He brushed the surface of the water, watching the colors shift and blend to the movement of his finger. "Everybody on the boat thought I'd gone nuts, they said it might've been a record for those waters, but I took one look at it and said to myself, this is a brave fish. He's fought his heart out and he deserves better than being stuffed and put over somebody's mantelpiece. He deserves to live out his life free. So I cut the line and watched him swim off and felt great about it. I still feel great about it. I hope he's still free, swimming out there in those Cuban waters someplace, remembering what a helluva fight we had."

That night at dinner I learned that it was not smart to stuff yourself on the first course of an Italian meal because they kept on coming; breads, pasta, fish, meat, vegetables, pastries and ices; one course after another was carried into the spacious dining room by uniform-clad servants, and by the time I'd pushed away from the table I could barely move. Across the table from me, Congressman Tom Creedy was fairly immobile too, but that came from getting shitfaced on red wine and stingers to the point where his wife was digging her elbow into his side every fourth or fifth word he uttered. Eventually, after he'd slurred and stammered his way through supper, he sunk into a quiet stupor, drooling down the front of his shirt like a kid with an ice cream cone on a hot Texas afternoon.

"I do believe that what the Congressman needs is a good cigar and a game of nine-ball," Nick suggested as we all rose. Now I am not unfamiliar with the game of nine-ball, and looking at the Congressman it struck me that he was hardly in any condition to hold a pool cue, much less focus on the stripes and solids and intricacies of the game, but I kept my mouth shut, and was secretly relieved when I was not asked to join them. I believed then that Nick Corsi was showing him kindness, much as he'd shown to that marlin fish down in Cuba, and I wasn't sure I had it in me to do the same. I had seen drunks before and was not disposed to judge them, but they had always been ignorant rednecks or homeless tramps, never men blessed with fame and fortune as the Congressman had been.

"You like him, don't you?" Molly asked as we sat outside on the patio, watching a yellow crescent moonrise over Long Island across the water.

"Nick? He's okay I guess."

"Not what you thought he'd be, is he?"

"A lot of folks don't turn out the way I think they're going to turn out."

"Like me?"

"I never said that."

"But you thought it."

I tracked a dark finger of a cloud drifting across the moon. "See how a big chunk of that moon's been bitten off? Back in Texas we say a coyote bit it off that way."

She gazed dreamily at it for a time. "I used to wonder what it would be like on the other side, the dark side we never see. I dreamed that maybe there were gardens with flowers and tall ferns, and waterfalls hundreds of feet high you could sit underneath and bathe your feet in the pools."

"Actually it wasn't a real coyote. It was an Indian brave who saw his tribe was starving and turned himself into a coyote so he could jump high enough to get a mouthful."

"You know how it is when you feel trapped; everything out there looks so much better than what you have. I knew the dark side of the moon was probably just the same as the side I could see, but there was no way to really know for sure. If they built a machine that could catapult you clear to the moon I think I would have been the first one to volunteer for a ride, even if there was no way of getting back."

"Why are we here?" I blurted.

"Because Nick invited us."

"No, I mean why would somebody with a place like this ask us here when he could probably invite anybody he wanted?"

"Like who, the Congressman in there?" She raised an eyebrow. "Did it ever occur to you how hard it is for a man like Nick to find friends?"

"Well I'd think he could do better than a Texas hillbilly."

"And a stripper."

"I didn't say that."

"But you thought it."

Nick came out on the patio and interrupted our jousting. "Didn't take you very long to put the congressman away," I noted.

"He's the one who put me away—took me for a bundle."

"How'd that happen? The man could hardly stand."

"Well, that's the way it goes. The Congressman always beats me when we play nine-ball."

"Hard to believe. I could give you a couple of pointers if you'd like."

"Thanks, but I don't need any pointers. I grew up in pool halls."

"Will they be with us on our picnic tomorrow?" Molly asked.

"No, they've already left. The game is the only reason the Congressman comes here in the first place. He's just putting up with the rest of it."

Later that night, lying in the most comfortable bed I had ever known, I thought about what Molly had said about how hard it was for somebody like Nick to find friends. That was a circumstance I had never considered, that a man could rise so high that the only friends he could find were ones who wanted the things he had. I understood that everybody wanted something, and that they were willing to put up with little lies to get it. Mama wanted nothing more than order in her life and she would abide marrying a phony old preacher to achieve it. Joe Carl had died wanting to be tall as me and I'd begrudged him even that small wish. Isaiah Balenkin had traded his genius for freedom, Shimmelman had abandoned all his friends so he could talk to the stars; and Molly was willing to overlook everything in life just to be dazzled by it all, and I was willing to go along, just to be dazzled by her. And the air was pure and salty coming off the water. Across the Sound a bell-buoy tolled, and the crickets and the peepers answered just like at home.

Seventeen

Nick was already up when I went downstairs. "You're an early riser," he commented.

"I'm a farm boy. Got a rooster in my head."

"You want some breakfast? I can have the cook whip up some eggs, waffles, you name it."

"Maybe just some coffee for now."

"How about some fruit? I get it right off the truck at the Hunt's Point Market, like you picked it fresh this morning." He rang the maid and ordered fruit without waiting for a reply. "You like to read the Sunday papers?"

"Only if they got comics."

He laughed. "Good idea. There's too much crap going on in the world anyway. Do you go to church? I can get somebody to drive you there if you want."

"I'm not much of a churchgoer," I admitted.

"Me neither, but I respect those who are."

"My mama's in the church choir back home. She's a Grand Matron of the Eastern Star."

"I don't know that. Is it like the altar guild or something?"

"I don't believe so. It's a Baptist thing."

"Your mother's a Baptist?"

"Everybody's Baptist where I come from."

"No Catholics?"

"Only Mexicans, I reckon."

He thought about it. "So how come you don't go to church if your mother's such a big Baptist?"

"Well to tell you the truth I'm sort've off God right now."

"Off God? Whatta you mean off God?"

"You know. Him and me aren't seeing exactly eye-to-eye right now."

Nick shook his head. "That's not right; you can't just go off God."

His reaction surprised me. I would have thought that being a gangster and going off God went hand-in-hand. "I don't have anything against him. It's just that he's made things pretty hard for me lately."

"Hard, huh? Let me show you something." He stood and motioned for me to follow him outside, where after a few minutes walk across the grounds we halted at the edge of a rocky bluff. "See that?" He pointed below where a very old woman dressed entirely in black was struggling up the incline toward us on her hands and knees. "That's my mother," he announced proudly. "Eighty-three years old."

"What's she doing?" I gasped.

"*Il viaggiare di dolore*, the voyage of sorrow, the voyage of pain. She does that every Sunday."

"Why?"

"It's the Way of the Cross, the way they did it in the old country. I had it built for her when we first moved here. It takes her about four hours to complete the circuit and by then her knees are tore up like hamburger."

I could see a series of cement monuments dotting the incline, one of them plainly her goal as she struggled upward toward it. "Aren't you afraid she'll hurt herself?"

"Hurting's the whole idea. She's atoning for Christ's suffering by repeating the journey of his crucifixion. Each one of those concrete stations marks another milestone on *il viaggiare di dolore*. He's scourged at the pillar, condemned to die, he falls three times, he's nailed to the cross, all that stuff. By the time she's finished all fourteen stations she'll have crawled all the way to Calvary. While we stand here women all over Sicily are doing that same thing.

"Do men ever do it?"

"It's a women's thing."

"My mama is married to a preacher."

"No shit? So how come you don't believe in God? "

"I didn't say I didn't believe in God, not exactly anyway. I just said I was off him for now."

"Because he's making it hard for you right now," Nick filled in. "You think that old lady down there is worried about how hard God's making it for her?"

"I don't know what to think about that."

"You know, except for weddings and christenings, I ain't been on the inside of a church in maybe thirty years. There's nothing personal in it; you just get to a point where you don't go any more, know what I mean? But even if I'm not what you'd call a religious man, I've gotta tell you I wouldn't have the balls to come right out and say I was off God. No way."

"I used to feel that way too, but I called him on it and he didn't come strike me down."

"Called him? Like in a poker game?"

"Something like that."

"So if you lose you've got to pay up, right?"

"Well nothing's happened this far, so I reckon I'm safe for the time being."

His face turned grave. "Let me tell you something. There's two things you don't fuck around with; gambling debts and God, and you done both. Either you got the biggest pair of *culiones* in the world or you're the world's biggest chump."

"I never thought about it quite like that."

"I watched you last night at dinner and you never took your eyes off the Congressman. He picked up a knife and fork, you picked up a knife and fork; that shows me you're a smart kid. When you don't know the territory you stake out somebody who does."

"I just didn't want to embarrass Molly. I figured he'd been at a lot more fancy dinners than me so I couldn't go too wrong doing what he did."

"But right away you figured out he was the one to watch."

117

"I reckon."

"The man does know how to eat proper, I'll give him that."

The old woman below had prostrated herself in front of the cement marker. Only her labored breathing indicated that she'd survived the ordeal. "You sure she'll be okay?" I asked.

"She'll be fine, and you know why? Because she believes in something. If you got something to believe in you can get through anything, but if you got no belief you're a shell, like that Congressman you think so much of. All he's got is what he can steal, everything else is gone, his pride, his manhood. He comes here so I can squeeze his stones, he leaves here a little richer and a little less of a man. That old lady down there's got more *coraggio* than he'll ever have."

It was then that I saw him for the first time: a man standing between us and the water with a rifle slung loosely on his shoulder. If not for his posture and his gait he might have been a hunter (he was too erect and stiff, and though his contours were pinched by the sun and wind it was plain that he was walking backward), but the only thing I'd seen that might be hunted there were seagulls, and hunting them seemed hardly sport. A man could drop a half-a-dozen with a single charge of birdshot the way they hung suspended in the breeze.

Harry Bailey could come home with them strung together, all the way the hound yapping at the string, and his brow creased and his blue eyes squinted against the sun as if he had something important on his mind and she would see him through the kitchen window and say that man's not bringing those birds into my house, and I would run out to greet him and the hound would lick my face.

"There's a man with a rifle over on the rise," I said.

"There's a few like him around."

"They hunters?"

"Bodyguards. They're there to see that nobody's here who shouldn't be here. You got nothing to worry about as long as you're with me." He walked to the edge of the downgrade where below the old lady had resumed her painful ascent. "You see, where she comes from all they've ever known is struggle. All their lives they had to scratch a living out of the rocks, to raise their children in poverty, to watch their husbands go off to war and never come back, and still they never lost faith. You see what it is I'm telling you?"

I thought of Mama, bereft on the Texas hardpan without a real man to see her through. Was that what she was doing, suffering for suffering's sake? If she had come with me to New York would she have needed to create another Eula in own mind, like the old lady needed *il viaggiare di dolore* to remind her of the struggle she had left behind? If what Nick was telling me was that too much of a good thing was bad and too much of a bad thing was good, I could not see how he could justify living the way he did. "What is it you believe in?" I found myself asking him.

"I believe in America," he said after giving it some thought. "I believe in a place where little Molly Cooney can grow up to be Mona Chalfonte and where a punk kid from Brooklyn can grow up to own cops and judges and congressmen. And I believe in him." He turned toward the sun, to where the solitary rifleman had disappeared behind the rim of the hill. "He's like God; even when I can't see him, I know he's there watching out for me."

Eighteen

The stool at the end of the bar was occupied by a woman in a dark wool dress, buttoned up in front to a lace collar stained yellow at the edges. Her hair was shades of gray, swept back in a bun and held together with a coarse hairnet that tied in the middle of her forehead. Behind her, the front window of the saloon looked out onto Third Avenue through hand-streaked wipings that made those passing look like folks posing in a carnival mirror.

"You old enough to drink that stuff?"

I pretended not to hear, hoping she'd forget about me.

Next to me, the Cajun studied a shot glass overflowing with Irish whiskey for what he reckoned to be a fitting amount of time before hoisting it to his lips and downing it in a single gulp. He replaced the empty glass on the pitted surface of the bar, grasped a freshly poured ale chaser with the tenderness one might show when handling a wounded bird, and drank it slowly, careful to leave a frothy drop or two at the bottom of the glass to prove he didn't need it. A simple twitch of his eyebrow told the bartender it was time to pour another.

"You heard me, kid. You ain't old enough, are you?"

Her upper lip curled into a toothless cavity when she spoke; and below, her few remaining teeth sprouted angrily from the jut of her jaw like tombstones in a poorly tended graveyard. I did not see her drink, but there was little doubt in my mind that it was a pastime she was familiar with. Rather she seemed settled in, as much a part of the place as the darkness, the music coming from the jukebox, the rutted moisture rings that had eaten through the cherry-wood finish of the bar.

Shimmelman had told me that generations of Irishmen had grown up in the grimy familiarity of the saloon - toddling beneath the stools and tables as infants while their parents sorted things out at the bar above them. They had celebrated their birthdays, First Communions, and Confirmations there; held their wedding receptions and mourned their dead there. They'd staked an early claim to their own stool at the bar and grown grizzled and toothless defending it. He'd told me that fights were commonplace there, as were outpourings of tenderness and affection. And in the back room where the chairs were almost always stacked top-to-bottom in the corners, and lifeless twists of crepe paper hung from one celebration to the next, young men and women danced to the bell-sharp tenor tones of Frank Parker, and dreamed of a place called Muvorneen they had never seen, and sometimes made love on the tops of tables.

"I know who you are. I seen you stealing food with Shimmelman."

"Why don't you leave the boy alone?" the Cajun growled.

"Why don't you go fuck yourself and the horse you rode in on?"

It was Aida, the woman who Shimmelman said had danced the fandango with the king of the Hottentots. By accident we had stumbled into another dimension of her narrow orbit, and just as in the E and B, she resented it.

"What's your name, kid?"

"You don't have to answer her," the Cajun said.

She eyed him scornfully. "Don't think I don't recognize you. I remember you from the hospital. Flak-happy's what you are."

"I never saw you before in my life, you old bat."

"Flak-happy!"

"What hospital is she talking about?" I rasped.

"The woman is bats."

"Flak-happy!"

'What's that mean, flak-happy?"

"It means he's crazy as a loon," she cackled. "Everyone in the hospital's crazy as a loon. McCracken was craziest of all and they let him out. Put the poor sap out on the street when he could hardly remember his own name. They didn't give a rat's ass whether he lived and died out there. Just needed the bed space, they did."

"Crazy old bat," The Cajun muttered.

"Flak-happy."

"Crazy old bat."

"Fuck you and the horse."

I did not know what to make of it all. New York seemed a place where people lived side-by-side with entirely different perceptions about the way things were. It was as if the world had cracked open and everybody's guarded secrets had spilled out; a world of Joe Carl's solipsisms tumbling all over one another and coming up addled. Instead of folks agreeing on the general outcome, the way a solipsism was supposed to work, they were ready to go to war to defend their own way of seeing things.

"McCracken was lost, he couldn't keep a job if his life depended on it," she went on. "People would hire him because he looked like he was getting ready to have an idea, but after a while they got tired of waiting for it to come so they shit-canned him. I'd send him off to look for work every morning carrying an egg salad sandwich in a brown paper bag. He'd take the subway uptown and wander around Grand Central Station all day, nibbling the egg salad sandwich and waiting for something to happen. He was run over by a Krug Bakery truck. I'll bet you didn't know that."

The Cajun shrugged. "It's of no concern to me."

"Got to playing in traffic, he did; darting in front of trucks and busses, then jumping out of their way at the last minute and giving them the finger when they drove past. The driver of the Krug's truck got so pissed off he doubled back and nailed the old fool on the second pass."

The Cajun hoisted the shot of Irish whiskey, downed it with a convulsive toss of his head, and held it to his lips for a few seconds before replacing it softly on the bar. He stared into the tumbler, inspecting the polished wood grain of the bar refracted through the empty glass as if he was watching grains of sand spill through an hourglass. "You have my condolences," he muttered.

"It was no matter to me, she shrugged. "McCracken was long gone before the truck squashed him. The army should've paid his death benefit when they mustered him out instead of waiting for him to croak. He was as good as dead anyway, couldn't make a decision if his life depended on it."

I thought of Isaiah Balenkin's Kuryokin wandering aimlessly through the shell-flattened forest, his mind benumbed by fear and shock. He had stumbled out onto a dirt road where a crude wooden sign directed him to the village of Lotsk, twenty-eight kilometers away. Obediently, he'd set out for Lotsk but he soon came upon another sign a few kilometers down the road which read, Volochisk 33 km, and without a moment's hesitation he had changed direction. He'd done the same at a sign pointing the way to Lvov, and again at one directing him to Drnin. Unconditionally compliant when it came to road signs, his shell-scarred brain was incapable of disregarding even the most obscure of them.

"I buried him in Holy Angels Cemetery out in Queens, consecrated ground. They said he was entitled to be buried in Arlington with full military honors but I told them to go fuck themselves. The army took everything from him that made him a man. I was goddamned if I was going to let them take his corpse." She scowled defiantly, yawned, and rested her head on the bar.

The Cajun sipped his ale chaser deliberately, siphoning the amber liquid through its frothy head in measured draughts. "It would have been better for McCracken if his body had been buried in a bomb crater in Europe," he whispered into the foam. "If the army took his mind, the Holy Angels are sure to play the old hoop-de-do with his soul for the rest of eternity."

"I thought you said you didn't know him," I recollected.

"Oh, I know him. I've known a hundred McCrackens, a thousand; flattened out over the generations, their blood thinned to water, their balls shrunk to BBs. They clung to God and milked him for all he was worth just to keep from shriveling up like rashers of overcooked bacon. Above all they needed order. Order relieved them of critical thought."

Isaiah Balenkin's Kuryokin had found order in signs, I thought. One after another they'd relieved him of the necessity of having to make decisions. When at long last he arrived in the city of Minsk he observed a message scrawled in chalk on the wall of a factory: SING THE PRAISES OF THE GLORIOUS RED REVOLUTION. Without hesitation he began to do just that, creating the words and tune as he went along:

"Praise the glorious Red revolution," he chirped happily as he trotted from village to village. *"...Eeeei-eeei-oh!"*

"Only men who turned their back on order were able to survive," the Cajun went on, staring through the rank of liquor bottles at his reflection in the back-bar mirror. "It's the ones whose minds constrained them to think about the senselessness and waste of it that ended up getting squashed by bakery trucks. They weren't killed by bullets, but by reality."

"Shimmelman says that reality is the hobgoblin of dolts and incompetents. He says that the only answer to it is to run away."

"That's because Shimmelman still believes in the world," the Cajun snorted, "Despite all his protestations to the contrary he can still be disappointed by it. He despises it because it's turned its back on him, because it refuses to recognize his genius. That's the difference between him and me. I believe in nothing while he believes in everything, and everything has let him down. It's no great feat to despise a world that's disappointed you. The feat is in despising it for the sheer joy of it."

"Do you think Shimmelman's a genius?"

"Do you?"

"I don't know, I guess I don't rightly know what a genius is. All that painting he does is hard to understand. Sometimes he stays up all night painting and the next morning all he's got done is maybe another inch. When I ask him about it he says an inch on the wall could be a thousand light years in the cosmos. Makes you wonder."

"Shimmelman's genius is in coping," the Cajun said matter-of-factly. "He paints the cosmos because it is his way of escaping the order of the world. The cosmos is a chaotic place, filled with unbelievable violence. Whether he knows it or not, he needs that violence. He keeps a pistol in the nightstand by his bed. Every night he takes it out and points it at a spot beneath his chin and cocks the hammer and asks himself, will this be the night? Shall I end it all now or suffer one more day of disappointment?"

"How do you know that?"

"I found the gun when I was spraying for bugs. The rest I assume."

The Cajun had sprayed the Soldiers and Sailors for cockroaches, using a vile-smelling concoction he said he'd learned how to make during the war. We were beginning to suspect that his account of shoveling seagull shit on an island off the coast of Louisiana was just another fantasy life he'd cooked up for himself, somebody else's story he'd heard in a homeless shelter or Salvation Army mission and adopted. Shimmelman said that a man without a past of his own did not need a conscience, and I'd thought about Harry Bailey disappearing the way he had and wondered if it was to keep from thinking about us. After covering his face with a surgical mask, the Cajun had prowled the halls and rooms of the Soldiers and Sailors with a flit-gun, firing it into closets, drawers and corners with all the relish of a combat-hardened Marine on Iwo Jima roasting Jap holdouts in caves with a flame-thrower. When he'd finished the rooms and hallways were filled with a trillion cockroach carcasses, the air inside reeking with their lifeless stink and the overpowering smell of the Cajun's concoction (like the outhouse at home after Uncle Mal had poured in a truckload of lime). All the windows had to be opened and what fans there were kept on high, and everything outside came in under the whirr of the fans and the scrape of us shoveling their cracked, hard shells off the tiled floors in the halls and stairways, and the elevated train rattling past every fifteen minutes or so, *take it to me, take it to me, take it to me.*

"Do you think he wants to kill himself?" I asked.

"I don't think he wants to. He just wants to know that he can. That's man's greatest luxury, power over life and death. Soldiers know that. McCracken must have known it, don't you think?"

I finished my beer warily, watching the sleeping Aida for signs of wakefulness and censure.

"It's hard for me to figure out. My daddy, Harry Bailey, was a soldier but I never got to see what he was like after he got back from the war. Folks who did say he drank too much and gambled too much and let his temper get the best of him sometimes, but I reckon he did all those things before he went away. I'd have to see him now to know what he feels about life and death."

The Cajun scooped up what was left of his money. "He killed a man with a knife, didn't he?"

"Might have," I conceded.

126

"Do you think he enjoyed it?"

"I don't rightly know. He killed game—deer and wildfowl, but he called that sport. I can't say whether he enjoyed it or not."

"Killing is killing. It's all a matter of controlling something that's supposed to be left to God. It gives men power, it gives then divinity."

Aida raised her head from the bar as we left and fixed the Cajun with a liquid stare. "Flak-happy," she grunted. "Better get yourself back to the hospital before you end up drooling all over yourself like McCracken."

"Old bat."

Outside the street clung to what was left of the afternoon, gleaning shafts of pale light from the trestle above as we walked toward the Soldiers and Sailors in a crisp October breeze. Back in Eula the last of the tall grass would already be cut and baled, and the windbreak elms would have lost most of their orange leaves, laying open the landscape to winter's bitter gales, but where Eula flattened out in winter, New York tightened like a fist. Folks braced against the chill that blew from the side streets and wrapped itself in tiny dust-funnels on the sidewalks, walking faster than they had in summer, keeping their chins tucked hard against their chests and their hands dug firmly in their jacket pockets. Fire escape landings that had been crammed with people looking to escape the heat only a few weeks ago were empty, hanging forlorn like empty saddlebags from the sides of buildings, and children did not dart in and out of doorways any more. Even the ever-present elevated railway seemed older and less comfortable, less able to cope. Steel I-beams shuddered and creaked long before the train arrived, and when it passed overhead the downward rush of air brought with it wooden slivers and metal shavings from the cross-ties, hot and glowing from the friction of the wheels, hovering in the shadows and glowing like nervous fireflies.

"You say he was in the war?" the Cajun asked.

"Who?"

"Your old man, the one who deserted you."

"He was in the army. I reckon he did some fighting."

"Do you know if he was wounded?"

"What difference would that make?"

"Because if he was wounded he'd be on disability. He'd be getting a check every month from the VA, same as me. That was my VA disability check we were drinking on this afternoon."

"What if he wasn't wounded?"

"Everyone was wounded in some way by that war. You'd have to be a wooden man to escape from it unscathed."

"So you think if I went to the VA they could tell me where to find him?"

The Cajun coughed a fruity cough that rose in vaporous clouds above his head as he walked. "They might not be able to tell you where to find him but they'll know where his paper went. Follow the paper, and if there's money follow that. A good gyp-artist could be collecting a king's ransom from the government."

"I don't think he'd gyp the government."

"Why shouldn't he? They gypped him. They took away his youth and his family and if he's still alive probably his sanity, things that most men would gladly trade for money but never get the chance. Harry Bailey's got everyman's God at his fingertips. If he's half the rogue you say he is he should be resting in the bosom of Abraham by now."

Nineteen

Molly had been away for a week; a vacation she said. On the spur of the moment she'd accepted Nick Corsi's invitation to go with him to Miami, Florida, where they'd lounged on the beach, gone swimming in the warm, green ocean, eaten in the finest restaurants, and even gambled some in an offshore casino. I wanted to grab her by the shoulders and shake her and make her tell me what they did at night when the swimming and eating and gambling were over; I wanted to warn her that she was throwing her life away on a guy who broke peoples' legs when they couldn't pay their gambling debts, who thought so little of women that he let his eighty-three year old mother tear her flesh to shreds in some monstrous ritual of atonement; I wanted to tell her that she was still young enough to make it on her own, that I would be there with her to see that we both made it, but I didn't. I was afraid of what I might hear, and I didn't want to foul her mood.

Everything, it seemed, was starting to break her way. Two of the regular Rockettes had come down with the flu and several more were beginning to show symptoms, just as rehearsals for the Christmas show were getting underway. Bertie's reserves were worn thin, his already fiery temperament strained to the point of hysteria, but despite the adverse circumstances, Molly was dancing. She was on-stage, in the line, tapping and kicking to his incessant shouting, hand-clapping and foot-stomping, his undisguised contempt for her inexperience, his apparent determination to humiliate her at any cost. Day after day he drove her, denounced her and ridiculed her until she was reduced to tears, yet I had never seen her happier. She'd also been accepted as a student at The American Dance Ensemble, the same troupe Bertie belonged to. It would mean hours of grueling training after hours of grueling rehearsals, leaving little or no time for anything else in her life, but it would all be worth it. Finally, after six years of rooting around New York for a break, she was realizing that dream she'd dreamt on her front porch back in Whitehall.

"It has to happen now," she stressed as we sat in the kitchen of her small Ninth Avenue apartment. "I'm twenty five years old!"

"I don't think twenty-five's all that old," I objected.

"It's ancient for a dancer. Most dancers start their training when they're eight or nine, when their muscles are still young and flexible. I've got to jam fifteen years of training into just one or two if I have any chance at all."

"You're already getting your chance. You're a Rockette. You said yourself it's the best job in New York."

"I know, and it is. Being a Rockette in the Radio City Christmas show is a dream come true, but ballet is more than just dancing; it's a form of creative expression, it's a way of life."

"Sounds to me like you've been listening to Bertie too much."

She frowned. "I don't care what you think about Bertie. He's a true artist, a genius at modern ballet. He's the heart of The American Dance Ensemble. Everything he does is absolutely perfect. Just watching him limber up at the barre is an inspiration."

"I'd think you'd be looking for reasons to spend less time with somebody who treats you as bad as Bertie does."

"That's because you don't know anything about dance."

I watched her across the kitchen table, her eyes cast downward to her lap where Trixie, her six-year-old Yorkshire terrier, responded to her affectionate stroking with soft, self-indulgent whines. Wearing no make-up, her skin glistening with perspiration and her hair disheveled from the morning's rehearsal, Molly was effortlessly provoking; as alluring as any seductress I might have conjured up in the privacy of my own thoughts. I could smell her skin, like cornflowers sprinkled with rose water (I had found them in an old album, pressed between brittle pages of photographs of when they were together; Mama curled demurely on a picnic blanket, her snapshot face yellowed by time and creased with a proprietary smile. And Harry Bailey there beside her with his shirtsleeve rolled high on his bicep, the tattooed spider peeking around the corner of his muscled forearm. He might have picked the cornflowers and given them to her, I'd thought, and she'd memorialized the event by pressing them in the album and sprinkling them with rose water, staining the pages with eternal substance, the life-blood of flowers, the essence of memory).

In truth, I was both resentful and relieved at Molly's backbreaking schedule. While it left her little time to spend with me, it freed me to continue my search for Harry Bailey without worrying that she was seeing Nick. At first, the Cajun's suggestion that I follow the VA paper trail had gotten me nowhere. Information about clients was held strictly in private, I'd been told by a pinched matron at the Veteran's Administration headquarters in downtown Battery Park. Only immediate relatives were entitled to see it. Without even a driver's license to prove my identity I was naturally at a loss to prove my kinship to him (I had a card attesting to my membership in the West Texas 4-H Club which had proved utterly useless), and so I was forced to phone Eula and ask Mama to send my birth certificate or a reasonable facsimile thereof. As I had expected she begged me to come home.

Thanksgiving was only weeks away, a time for family to be together, she said. There would be roast turkey and stuffing, baked yams and creamed pearl onions and pumpkin pie with ice cream, all things I had a hankering for; but what she did not say, and what I knew to be the fact of the matter, was that the Reverend Harley Brown would keep us at the table for most of the day while he jawed on about giving thanks for the Lord's bounty to the Hebrews during their desolate flight from Egypt. God rained down manna that tasted like biscuits and honey, the story went, and the children of Israel ate it for forty years until they stumbled onto the Promised Land. I was not secure enough in my disbelief to challenge the scriptures altogether, but it did seem to me that entirely too much time was spent thanking the Lord for something that should have been settled a few thousand years ago. A lot of Hebrews had starved to death since then, and the skies hadn't exactly been raining biscuits and honey for any of them.

(In *Womb*, Kuryokin had wandered into a village where Cossacks had confiscated everything and left the population without food. The streets were littered with the dead. Buzzards fought with mongrel dogs over their bloated remains, and the handful of emaciated zombies who were left alive subsisted on the carcasses of the dogs. "Sing the praises of the glorious Red revolution," Kuryokin sang as he walked among them, "eeeei-eeei-oh;" and those who had the strength pelted him with rocks).

I did not exactly promise to be home for Thanksgiving if Mama mailed me the birth certificate, and Mama did not exactly confirm that she would send the birth certificate if I promised to be home for Thanksgiving, so I'd been happily surprised when it arrived in the post a few days later, and made a decision to go back for Christmas when Harley Brown's dinner table rambling would be the far more familiar story of the manger in Bethlehem.

"Come downtown to the Veteran's Administration with me," I urged Molly.

"Why, afraid of what you might find out?"

"Maybe. Maybe I just want to be with you."

"I wish I was up to it, but I need to get some sleep before I go to the studio."

Leaving her to sleep, I traveled downtown by subway to Bowling Green at the tip of Manhattan and made my way to the Veteran's Administration building, a low, brown, decrepit structure of crumbling brick and peeling plaster and the penetrating odor of decay locked in its narrow corridors. The solitary clerk in the Department of Pensions and Benefits was the same woman who'd confronted me my first time there:

"I'm Chance Bailey," I informed her, sliding my birth certificate across the chest-high partition. "I was here before and you told me I had to come back with proof of who I was."

She scrutinized the document. "And what is this in reference to?"

"To my daddy, Harry Bailey. I'm trying to find out if he's on disability."

"Your father is a veteran?"

"Yes ma'am."

She donned a pair of brown-rimmed spectacles and squinted again at the birth certificate. "And you think he might be receiving disability payments?"

"Well I'm hoping he is."

"Do you know the nature of his disability?"

"No ma'am, I can't say that I do."

"Do you know how long he's been receiving benefits?"

"I'm afraid not."

"I don't suppose you have any idea what branch of the service he was in?" she asked irritably.

"Yes ma'am. He was in the army."

"The United States army?"

"Yes ma'am."

She scribbled something on a sheet of yellow paper and handed my birth certificate back over the partition. "His name is Chance Bailey?"

"No ma'am, I'm Chance Bailey, he's Harry Bailey."

"Middle name or initial?"

"If he has one I don't reckon I know it."

"And is there a problem with his payment?"

"I don't know for sure. I don't know if he's even getting a payment for sure. I'm just trying to find him."

"You're his son?"

"Yes ma'am."

"Are you planning on making a claim against his disability award? Because if you are, you're in the wrong department; you'd want Legal Services downstairs."

"I'm just trying to find him, ma'am."

"Harry Bailey"... She muttered the name under her breath as she went to a row of metal filing cabinets behind her. "Would that be Harold or just Harry?"

"I can't say for sure. Harry's all anybody ever called him."

"I don't suppose you know his date of separation." It was a statement, not a question.

"Sorry about that."

She nodded, confirming her own conviction that she was dealing with a half-wit, and began riffling through the files. After several minutes she returned to the partition with a stack of manila folders. "We have six

Harold Baileys on record," she reported. "You'll have to identify him from his photograph. Do you think you can do that?"

"He's my daddy."

She extracted a single cover sheet from the top folder and handed it to me. Across the top, the name Harold Edward Bailey was typed in an irregular line along with his serial number, and stapled to the side of the sheet below was the photograph of an older man with graying hair and an overhang of dark brows framing two angry coal-black eyes.

"It's not him," I told her.

Harold Thomas Bailey, Harry B. Bailey, and Harry Custis Bailey were not him either, the last being a colored man, of all things. Horace Bailey was not Harry Bailey at all, but simply somebody who'd gotten misfiled, and although he seemed like a decent sort, the fact that he'd got stuck in a place he shouldn't have been seemed to cause her no end of aggravation. She shoved the final cover sheet across the partition with venom.

Harry (nmi) Bailey. U.S. 414-22-809: There was no mistaking his Comanche cheekbones and blue, blue eyes, even though they showed pale gray in the black and white photograph. He was older than I remembered, his face slightly thinner with a touch of hardness I could not recall having seen before; but even through his unsmiling gaze I could detect an undeveloped set to his jaw that told me he was choking back a belly laugh (He would make fun of her with his eyes at the dinner table when she fussed over little things like unwashed hands or careless posture, and when he saw it upset her he would flatten out his visage like a mask and the laugh was still there but she couldn't pry it loose).

"That's him!" I fairly exploded.

She took the cover sheet from me and matched it to its folder. "Your father's been diagnosed as suffering from a stress-related disorder," she read from the information inside. "He's been receiving a monthly benefit of eighty-eight dollars and sixty-three cents since July of nineteen forty-seven."

My heart raced. After months of fruitless searching it looked like I'd finally hit pay dirt. "Is this where he gets the money?"

She scanned the sheet. "The check is sent to him at home. Actually your mother is listed as the recipient."

"My mother gets the money?"

"If your mother is Glenda Louise Bailey, she does."

"There must be some mistake. That's my daddy but I don't know any Glenda Louise Bailey. My mother is Addie Bailey."

She reread the information carefully. "Glenda Louise Bailey residing at 181 West Sixty-third street in Manhattan?"

"My mama lives in Eula, Texas."

"And you're certain the man in this photograph is your father?"

"It couldn't be anybody else."

She stepped back from the partition, the taut angles of her face softening.

"I'm sorry but there's nothing else I can tell you. I'm sure there's a logical explanation for this. I'd suggest you have a talk with your mother and straighten it all out."

The face in the photograph stayed with me as I exited the building, gaunt with that budding grin of his, and I knew that of all the pictures I had seen of him, it was the one I would always remember.

(I had removed the snapshot of the picnic from the album along with the cornflowers and wrapped them in a handkerchief in my dresser drawer where they remained unmolested for many months, and later when I thought to look at them the scent of rose water was gone and the flowers had disintegrated to fine, dry dust.)

Shimmelman had said that the only sane response to reality was to flee from it, and more than anything I wanted to escape from it then. If there was a logical explanation, then logic would tear me apart, and so I ached for the release of the illogical, the preposterous, the world of derelicts and dreamers where all the eons of creation could be captured in a few deft brushstrokes and people invented their lives as they went along.

LeMoult

Twenty

One-eighty-one West Sixty-third Street was four cement steps rising from the dusty pavement between a dry cleaner and a florist shop, a battered metal door painted black that opened reluctantly on rusted hinges to an unlit foyer smelling of grime and neglect. A row of copper-colored mailboxes were set against the entrance wall, some hanging open, and above, the names of tenants scrawled on strips of adhesive tape: Calish... O'Connor... Regimenteri...Bailey — 2C; small and neatly scripted in a woman's handwriting. A flight of wooden stairs in the back took me to the second floor where I found apartment 2C and nervously rang the bell.

"Yes?" An eye, a strip of shadowed skin showed in the partially opened doorway.

"Is this Harry Bailey's apartment?"

"Who wants to see him?" The voice was soft and throaty, a British accent.

"I'm Chance, his son."

The door strained at the chain, as if she had given it a sudden, reflexive yank before she slammed it shut, leaving me alone in the hall with my stomach doing flip-flops. I was about to ring the bell a second time when the door opened again, and a woman appeared partially silhouetted in the doorway, nervously smoothing out the wrinkles in her house dress with open palms. "Harry never mentioned he had a son."

"Is he here?"

She shook her head. "I haven't seen him in almost a year."

"I was six last time I saw him."

She stepped back from the door, showing me her profile in the light behind her—slim and fine-featured like Mama. "Do you want to come in?"

"I don't want to be a bother," I said awkwardly. "Maybe if you could just tell me where to find him..."

"Come on inside." She shrugged and laughed nervously, hoarse like a whimper. "I'm Glenda, but I guess you know that by now."

"Yes'm"

She was older than I thought she'd be, with pale yellow hair tied on top with a flowered kerchief and blue eyes, darker than Harry Bailey's, the skin around them creased with tiny wrinkles she had tried to cover with makeup. "Cigarette?"

"No thanks. I don't smoke."

She took one herself from a pack of Lucky Strikes on the coffee table and lit it. "Something to drink—you old enough for a beer?"

"I'm fine, ma'am."

I sat on the sofa and she sat in a straight-back chair in the center of the room, each of us sizing up the other. "You do look like him," she said after a while; "a little taller perhaps, a little broader."

"I been told I favor him some."

"You have his eyes."

"Yes'm. They say that." My mind had gone blank. I'd spent hours rehearsing what I would say to her when I saw her but the words had deserted me before I ever set foot in the tiny apartment.

"Well, this is quite a surprise, learning that Harry has a grown son and all. Is your mother still alive?" The question hung weightless in the air with the smoke from her cigarette.

"Yes'm."

"I wish you'd call me Glenda, or Glenny. Harry always called me Glenny."

"Didn't he ever tell you about us?"

"He told me he'd been married and divorced. He never mentioned having children. Do you have any brothers or sisters?"

"No ma'am, and there never was a divorce. Harry Bailey went off to the war in nineteen-forty-two and that was the last we all heard of him until he called last spring and told us he was working at Radio City Music Hall, but by the time I got here he'd gone somewhere else. I've been looking for him ever since."

The mention of the Music Hall brought a spark of recollection to her face but it quickly lapsed back into static curiosity. "Did your mother come to New York with you?"

"No ma'am, she's back in Eula, married to the Reverend Harley Brown, and the less said about him the better."

She smiled, but it was hard to tell whether she was amused by me, or just filling in the gaps. "And Eula is?"

"In Texas, ma'am, west Texas actually, out on the hardpan."

"Harry mentioned having a brother in Texas."

"That would be my Uncle Mal. He and Daddy ran the farm before the war. Now Uncle Mal runs it by himself. I help some."

That seemed to surprise her. "It's hard to imagine Harry a farmer. I wouldn't have thought he had the discipline for that."

"I don't think he cottoned to it much," I allowed.

Glenda ground her cigarette out in an ashtray and immediately lit another, punctuating the awkward silence with a breathy exhalation. "So here we are," she acknowledged with a shrug. "I'm sure you have questions of your own."

I had a million questions, all the questions I'd been asking myself since I'd been old enough to wonder why he'd left us, since I'd tracked him in Mama's careworn eyes, in the bushes, creeks and arroyos, in the plaintive howls of wolves. Did he hitch his thumbs into his belt when he walked the way I remembered? Did he strop his razor with smooth, measured strokes until the steel blade sang on the leather? Did he still carry a stag's-horn knife? Did he drink in saloons, play cards with tinhorns, visit whores at night and throw his trousers over the bedpost and tuck his socks and shorts into his boots the way he did at home? And was he brave; was he brave ever?

"How did you meet him?" I asked instead.

"It was during the war, in England. I was driver for a colonel in the RAF and Harry was a Yank sergeant. We met at a pub, sang some sad songs and cried a bit, and two weeks later we were married."

"Didn't you ask if he was already married?"

"No, I didn't ask, but I don't think it would have mattered if I'd known. Not much about the past mattered in those days; everybody was falling in love, total strangers, people who'd met the night before and who knew they'd probably never see each other again after the war were getting married. It didn't mean the same thing it meant before the war, or maybe it meant much, much more. All everybody knew was that it was important to have someone to hold onto while the world was blowing up." She smiled a sad, dreamy smile. "I'm having a beer, sure you don't want one?"

"Maybe just a glass."

She went to the kitchen and returned shortly with an unchilled bottle of Rheingold's and two glasses, picking up the account where she had left off: "Harry shipped out four days after the wedding; D-Day. I never knew he was leaving. Everyone knew it was going to happen soon but it was still a shock. We needed another day, another few hours but all of life was so temporary then." She poured the warm beer equally into both glasses and handed one to me. "He was in the Infantry, at the Battle of the Bulge, did you know that?"

"No, he never wrote after he left."

"Harry wasn't keen on writing. I got only one letter whole time he was away and most of it had been inked out by the censors. He said he thought about me, promised to live through the war and come back when it was all over. I don't think I believed he'd come back even if he managed to survive. England was full of war brides whose husbands had gone back to their old lives after the war. It was just the way of things. Everything we were about was immediacy and need. There just weren't any percentages in thinking about the long haul. Looking back on it, I think the ones who were abandoned might have been the lucky ones after all. The Yanks who came back were changed, not at all the dashing young men who'd marched off to save the world. They'd fought a war, bloody killing and all. Some of them would never get over it."

"But he came back to you."

"Yes, he did." She eyed me with a mixture of pity and regret. "I don't suppose it would be any consolation to you or your mother to know that the man who came back was a different Harry Bailey from the one who went away."

"Probably not," I conceded. "I think Mama would've wanted him back no matter what shape he was in."

"That's the way I felt about it in at first. We came to America to make a new start of it and on the surface everything seemed to be going rather well. Harry joined the Fifty-two-twenty Club; the government paid every returning veteran twenty dollars a week for fifty-two weeks to keep them on their feet until they could find jobs; we were able to rent an affordable flat, we made a few friends and generally kept up appearances, but from the start I knew something was terribly wrong. There was a restlessness about him; nothing obvious mind you, but something coiled and brooding, something very frightening."

"Folks back home say he was like that before he ever went away," I broke in. "They say there were times he was like a caged panther. He'd have to go off in the brush by himself and shoot a mess of quail or bag a pronghorn elk or snatch a jackrabbit by the ears before the feeling left him. He had an awful bad temper. Guys'd look at him cross-ways and like as not he'd beat the tar out of them."

"I think I might have preferred his temper to his demons, at least it would have shown me there was something left inside to care about."

"Did he ever talk about the war?"

"Very little. I didn't even know he'd been decorated until I came across his medal accidentally when I was cleaning..." She excused herself and went into another room, returning shortly with a small velvet-covered box neatly tied with a red ribbon. Carefully, she undid the ribbon and handed the box to me. "I think he would have wanted you to see this."

The medal was a silver five-pointed star nestled in a background of dimply red, white and blue ribbon. A folded parchment citation underneath the medal detailed the circumstances that had led to the award:

"FOR GALLANTRY ABOVE AND BEYOND THE CALL OF DUTY:

The President and Congress of the United States hereby acknowledge that Staff Sergeant Harry Bailey, assigned to the One Hundred-First Airborne Division, did on the twentieth day of December in the

Town of Bastogne, Belgium, conduct himself in the finest and most valorous tradition of the Unites States Armed Forces. While under fire from an overwhelming enemy force, Sergeant Bailey repeatedly left his fortified position with selfless disregard for his own well being to remove his fallen comrades from the open battlefield and return them to positions of safety. As a direct result of his courageous actions in the face of extreme danger, the lives of thirteen of his comrades-in-arms were saved. In recognition thereof, Sergeant Harry Bailey is herewith awarded the Silver Star for uncommon valor.

Henry L. Stimson, Secretary of War"

I handed the box back to her. "Don't you think he'll be back for this? It's not everybody who gets one of these."

"The medal never meant anything to him. It was as if he'd never heard of that hero who saved all those wounded men in Bastogne."

"They said at the VA that he had a stress disorder."

She shrugged. "I guess that's just a more scientific way of saying he couldn't lick the demons. He's been in and out of hospitals for years. The last time I heard from him he was in a VA hospital out on Long Island. He wanted me to send his shaving kit. He said he'd be home in a week or so." Her voice caught and she swallowed hard. "That was almost a year ago."

"Is he still there?"

She shook her head. " When I called they told me he'd checked himself out against medical advice."

"Did you try to find out where he went?"

"I tried to stop missing him. It got easier after a while."

"I'm sorry about what he did to you."

"It's not your fault. I'm sorry about what he did to you and your mother."

"That's not your fault either."

"Maybe contrition all we have. Maybe it saves us from our own demons."

I stood to leave. "You know I have to keep on looking for him."

"I know you do." She handed me the velvet box. "You keep this. I think it's fitting that you have it."

"Thanks. I'll give it to him when I find him."

"Will you tell your mother about me?" she asked as we stood in the outside hallway.

"I don't think so. She's got problems enough."

The laugh was genuine, a laugh of relief. "Is there someplace I can reach you if I hear anything?"

"I'm at the Soldiers and Sailors YMCA over on Third Avenue. I don't know the number but it's in the book."

"Well..."

Without thinking I gave her a clumsy hug and felt the brush of her tears against my cheek. "I'm sorry if I stirred things up for you."

"I just wish you didn't look so damn much like him." She turned and went back into the apartment.

LeMoult

Twenty-One

I clutched the medal in my pocket and headed across town to the Soldiers and Sailors in a brisk, gusting wind. Above me, a leaden swath of sky hung between the rows of buildings, pinched and ominous, reminding me that the earth had taken another quarter-turn away from the sun and was getting ready to face winter head-on. Back home there would be chores to do, the endless, repetitious tasks of haying and forking and gathering wood and cow patties for fuel, and the swoosh of flat air across the prairie warning us that there was never enough time. She would open the chest she had brought with her from New England smelling of moth flakes and cedar bark and remove her winter things and air them out on the porch wistfully. As if each garment held a memory, she would unfurl them and examine them in the light of day, looking for holes, for seams that had come unsewn, the unraveling of overuse and time, and hang them over the porch railing or out back on the line she'd strung between the apple trees where the autumn chill would cleanse the smells of confinement in them. Digging in; curling up at the corners.

Old black chest at the end of her bed, nicked at the corners. Everything she had been before she met Harry Bailey had come with her to Texas in that chest. Brave like the eagle carved into its facade (a portion of the beak chipped off by careless railway men), she would sit cross-legged on the floor and inspect its contents, gathering remembrances from the sturdy, oiled mahogany, folding and rearranging the articles inside to bring variety to her unchanging life. And at night when he would take her upstairs and love her it would be there at the end of the bed imparting strength to her, making her forget how much he had disappointed her.

I ran my finger across the soft velvet cover of the medal case. He was a hero and she'd never known it. He'd saved the lives of thirteen men on a battlefield in a place called Bastogne in Belgium, surrounded by an overwhelming enemy force. Somewhere out there he had watched them, tracked them across the barrel of his rifle and picked them off one by one. Had he enjoyed it? Did his heartbeat quicken and his breath become shallow the way it did when he killed an antelope? That would convince the world of his bravery; that would be better than any medal that would lie at the bottom of that mahogany chest when the Reverend Harley Brown climbed on top of her and pulled the comforter up over her and violated her in the dark. He could not be there to stop that. His uncommon valor was spent in war and the sickness that came from war.

Molly had left a telephone message with Shimmelman while I was gone. I dialed her number and she answered after the first ring.

"How'd it go?" Her voice was tentative, expectant.

"Okay I guess. Actually she's a pretty nice lady."

"Was your father there?"

"No. He left her almost a year ago."

"Any idea where he went?"

"Could be anywhere. I don't know any more now than I did before I got there."

She sighed over the receiver. "I'm sorry, Chance. I know how much you were counting on this."

"She gave me his medal. He was a hero in the war."

"I'd like to see it. Suppose I come over and we take a taxi up to Central Park? This might be the last chance we get to see the fall foliage"

"No rehearsals? No school?"

"Everybody needs a day off. See you in a half hour."

I knew she was doing it to lift my spirits, and I knew I should be grateful, but for the first time since I'd met Molly I was not looking forward to seeing her. Maybe it was because I was afraid she would lift me out of my despondency. Maybe I was afraid that when the gloom lifted I would be relieved of the need to find him. The memories and the medal would be enough, everything else only tarnished my image of him. I decided then and there that I would not send his Silver Star to Mama, or even tell her about it. She needed to believe that everything about him was a reflection of his flawed nature; his broken promises, his abandonment of her, even his ill-gotten money, were all proof that his soul was unsalvageable. No medal or ringing citation of his heroism would change that. If she thought for a minute he was gallant she could not live with having lost him, so she would let the Reverend Harley Brown convince her it was nothing more than a token of his savage Comanche bloodlust, and I could not let that happen. The medal was mine, along with everything that went with it. Blood and bravery were our heritage, his and mine.

I heard a faint humming coming from Isaiah Balenkin's room as I passed it in the hall, and the unfamiliar sound of someone moving about inside. "Is everything okay in there?" I shouted through the closed door.

There was a momentary fumbling with the handle before the door opened and the Nobel Laureate appeared, dressed only in his nightshirt, seeming even more frail and diminutive than he had in bed. "I've been trying to open the window but it seems to be stuck, he said haltingly. Perhaps you could give me a hand with it."

"Are you sure you should be out of bed?"

"Why shouldn't I be out of bed?"

"Maybe I should get Shimmelman."

He gave me an appraising glance. "You seem like a capable young man. Surely Shimmelman isn't the only one in the Soldiers and Sailors able to open a stuck window."

"You know where you are?" I gasped.

"Of course I know where I am. Why shouldn't I know where I am?"

"Well, it's just that for a while there you seemed to be a little..."

"Mad?"

"Well not exactly mad. Confused maybe."

"Oh I think I was quite mad; or maybe I was pretending to be mad." He rubbed the stubble on his chin with a bony finger. "Then again, perhaps I'm simply pretending to be sane now. It's all very interesting. Did you know that madmen were worshipped as gods in some ancient civilizations? I believe even your own American Indians held the mad in great esteem. They believed they had special powers to intervene with the deities."

"I have Comanche blood in me," I volunteered.

"Good for you. Then I can tell you where I've been these past months, or years. I don't really know how long I've been away."

"Shimmelman says he found you wandering around in Bryant Park a couple of years ago."

Balenkin nodded. "Yes, I met my grandfather there. He told me a fascinating story about how he survived the siege of Sevastopol during the Crimean War. He was already an old man then, well into his eighties, as were his two closest friends, Gretchko and Miskovitch. But their hearts beat with patriotic fervor and they decided they would do what they could to protect their homeland from the invading Turks, even to the point of sacrificing their own lives..."

The window had been painted shut. I managed to loosen it some by banging on the frame but I was unable to raise it an inch. "I think I'll have to get the Cajun in here with some proper tools," I said.

"The three old friends got drunk on homemade vodka and marched through the silent streets of the city, carrying garden implements for weapons. The streets were almost empty. Everyone knew the invasion of Sevastopol was imminent and they had all fled the city. There was not a sound, not even a barking dog, since they had all been eaten by the starving population. They marched until they reached the outskirts of the city where they sat, surrounded by the tall grasses of the Russian steppes, waiting to meet the Turkish cavalry charge. Three old men with hoes and rakes prepared to meet the entire Turkish cavalry head-on. Think of that!"

I took Harry Bailey's Silver Star from its box and showed it to him. "My daddy was a hero in Bastogne, Belgium. He faced an overwhelming enemy force and skinned them all alive."

"As well he should have. They had no right to march on a helpless city, butchering innocent civilians in their way—barbarians, all of them."

"He saved the lives of thirteen other soldiers."

"There were no lives to be saved in Sevastopol. My grandfather and his two companions, Gretchko and Miskovitch, marched proudly into the cavalry charge; ten thousand screaming Uhlans mounted on steeds breathing fire, carrying scimitars and flag-draped lances. The three old men stood at rigid attention as the Uhlan columns engulfed them, blinded by the blur of horses and choking dust, and when the last of the Uhlans hoofbeats receded into the distance they realized they had been left untouched. Not a single scimitar had scored their skins, not a single lance had left its mark on them. Triumphantly, they sat down on the steppes and built a bonfire and watched while the city of Sevastopol burned around them."

Balenkin thought for a moment, making sure he'd remembered all the details. "That's the story," he said finally. "It would make a good book, don't you think?"

"Your grandfather told you this story?"

"Almost word-for-word," the author affirmed.

"When you were mad?"

"I believe so, although I could be mad now. It's hard to tell."

The window jiggled some when I hit it at the top with my elbow. I braced the heels of my palms underneath the crosspiece and using all my strength, forced it upward until it slammed open, ventilating the stuffy room. Isaiah Balenkin stood in front of the window, expanding and deflating his bony chest with each exuberant gulp of air, humming the same tune I had heard when I first passed his door.

"What's that song you're humming?" I asked him.

"It's an old Russian lullaby, Mothers sing it to their babies before they're old enough to open their eyes. I don't think it even has a name."

"It sounds sad."

"It is." He inhaled greedily. "There was a forest surrounding the gulag. I remember the air was like this, cold and exhilarating. We would line up outside our barracks every morning before the sun was up and listen to the wind whistling through the dry branches and smell the camphor smell of evergreens."

"Why would a mother want to sing a sad song to her baby?"

"How else is he to know he is a Russian?"

The elevated train roared by above us and I saw him stiffen, like his grandfather must have stiffened when ten thousand Turkish Uhlans charged him on steeds breathing fire. He would not falter, he would not

LeMoult

give an inch.

"How long since you've been outside?" I asked him. "How long since you've seen a tree?"

"A day, a week, a lifetime."

"If I got you dressed could you manage a walk in Central Park?"

He shrugged. "I walked all the way to Finland. A few more miles won't make much difference at this stage of my life."

Twenty-Two

The taxi let us off at Central Park South and we entered from Fifty-ninth Street, emerging from the angled, noise-filled corridors of the city into that tranquil world of tree-shaded walks, ponds shimmering through the orange overhang, and rolling, granite-dappled hills where children played in new-fallen leaves.

Isaiah Balenkin made his way slowly at first. Braced at the elbows by Molly on one side and me on the other, he set one foot cautiously in front of the other with great concentration, perhaps trying to remember the simple mechanics that had taken him across the continent of Asia to Finland, until augmented by the breeze and autumn color his strength and confidence gradually returned and he began walking at a brisk pace.

Molly watched him with a mixture of awe and concern, always seeming ready to spring to his aid if he stumbled, but admiring enough to afford him a respectful distance. Outside of the poet Frank Lupo (who hardly anyone outside of Bertie's immediate circle of friends had ever heard of), she had never been introduced to a writer of any kind, let alone a Nobel Prize winner, and the idea that I had been living upstairs from one and never mentioned it before must have persuaded her that I was either hopelessly uncultured or far more worldly than she'd previously suspected.

To impress her, I'd told her I was reading *Womb*, the old man's heralded masterpiece. I told her about the simpleton Kuryokin's solitary journey through Czarist Russia, his will shattered by the horror of war, helplessly guided by signposts and slogans, merrily singing the praises of the Red revolution in the midst of ruin and starvation. I told her of his arrest by Czarist police for being a Bolshevik agitator; that he had been thrown into a dismal prison in Kiev where an earlier inmate had scratched the single word REPENT into the damp cell wall, and how that scrawled injunction had convinced him that, should he survive his imprisonment, he would be obliged to make amends to everyone he had ever offended in his lifetime.

"What do you think it means?" Molly asked as we emerged from the trees into the Central park zoo. By then Isaiah Balenkin was well ahead of us.

"It's a story. Why does it have to mean anything?"

"It wouldn't have won the Nobel Prize if it was just a story," she scoffed. "All great literature has meaning."

"Maybe he'll say what it is at the end. I haven't gotten that far."

Ahead of us, Isaiah Balenkin had pushed himself to the front of a crowd gathered around the Seal Pond watching a brown-uniformed zoo attendant toss small sacrificial fish into the mouths of waiting seals. He followed the flight of the fish as they arced through the air in graceful parabolas, clapping like a delighted child when the seals intercepted them in mid-flight and downed them with satisfied barks. Molly took my hand and snaked through the throng until we stood next to him at the railing. "I'll bet there are lots of seals where you come from in Russia," she said.

"I don't think so. These are the first I've ever seen." He glanced down at our clasped hands. "It's good to see young people in love again. It reassures me that perhaps there's still hope for this sorry planet of ours."

Molly reddened. "We're not in love, Chance is like a kid brother to me."

My throat tightened but I caught the gulp before it betrayed me. "Yeah, we're just real good friends."

Balenkin eyed us indulgently. "Why deny what's so perfectly obvious? Being in love is no crime. Young people are supposed to be in love."

I shot a sideward glance at Molly, torn between wanting to set her at ease and wishing it was true, but I did not release her hand and she did not ask me to, and either out of deference to his notion or out of inestimable need we held on, twining our fingers together in a kind of desperate tactile probe of one another, closer then than we had ever been. I ran the tip of my thumb down into her palm, absorbing her warmth, her moisture, kneading the swirls and protrusions and the soft skin between

152

her fingers like moments in a dream, and she held on still, still afraid but committed. We explored the monkey house and lion house holding on; the polar bear den etched out of solid rock, the elephant and rhino enclosures, all the poultry, marsupial and ungulate pens along the way, until Isaiah Balenkin fairly sagged from exhaustion on an unoccupied bench by the donkey path. "You two young people go on ahead and let an old man get some rest," he wheezed. "I'll be here when you get back."

If either of us felt guilty leaving him there alone we did not mention it. Hand-in-hand we walked the leaf-strewn paths until we came to an immense open field where a few dozen hardy New Yorkers were sprawled about on blankets and chairs in the chill wind; reading, talking, listening to music on small radios or simply lounging with tinfoil reflectors tucked under their chins, capturing the last rays of autumn before winter set in. Molly selected a spot and we curled down into it. "If I'd been thinking I would have brought a blanket," she apologized.

"It's okay. I like sitting on the ground." I ran my fingers through the close-clipped blades of grass. "Back home I'll go off by myself sometimes and find a spot and just plop down in the grass for hours, not doing much of anything but thinking."

"What do you think about?"

"Lots of things, I guess. Thinking's a hard thing to explain. Sometimes I can just think about the farm, that's easy enough; about crops to be brought in or livestock to be fed or fences to be mended, but there's not much thought in any of that. A farmer just does what comes next. Where it gets complicated is when I start thinking about all the things I could be doing instead, sort of let my mind run off and spin away faster and faster until it makes me dizzy just trying to keep up with it. Times like that I think it might be better off if I was like poor old Kuryokin; no questions, no decisions to make; just wait for the next signpost to point the way."

"Maybe that's what Isaiah Balenkin meant after all, that too much thinking gets us in trouble."

"That sounds like the Reverend Harley Brown. He thinks learning anything but the Bible is a waste of time. Kuryokin would have been just his kind of crony; somebody so addled they'd follow the word whether it made sense to them or not."

"Wasn't there somebody named Isaiah in the Bible?"

"The Prophet Isaiah. 'And I will set the Egyptians against the Egyptians, and they shall fight every one against his brother, and everyone against his neighbor; city against city and kingdom against kingdom.' Old Isaiah the Prophet knew all about getting even I reckon."

Molly raised an eyebrow. "Now I'm really impressed. I had no idea you knew so much of the scriptures."

"You live with a Baptist preacher long enough and it sticks whether you want it to or not, like cow patties on your boots."

She leaned back on her elbows and spotted the moon rising pale and gossamer above the trees. "There's my moon. You can make a wish on it if you want."

"I thought stars were for wishing."

"They are, but the moon is a kind of star, especially when you see it in the afternoon sky; then it's a wishing moon."

"It's a hunter's moon when it's full like that and the sun is still shining. You can raise a flock of doves and they'll head straight for the sun so's to blind you, but a hunter's moon fools them and they head for that instead. That gives the hunter the advantage."

She made a face. "I can't think of a time when a poor bird would have an advantage over a man with a gun anyway."

"When they're flying against the sun, they do."

"Maybe back in Texas, but this is Central Park and it's my moon so I can make it anything I want; and I say it's a wishing moon. So go ahead and make a wish, my treat."

"You first."

Molly closed her eyes and concentrated, forming the wish with her lips as she constructed it in her mind.

"What'd you wish for?" I asked when she was finished.

"I can't say. It won't come true if I tell you."

"I can tell you what my wish is. I wish you thought I was more than just a kid brother."

"I do. I think I feel closer to you than anybody else in the whole world," she insisted.

"Close enough to love me?"

"I'd be crazy not to love you, you're a beautiful boy." She closed the space between us and kissed me on the lips, lightly at first but growing in intensity with my participation; and she moved into me with her breasts all heaving and I heard her husky breathing and smelled her perfume, and then she pulled away, flushed and perplexed. "I'm sorry, that was selfish of me."

"It was wonderful!" I gasped.

She stood abruptly. "We'd better go see to Isaiah. There's a chill in the air and we wouldn't want him catching anything."

We walked without speaking, not even daring to look at each other, until we reached the bench where Isaiah Balenkin sat huddled against the wind with his chin tucked into his chest. "Time to go home, sir." I shook him gently by the shoulder.

He awoke with a startled grunt. "Where is this?"

"Central Park, sir."

"Central Park?"

"Yes sir, at the zoo. We were looking at the animals, remember?"

The animals?" His brow furrowed. "They ate a rat, you know."

"Who's that?"

"Gretchko, Miskovitch and my grandfather. They skinned it and roasted it over the fire and picked its bones clean. It was all there was."

He was back on the killing fields, gone again into that world of bugles, smoke and cordite; the frenzied charge of ten thousand Uhlans with scimitars bared and lances poised and horses breathing fire from their nostrils, and three drunken old men with garden tools who faced them down and lived, and ate a rat while Sevastopol burned around them; triumphant, he'd said; more for their madness than their judgment, less for their bravery than their survival. It was all there was.

Twenty-Three

He slipped in and out of madness the next few days, sometimes teetering on the edges of both worlds, not quite sound, not quite mad, abiding it seemed in a halfway state of mind where he was able to exist in both conditions. Although Shimmelman told me it had been the old man's recurring pattern for years, I could not help but think that our outing in Central Park had sprung a seed of rationality in him that had been dormant before. For one thing, he was now able to recognize me and call me by my name no matter which state he inhabited. It was as if I had somehow become his bridge to both worlds; as real to him on the smoking battlefields of the Crimea as I was in the confines of the Soldiers and Sailors. Now, instead of simply living in his past he became an instructor of it, weaving me through the circumstances of his early life as deftly as Molly guided visitors through Radio City Music hall.

In fact, Molly had become the surrogate wife and lover of his intricate narration. She was Anya, the daughter of Mishkin, the fat banker in the town of Vilyuisk where the author had grown up (in the telling he had embodied her with Molly's red hair and freckles). Isaiah Balenkin recounted the story of Anya and his older brother, Sergei, who had fallen in love. Naturally, because Sergei was the son of a schoolteacher and Anya the daughter of the wealthiest man in town, a social chasm existed between them that prohibited them by station from ever marrying, and so in the beginning their love remained a secret, manifested in quick, nervous glances when they passed one another in the street, the open-air marketplace, or the *shul*; realized after a while in a few precious moments of stolen romance, scattered over time and opportunity and the constant, awful fear of discovery. Finally, when he could no longer accept the deception, Sergei had gone to Mishkin and poured out his feelings for the banker's daughter. His family was virtually penniless, he admitted, but

157

his birthright was something more valuable than all the rubles in Russia; he had inherited character, and an indomitable will to succeed. Chortling at Sergei's arrogance, Mishkin had pointed out that character was not worth a single kopeck in the marketplace, that it would not buy a fish or a chicken or a loaf of challah in the town of Vilyuisk, and that will, God save us, was in the hands of the Almighty. If God willed that Sergei was to have a beautiful red-haired wife, he would provide one, but she would not be Anya, the beautiful red-haired daughter of Mishkin, the banker, and that was the sum total of that. Mishkin did however leave Sergei with one unlikely possibility. Were he somehow able to translate this character and will of his into hard currency, he could come again to seek Anya's hand.

Sergei had left home embittered, and joined the Bolsheviks, where his quick brain and determination won him a position of power, and after the Reds had taken over the reins of the country, he returned triumphantly to Vilyuisk, only to find that Anya, rather than be forced into an arranged marriage with a prosperous landowner named Homulka, a man twice her age, had killed herself. Enraged with grief, Sergei reported both Mishkin and Homulka as capitalist exploiters to the Red Regional Committee, which promptly arrested them, along with prominent intellectuals in the area who might have posed a threat, among them Sergei's and Isaiah's own father, Ivan the schoolteacher, who was taken away and never seen again.

Years later when Isaiah Balenkin was himself imprisoned in Moscow for writing anti-Soviet propaganda, Sergei, who was by then an important Communist official, visited him in the Lubyanka. He could help his brother obtain a lighter sentence, he promised, or even have his sentence commuted altogether if the author was prepared to repudiate his novel *Womb*, and renounce the Nobel Prize for Literature he had been awarded in absentia. Naturally Isaiah refused. He welcomed the chance to go to the gulag and search for the father who had been betrayed by his own flesh and blood, he asserted; then he spit in Sergei's face for emphasis.

The story seemed as melancholy to me as the rest of Isaiah Balenkin's life. Jumbled as it was, with characters and events from the present overlaying those of his childhood, it stretched across the span of deprivation and betrayal, courage and monumental achievement, but for all of that there was no love. As if he'd been compelled by fate to atone for Sergei's treachery, or to share the pain of his tragic loss of Anya, Isaiah Balenkin had never married; never even fallen in love. Now in the meandering of the old man's mind, Molly had become all the young girls he had ever lusted after, all the women of wealth and status he'd felt were beyond his reach, all the toothless old babushkas pushing twig brooms in the squares of Moscow who put the lie to the promise of youth; his eternal vision of women encapsulated in Molly's cascading red hair, her pale, freckled face and emerald eyes.

"You will take care of her," he'd made me promise, and I'd told him that I would, even though I had no idea how I'd go about doing that, or even if she wanted to be taken care of, especially by me. I had not seen her since our trip to Central Park, and although she had given me no specific reason to think so, I was beginning to suspect she was avoiding me. I'd asked her about it, cautiously suggesting that our solitary kiss was not important enough to wreck a really good friendship (in truth it seemed the most important event of my entire life up to that point), but Molly had assured me that was not the case. The kiss we shared had been a sweet, impetuous thing to do, in her words; not exactly the breathtaking sexual experience I remembered. She vowed she still cared about me and that we'd be able to spend more time together once her hectic schedule of rehearsals and dance practice evened off. There was little I could do besides wait and sulk, believing in my heart that I was destined to spend the rest of my life like Isaiah Balenkin, loveless and unfulfilled, until something happened to persuade me that I meant far more to Molly than she'd admitted to me; that something was Nick Corsi.

I was helping the Cajun heat up some pipe joints for the pool (he called it sweating them) the afternoon Nick showed up at the Soldiers and Sailors. "I was in the neighborhood," he said unconvincingly. "You had lunch yet?"

"I was just helping with the plumbing here."

"Forget the plumbing. I know a little Italian place down on Twelfth Street—best veal napolitano in New York."

"I don't think I ever had that," I admitted.

"Well you will now." He put a fraternal arm around my shoulders, shot the Cajun a look that said don't ask, and steered me outside to a waiting limousine.

"How'd you know where I lived?" I asked him as we drove downtown in the shadow of the El.

"It's my business to find out about people. The more I know about the people I deal with, the better it is for me; kind of like a shrink or a priest, you know what I mean?"

"Not exactly."

"Well look at it this way. Let's say you go to a shrink or a priest for help or advice. He ain't gonna be much help to you if he doesn't know where you're coming from. Now me; people come to me for things too; money, favors, all kinds of things, and I wouldn't be much of a businessman if I didn't find out everything I could about them just to protect my investment. That make sense to you?"

"I reckon, but what's it got to do with me? I don't need any money or favors or anything like that."

"Everybody needs something, everybody wants something." He stared moodily out the car window. "Everybody you see out there is on the make. Maybe it's money they're after, maybe power and prestige, maybe sex, maybe love, whatever, they wouldn't be human beings if they weren't whoring after something. You wouldn't have come all the way to New York from East Asshole Texas if you weren't looking for something, right?"

"It's Eula."

"Yeah, Eula; must've slipped my mind, but you know what I mean. You came here to find your old man. You came here because you couldn't stand it back there any more. You came here because you had an idea life might be better. Those are all good things; New York is still the melting pot, still a place where kid with nothing but balls can end up rich as a fucking sultan. It happened to me, it can happen to you too." He directed the driver to pull to the curb in front of a restaurant named Colanani's. "You'll like the food here, all homemade. You ever eat Italian food before?"

"I've had spaghetti and meatballs."

"Out of a can, right?"

"Reckon."

"You're in for a treat."

Colanani's was small and dimly lit, with ceramic tiles on the floor and lower walls, the upper portions being covered with hand-painted murals of scenes from Italy: tree-dotted hills, mountains, lakes and canals, bearing exotic faraway names like Abruzzi, Genova, and Venezia. A fat, balding man with a black handlebar mustache hurried from the back of the restaurant when he saw us enter. "Signore Corsi!" He bowed stiffly from the waist. "How can I be of service to you?"

"How's the veal today, Vittorio?"

He smacked his lips. "*Delizioso*, Signore. The best ever!"

"And the clams?"

"*Grasso e succoso*," he grinned.

"Then bring us some veal, and some clams, and anything else you think is good."

Vittorio fussed with our seats and rearranged the objects on the table. "It is my extreme pleasure to serve you, Signore Corsi. I hope you will accept a bottle of my best wine as a small token of my friendship."

"You make it in the cellar?"

"Where else?"

"Then *grazie* my friend."

"You must come here a lot," I said when we were alone.

"Not for a while now." Nick tucked his napkin into his shirtfront. "Vittorio is from the old neighborhood. Our fathers came over from Sicily on the same boat."

"He seems real glad to see you."

"He's grateful to me. A few years he ago was having trouble with the health department; an inspector was threatening to shut him down unless he kicked back most of his profits, so he asked for my help."

"What'd you do?"

"I made the inspector see the error of his ways. You see, most people are willing to listen to reason if you just put it to them in the right way." He tore a thick slice of bread from a loaf on the table and saturated it with olive oil. "Try some of this bread, it's homemade. I have a couple of loaves delivered fresh every morning."

"What way did you put it to him?" I asked cautiously.

"What way do you think?"

I shrugged, afraid to suggest what I thought.

"Whatta you think!" Nick insisted.

"I dunno. You threatened him?"

He leaned back in his chair and wiped his chin with the napkin. "You know you disappoint me. You think I got as far as I did just by muscling people?"

"I didn't mean that."

"Sure you did. You saw a wop from Brooklyn swimming in dough and you said to yourself this guy's a gorilla, admit it."

"Not exactly that way."

He smiled. "It's okay. I won't lie to you and tell you I didn't have to bust a few heads along the way, but for everybody I had to muscle, there were a dozen more I outsmarted. Nobody makes a million bucks with their fists unless he's Rocky Marciano. You take that health inspector who was putting the arm on Vittorio. You see I knew this guy. I didn't actually know him, but I'd known a million guys just like him; small-time punks with hardly any vision. I figured that he was pulling in one-two hundred a week from local store owners and that was more money than the dumb shit ever thought he'd make in his life, so what I did was convince him to go to work for me. Vittorio was off limits but it was understood by everybody else that the inspector was now my agent, and being that he was no longer had to worry about actually inspecting these places he was able to triple his route, up the weekly take from everyone he saw based on our new affiliation, kick half of his earnings back to me and still end up doubling his income. Everybody was happy and nobody got hurt. See what I mean?"

I tore a hunk of bread from the loaf and nodded uncertainly.

"You see, everybody's got his weakness; money, sex, power, whatever. It don't make no difference how much he's already got; the laws of nature say he wants more, and the more he gets the greedier he gets, and greed makes a man weak. If you know a man's weakness and you can satisfy that weakness, that puts you one up on him in any situation."

I'd grasped the notion that he wanted to make a point, but so far it had eluded me. Vittorio arrived at the table with a straw-wrapped bottle of red wine and poured two glasses.

Nick tasted it, nodded approvingly and dismissed him. "Actually the wine isn't that good," he confided in a hoarse whisper, "but it wouldn't do to hurt Vittorio's feelings."

I took a sip. "Tastes okay to me. Back home we drink home-brewed corn that's like to take your head off."

"Well this won't do that, but it'll probably give you the shits."

"Reckon."

"Anyway, the point I'm trying to make is that I'm a reasonable man, and when I have problems I try to resolve them with reasonable solutions. Take this business with you and Molly. I'm sure there's nothing there that can't be worked out with a little reasonable negotiation."

"What business with me and Molly are you talking about?"

"You know; the walks in the park, sneaking kisses when you think nobody's looking."

"How do you know about that?"

Nick shrugged it off. "It doesn't matter how I know. The point is I do know, and you know, and you and me have to figure out what we're gonna do about it."

"What we're going to do about what? There's nothing to do anything about," I objected. "Molly and I are friends; we gave each other a little friendly peck in the park. I don't see what's so wrong about that. And what business do you have following us anyway?"

He held his wine up to the light, examining the dark residue at the bottom of the glass. " A man in my position has to know things to protect his investments."

"Is that what Molly is to you, an investment?"

He slammed the glass down on the table and I winced. "What she is to me is none of your business. All you have to know is that she's important to me, and that I'm willing to deal."

"To deal what?"

"Whatever it takes to make you to disappear."

"Is that what Molly wants?"

"It don't make any difference what Molly wants, it's just you and me here. Now I just got finished telling you that I try to be a reasonable man. What I didn't tell you was that I'm not a very patient man. I don't have a lot of time to explain the way things are to a lovesick teenager who's in way over his head. Enough to say that I like you, and I wouldn't want to see you get hurt. Suppose you tell me what you're gonna want to make us all happy here, money, a job? I know you've spent a lot of time looking for your old man. I've got people who are very good at finding people who I can put at your disposal. Just say the word."

"What if I just say no?" I choked.

Nick spotted Vittorio approaching us with a steaming tray of antipasti and grinned. "No is not an acceptable answer among reasonable men. You're very young so I'll overlook it just this once." He inspected the appetizer and inhaled its rich aromas, gathering the fragrant steam in greedy gulps with his cupped hands. "Try the clams casino," he urged. "You'll think you died and went to heaven."

Twenty-Four

He would give me money, he would give me power, he would send his agents to find Harry Bailey if I wanted. All down the whistlings of my thoughts he would give me things I did not have, things I wanted. How much money? We had never discussed it; and power, what was that? Would I be given power over the sun and stars? (Shimmelman maintained we were the stars and that opened up another whole can of worms). Would I have power over death like Lazarus or be able to split the sea like Moses? The Reverend Harley Brown said that all power came from the Lord, filtered down through the unworthy like rainwater seeping through the dry earth to nourish the roots of trees. It was called Grace; not the power to bend others to your will that men really wanted, but the power to endure suffering that they needed, that old fart-blowing phony of a preacher said. *Blessed are the meek for they shall inherit the earth, Blessed are the poor in spirit for theirs is the kingdom of Heaven.*

New York City was teeming with the meek, the poor in spirit, the abandoned, the bereft. They filled the streets and alleyways, huddling together out of the cold making up lives for themselves and cadging cheap meals at the E and B and munching donuts in the Salvation Army shelters. They felt all blessed and infused with the power of the Almighty, I'll bet. I'll bet they never wanted to ride in the back seat of a Cadillac limousine, or leave a hundred-dollar tip in an Italian restaurant, or sail their yacht through the Marshmallow Islands, or own a Congressman of their own, I'll bet. In New York City their power abided in the vaporous, shifting solitude of their own minds. In their delusion they danced the fandango with the king of the Hottentots and shoveled seagull shit for the government and captured exploding galaxies in space, the underpinnings of life's voyages, *il viaggiare di dolore.* And they dreamed of dancing on a stage in front of a million people and hearing their applause.

165

How much money? We hadn't gotten down to that.

Maybe he would give me a thousand dollars, maybe ten thousand. I could buy a lot of weeks at the Soldiers and Sailors for that, or maybe I'd move to swankier digs; start eating at restaurants with pictures of exotic foreign places on the walls where I could order things like *zuppe di pesce* or *calamari fritte*, and drink sour red wine with the skins of grapes still floating in the bottom, and slide a crisp hundred-dollar bill underneath the plate when it was over.

Back in Eula, ten thousand dollars would buy a fair-sized ranch and a dozen head of the finest breeding stock. A man with that kind of money could walk into that dusty shit-hole of a town and know every eye was watching him, tracking his every move. He could go into the bank to make a payment on his note and they would bow and scrape and call him Mister this or that, and it wouldn't make any difference in the world what he'd done back when he was a wild-eyed kid with a temper like a bull-whip who'd cold-conk you soon as give you the time of day, I reckon.

He would help me find Harry Bailey.

That would be along with the ten thousand dollars, maybe. Nothing wrong with Harry Bailey that ten thousand dollars couldn't fix; nothing a little rest and sunshine and the best medicines wouldn't set straight in a jiffy. Man had too much war, plain and simple, like poor old Kuryokin whose brain got so addled from cannon fire that he'd lost everything but the will to follow signs. Maybe that's what Harry Bailey had been doing all these years, just following the next sign in the fork of the road, look-ing to catch a break any which way he turned. Never had an easy time of it from the day he was born, Harry Bailey; never had two nickels he could rub together and call his own, except what he stole, and he ended up on the chain gang for that. They'd set up and take notice if he climbed off the bus in the middle of town checked out that sorry place this way and that with ten thousand big ones in his jeans, you bet. They'd be lining up to shake his hand and carry his satchel and tell him what a good old boy they'd always thought he was. Ten thousand dollars can make folks take a better look at you.

Maybe Harry Bailey would just ride into that poor excuse for a town in a Cadillac automobile; no bus for him. He'd drive like a demon on those dusty dirt roads out of town so's they could see him coming from the farm and know that he'd come back for what was rightfully his. He'd pull up right next to that sorry Nash car of the Reverend Harley Brown's and give his brother Mal a nod and climb up on the front porch and set in his favorite rocker like he'd never left and smell the apple scented air and kick his boots off on the wooden railing and take himself a nap.

I would never be able to see Molly again, that much was plain.

There were cheeseburgers frying behind the bar at the saloon next door to the Soldiers and Sailors—dark brown meat patties sizzling in on the grill, wafting thick, greasy emissions from the exhaust fan in the back. I could smell them when I lay awake in bed at night, not really cooking but what was left over from the cooking after the bar had been shut down for the night and everybody had gone home. Where was home?

Aida McCracken was at her usual stool near the door, drifting in and out of sleep or thought, ironing out her solipsism. A few stools down sat a man I had come to know only as the Wizard, apparently because he claimed to have once been an important scientist of some kind, and further down still a man named Beano Larkin, who would do a loose-limbed jig if he'd had enough beers, or fart a boiled egg fart on cue if you yanked his forefinger.

I would only be able to think about her; about her soft, satiny skin, her breasts webbed with tiny blue veins rising to my touch.

The farm in Eula rightly belonged to Harry Bailey, as much as it did to his brother Malachai; passed down through the generations from their great grandfather, Ezra Bailey who had first developed the land in the 1800s. Ezra Bailey had held off a Comanche raiding party single-handedly, the story went; picked them off one-by-one with a Buffalo pistol until them that were left raised their war bonnets in salute and called it quits. Next day they brought him a half-breed squaw in tribute, and before he got himself killed in the Mexican War he had four sons with her, and one of them was my grandfather, Elijah Bailey, who'd kept the farm going after the others had scattered to the four winds.

Three generations clawing at the dry earth, and I would be the fourth, Chance Bailey, the fourth generation proprietor of a piss-poor speck of dust in the middle of a bad joke on the world, that's what I would be. Better we had all stayed wild, riding the wind on bareback stallions. Better we all wore loincloths and chewed loco weed and upped and

167

moved away whenever the land wore out or the buffalo vanished or we just plain got tired of looking at the same old buttes and mesas.

I could take the money and buy a house in Boston or Chatham or wherever those folks of hers who had disinherited her came from, and I would allow as how we shared some blood, but blood was all we shared because they had missed out on the chance to share my wealth the very second they had kicked her out. And I would sit on my front porch with my boots off and my feet crossed on the railing and watch them go by and say, See, y'all never reckoned on this, did you?

You never reckoned that a son of Harry Bailey, who you believed to be a redneck and a rowdy, would come back here and own the best house in town. That's what Harry Bailey's been doing all this time you thought he was raising hell in saloons and ruining your daughter's life. He was teaching his son the way of the Comanche; how to track an elk and catch a jackrabbit by his ears and put on war paint and mount a pony without a saddle and ride the wind and kick the Germans' asses at Bastogne. That's what that man you thought was such a loser was doing all that time. If I did the right thing I'd gut you all with my stag-horn knife and salt your pelts and hang them out between the apple trees to dry. They'd give me a medal for that, I reckon. A Silver Star with red-white and blue ribbon— that would be about right.

No is not an acceptable answer.

Nick would find out everything there was to know about you in order to protect his investment. He would learn what you wanted more than anything in the world, what you lusted after in the depths of your own soul, and knowing that gave him power over you because greed made a man weak. Greed convinced him that what he wanted was more important than standing up for what he had, what he knew to be right, so he was willing to give up everything that mattered for the promise of something better down the line.

Gretchko, Miskovitch and Isaiah Balenkin's grandfather would never have had the courage to face ten thousand Turkish cavalrymen armed only with garden tools if they had been blinded by greed. Ezra Bailey would have pulled up stakes at the sight of the first Comanche brave hooting and hollering outside his cabin instead of standing his ground and winning my great-great grandmother for his stubbornness, and those thirteen soldiers would be stone cold dead by now, pushing up daises in some sorghum field in Bastogne if Harry Bailey hadn't decided to flat out say no, not now you bastards, not ever.

And all the pain that meant, knowing that everybody was right and everybody was wrong and none of them could help me but me. She will never lie asleep next to me and I will never hear her even breathing and feel her moving to her dreams and I will turn like Sergei against the world because the only love that I will ever know is dead.

Twenty-Five

The practice hall at the American Dance Ensemble was a huge, empty, cavernous space where waist-to-ceiling arched windows overlooked an unbroken expanse of polished oak floor, and dancers in practice costumes fluttered to silent rhythms or contorted their bodies at the barre along the wall. A single upright piano stood in the corner, and on the stool a female piano-player, seemingly without direction, plunked out tunes of a highbrow nature while Bertie, far less combative that he was at the music hall, strode among the dancers offering encouragement or mild rebuke. Molly had taken me there one day to watch her practice, but even though she had explained the *entrechats* and *fouettés* and arabesques to me like a patient schoolmarm lecturing a wayward child, I knew I was in way over my head; a Texas hillbilly in a place where he had no right being. I'd made up my mind then and there that I would never again question Molly's dancing. It was something I could not hope to understand, I could never let her know that as close as we seemed to be, we inhabited different galaxies.

The dancers dispersed to the edges of the hall, making room for a single ballerina wearing a skin-tight body suit, who drifted into the center and began to writhe on the wooden floor. Except for a small lamp on the piano and a single spotlight in the ceiling that bathed her in a circle of pale blue, the room was dark. Even the enormous windows had been shuttered to keep out the ochre light that filtered through the soot-smeared glass. Although I might have thought at first glance that the girl in the center of the room was in some difficulty, I had attended enough of Molly's practice sessions to know that what she was doing was called interpretive dancing. She was acting out a story that Bertie had dreamed up for her, alone in the circle of light while the rest of the American Dance Ensemble troupe sat around her in the dark, slowly swaying and

171

clapping their hands in rhythm to the discordant plunks of the piano keys.

A young man entered the circle of light, dressed much the same as the girl. At first he hovered over her; seeming unsure, he rocked back and forth on his heels as the music grew louder. He reached down and touched her hair, twining the yellow strands in his fingertips while the rest of the troupe rose and began to close in, chanting as they moved: Oooooom, oooooom.

I did not try to understand it. By then I'd learned that there were parts of Molly's world that would forever be beyond me. I could sit in that darkened corner watching those interpretive dancers wriggle and writhe for the rest of my natural life and by the time I'd been called to judgment, it would all be still as baffling to me as one of Frank Lupo's poems, still as much a mystery as why she'd danced naked in front of men, why she let her life be dominated by a man like Nick Corsi.

Greed made men weak, he'd told me, but he hadn't said anything about women, and I struggled against the thought that greed was what bound her to him. Everybody wanted something, he'd said, they were all whoring after something that was so important that they'd be willing to give up almost anything to get it. That was what gave him an advantage over them; knowing what it was they wanted and being able to provide it. More than anything Molly wanted to be a dancer, and she was willing to endure whatever it took to make her one: the endless hours of training, Bertie's constant criticism of her, the unceasing pain of muscles stretched beyond their natural capacity, blisters, bone spurs and torn, abraded flesh. Dancing was her own journey of pain, I knew; not a journey of atonement like *il viaggiare di dolore* but one just as committed. Just as the old lady in Nick Corsi's manufactured grotto suffered for salvation, Molly endured for that dream she'd dreamt on her front porch in Whitehall. Nick knew all about her dream. It was his business to find out about people.

The dress rehearsal ended and Molly plopped next to me on the floor, out of breath and glistening with perspiration. "What'd you think?"

"Interesting."

"I mean it. Did you think it was good?"

"I reckon. I'm not the best person to ask about it though."

She wiped her head with a towel, wringing the ends of her hair like wet laundry. "I could have had a bigger part if I'd wanted it; Bertie said I was ready."

"So why didn't you take it?"

"I don't know, scared I guess."

"You could do what that girl in the middle of the floor was doing."

She shrugged and took a sip of water from a paper cup. "I didn't expect to see you here today."

"I didn't expect to be here, but there's some things we ought to talk about. Nick Corsi came to see me yesterday."

"Nick? What on earth for?"

"He knows all about us going to the park together, about the kiss and everything."

"How could he possibly know about that?"

"He must have been following us, or somebody who works for him was following us."

"That's crazy." Molly shook her head in disbelief. "Why would Nick want to have us followed?"

"To protect his investment, I reckon."

"What investment?"

"That's what he says you are to him, an investment."

"Nick said that?"

"Well maybe not exactly that way, but that was what he meant."

Some of the troupe approached us on their way to the door. "We're going to the Automat for some hot water and ketchup," one of the male dancers said as they passed. "Want to come along?"

"No thanks." Molly flashed an unconvincing smile. "Some other time."

"What'd he mean, hot water and ketchup?" I asked her after they had gone.

"They're both free at the Automat. You put some ketchup in a cup, pour in a little hot water from the tap and you've got tomato soup, sort of."

"Sounds awful."

"But it's cheap and not fattening. Dancers are poor and they can't put on any weight so everything they eat tastes awful. Actually it's not all that bad if you just close your eyes and pretend it's *potage au tomate*."

"If you say so." I made a face. "Did Nick ever take you to an Italian restaurant?"

"Sure, but I could never eat any of the food. Everything's about a billion calories."

"He took me to one called Colanani's yesterday. We had clams and mussels and shrimp and veal, and wine from a bottle with straw all around it."

"You're a growing boy; you can take it. Besides, you don't have to look beautiful all the time."

"The owner was a friend of his; they grew up in Brooklyn together. Nick told me about how this guy, his name is Vittorio, how he was having trouble with an inspector from the Health department, and showed the inspector the error of his ways and how the inspector went to work for him and doubled his salary and nobody got hurt and everyone ended up happy."

Molly eyed me quizzically. "I'm not sure I get the point."

"Well the point is this inspector was a problem for Nick, or at least for Vittorio, so instead of hurting him Nick gave him a job."

"And what's so wrong with that? I've been telling you all along that Nick's not the goon you think he is. He's helped a lot of people. He certainly helped me."

"I don't know, I don't know. It's a hard thing to figure out. Vittorio got his restaurant and the inspector got a job, and I reckon the both of them are in debt to Nick forever. That's what Nick does; he gives people the things they want and then he ends up collecting interest on them for the rest of their lives."

"Don't you think you might be making too much of this? Isn't it possible that he does things for people just to be nice? Don't get me wrong; I'm not completely naive. I worked for Nick; I know how he earns his living. I'm not saying he's a saint, or even an upstanding citizen by most peoples' standards, but he's no monster. He's not even as calculating as you make him out. I know Nick. He's got a soft streak a mile wide."

"Yeah, maybe you're right. He offered to help me out yesterday."

"Is he giving you a job?"

"Well I reckon if a job was what I wanted he'd give me one, as long as it was a job that kept me away from you. I think he'd like it better if I took money though; that way I'd just hightail it out of here and he wouldn't have to worry about you and me sneaking kisses in the park any more. It looks like that soft streak of his ain't wide enough for us both to fit in."

"He offered you money not to see me?"

"Money, power, whatever. He even offered to find Harry Bailey for me if that's what I want."

"How much money?" Her voice was a rasp.

"We never did get right down to it, but Nick's a businessman. I expect he'd pay whatever it took to protect his investment."

Molly took a deep breath and sagged against the wall. "This is ridiculous, this whole thing has gotten out of hand. I'm going to call Nick as soon as I get home and explain to him that there's absolutely nothing between you and me, and even if there was I'm not a commodity to be bought and sold. I'll see who I want when and where I want to see them, and I won't be spied on. If you're telling me the truth about him having us followed, he's got a lot of explaining to do."

"He's just protecting his investment."

"I wish you'd stop saying that."

"I can't stop saying it because it's true; at least Nick thinks it's true, and he's the one holding all the cards. Truth told, if I was Nick and I felt about you the way Nick feels and I saw somebody like me coming along, I'd probably do just what he's doing."

She stared in amazement. "You think it's right? You think it's perfectly okay to pay for me like a piece of material?"

"If I was Nick I would. He's not stupid, he wouldn't have gotten as far as he has if he was. He might know all you feel for me is I'm some cute, wet-behind-the-ears schoolboy from Eula, Texas; but he sure as hell knows that's not what I feel. All he's got to do is take one look at me to know how crazy in love I am with you, and if you hadn't been so busy becoming the most famous dancer in New York you would have seen it too."

I could hardly breathe; my heart was pumping wildly, like all the Comanche tom-toms in the world beating at once. "He'll find whatever it is I can't turn down and give it to me never to see you again; and if he can't find it he'll do the next best thing."

"I can't believe it," she muttered.

"You better believe it."

"Did you give him an answer?"

"I don't know what my answer will be. I thought I'd leave it up to you."

"To me?"

"Why not you? You're in the middle of all this. All you've got to do is tell me you could never feel the same way about me as I feel about you."

"What would that accomplish?"

"It'd free me up to take Nick's money and run."

"Is that what you want?"

I swallowed hard. "What I want is for you to love me the way I love you. Don't tell me about how much older than me you are; don't tell me I'm just a hick from the sticks who's reaching way higher than he's got a right to reach. Just say you love me, say it."

"What then?"

"Then you've chosen me over him. Then I can deal with anything he's got up his sleeve."

She remained silent for a long time, and when she finally spoke her words were slow and measured, like a gramophone whose spring had started to run down. "Even if I believed that, I can't make that choice. You have no right to ask me to make that choice."

"If I leave here I can't come back, not ever."

"You're still a kid, I can't tell you what to do with the rest of your life. I'm too far along with mine to change it now." Molly wiped a tear from her eye, stood unsteadily and headed for the door. "Thanks for loving me, Chance. I wish it all could have worked out differently."

I sat alone for a long time after she had gone, running it all through my head until I finally realized she'd done the only thing she could. I was a teenage hayseed with hardly any education, no prospects, and no class. All she could ever get from me was more of what she'd grown up with, poor and poorer, and then a little poorer yet; all I could ever do for her was dash her dreams. Nick Corsi offered her the dark side of the moon where there were gardens with flowers and tall ferns and waterfalls hundreds of feet high that she could sit underneath and bathe her feet in the sparkling pools. She'd be some kind of fool not to go for a deal like that.

LeMoult

Twenty-Six

I was there when the old man died, kneeling beside him in the ambulance when he drew his last breath. It was more of a sigh than a death rattle, as if the great author had expected so much more out of the experience than it was that he'd died disappointed by the banality of it all. The ambulance attendant crouched next to me shrugged and covered Isaiah Balenkin's craggy face with a sheet and muttered something about being sorry and knowing how I felt, which of course he didn't since he saw death every day and the death of one more old man in a city of millions could hardly have affected him the way it did me. Then the siren ceased to wail and we were alone in the silence; and I cried, I don't know why.

He had never spoken to me; never even opened his eyes after Shimmelman and I found him sprawled on the floor beside his bed that morning. I'd been up most of the night before, lying awake in bed with only the periodic clamor of the elevated train outside and the smell of greasy cheeseburgers from the saloon next door to remind me I was alive, running the whys and wherefores back and forth in my mind, trying to figure how I could have done things differently; but it stayed the same, always, no matter which way I turned it.

Molly was gone—she would not be back. I could kick and scream and curse the world around me and she would not be back. I could get rip-roaring drunk and pick a fight in some saloon with the first guy who looked cross-wise at me, and beat him to the floor and kick him in the balls and squash his face with my boot heel until it looked like corn mush and she would not be back. I could get a whore and fuck her every which way to Sunday until my body ached and my ears rang and my brain was too befogged to care any more, and she would still not be back. I could set a spell with smoke and fetishes, and track her at night the way Comanche did, and snatch her shadow framed against the moon, but it would slip away like water through my fingers, and she would not be back.

Shimmelman said the old man probably didn't suffer.

The next morning we'd found him, still alive but barely. I'd asked if I could ride with him in the ambulance, thinking that somehow he might still be able to use me as a bridge to that other world of his, that intense, passionate world of war and love and betrayal that had kept him from withering up and blowing away, but he'd never opened his eyes. Shimmelman had followed in a taxicab and I gave him the bad news when he got to the hospital. He'd simply nodded, then spoken some to a hospital official who told us to wait while they processed Isaiah Balenkin's body to the morgue. There were some papers we would have to fill out, he told us.

"What do you think it was?" I asked Shimmelman as we sat in the hospital waiting room.

"Old age I guess."

"How old was he?"

"Ninety maybe, it's hard to tell. He had one of those ageless faces."

"He had no toes, did you know that?"

"I think he had a few toes."

"None. They took his socks off in the ambulance and there wasn't a toe."

"Probably lost them from frostbite when he trekked across Siberia."

"Reckon; or maybe he was born that way."

"Not likely."

"I seen a calf once was born with six legs."

"Anything can happen."

"There was a half man-half woman at the State Fair up in Lubbock. Had both a dangle and a kootch."

"It's a strange world."

"You think a man like that would be able to do himself?"

"I think it would be difficult."

"He never said anything in the ambulance, never even opened his eyes. He was breathing, but then he just kind of sighed and that was it."

"He probably just let go. Sometimes it's better than holding on to a life that's not worth living."

"The Cajun says you have a gun in the nightstand by your bed; that you point it at your head every night and think about pulling the trigger. Is that true?"

"It could be me, it could be someone else."

"He said for a fact it was you."

"The Cajun says a lot of things."

I thought about it some. "How do you know he had a life that wasn't worth living? Most of the time he was living in the past, so it couldn't have been all that bad."

"Did it ever occur to you that these past few years were the only peaceful years he had ever known?" Shimmelman shot back irritably.

"Peaceful maybe, but I don't think they were much fun for him; sitting alone in his room the way he did, eating scraps from the E and B."

Shimmelman heaved a sigh. "You wouldn't make such a shallow observation if you'd read even a single page of *Womb*."

"I read it, at least most of it. "

"And you didn't understand that his search was not for fun, not for adventure, but for peace?"

"That was Kuryokin, not Isaiah Balenkin."

"Kuryokin is Isaiah Balenkin, just as the author is the simpleton Kuryokin. They are one and the same, inseparable for all time and eternity."

"I don't see how that can be," I objected. "Balenkin sure wasn't a simpleton, a little touched maybe but basically sharp as a tack. He told me all about his life and he never said anything about the first World War. No way he could have done all those things Kuryokin did."

He rolled his eyes. "Kuryokin is a metaphor. Do you understand what a metaphor is?"

"I don't believe so," I admitted.

181

"Try to imagine the moment of your birth, try to describe it."

"Well I can't remember that."

"But you were there, you were conscious the entire time."

"Nobody can remember when they were born."

"But they can describe it, based on what they've heard about birth from those who have seen it. Try to imagine Isaiah Balenkin struggling to describe his search for the greatest singularity in the explosion of human experience, his search for peace. Since he knows what it is but has never experienced it, he can only depict it through the eyes of someone who has, someone entirely pure, someone uncorrupted by cruelty and greed and violence, someone newborn to the world, like Kuryokin."

"Maybe it'll make more sense to me after I've finished it."

"I doubt it. I'm not sure it even made much sense to the author himself. He seems to have concluded that the search is doomed to failure, that the best we can hope to do with this world is tolerate it; which is probably why Stalin had him thrown in the gulag in the first place. It flew in the face of his perfect Communist paradise."

"So if he's doomed to fail what's the point of the whole thing?"

"Perhaps there is no point; perhaps the search is all we've got. Maybe the idea is to write and paint and posture our way through until the exertion of the voyage becomes too much to bear and we're blessed with the wisdom to say, enough! I've had enough."

A white-uniformed orderly arrived with some papers for Shimmelman to sign. "Are there any relatives who can claim the body?"

"He had no relatives. Except for us he was alone in the world."

"How do you want to handle the disposition of his remains?"

"He was a Nobel Laureate. Do you suppose it would be possible to donate his brain to science?"

The orderly shrugged. "What you do with his brain is your business. I get a dozen like him in here every day and I'm sure science is dying to get ahold of all their brains, but it's a pain in the ass for the medical examiners. There's a million forms they've got to sign if they take a part out and don't put it back; plus, you'll have to pay whatever cost is involved."

"Can we just have him cremated? I can't bear the thought of him lying in a pauper's grave."

"Cremation's thirty bucks. A brass urn'll set you back another ten."

We took a taxi back to the Soldiers and Sailors where the Cajun was waiting for us in the lobby, his one good eye fiery and menacing. "Some bum was here to see you and I threw his ass out, he told me. He left this card with his number if you want to call him."

"You threw Nick Corsi out?"

"Why not? He looked like a punk."

"Jeezus! And he didn't do anything?"

"What was he gonna do? He's a little punk. I knocked punks like him around all my life."

"And you had no idea who he was?"

"I don't care who the hell he is; I didn't like his looks is all. Little wop was what he was."

"Yeah, well that little wop can get your knees broken."

"I'd like to see him try." The Cajun stormed off in the direction of the pool.

I dialed the number on the card and Nick answered. "You did the right thing the other day," he said when I identified myself. "Did you give any thought to what we talked about?"

"What'd we talk about?"

"You know; about what you want to back out of the picture."

"I don't want anything."

"Whatta you mean, you don't want anything? I thought you were starting to show some sense here."

"If you're talking about my seeing Molly, don't worry. It's all over, not that there was anything to get over in the first place."

The phone was silent for a moment. "Okay, I got no reason to doubt you, and you got no reason to disrespect me."

"I'm not disrespecting you. I told you I was out of the picture."

"And I told you that in return you could name your price."

"There isn't any price."

"Everything's got a price."

"Not this."

Another silence. "Okay, just what kind of game are you playing here?" he asked finally.

"No game. I'm too wore out to play games."

"And you're outa here, no matter what?"

"I know when I've had enough." The wind was gone out of me. I do not know whether what I felt was the end of adventure or the beginning of wisdom, and right then it didn't seem to matter.

Twenty-Seven

I should have known Nick Corsi would never let it go. In his world everything had a price, no matter which end of the bargain you found yourself on. If you needed something from Nick you gave something in return, and if he needed something from you he gave something in return. I had given him what he'd wanted but he could not claim victory until I'd balanced it off by taking something back. Like the spiraling stars in one of Shimmelman's galaxies, all of them circling one another warily, giving no more than they were taking, it was a fragile balance of strength and weakness, power and submission. The only circumstance that could disrupt his carefully constructed orbit was a debt unpaid. The only sin was owing somebody.

Nick's payback came in the form of a Western Union telegram delivered to the Soldiers and Sailors a few days after Isaiah Balenkin's death. "S/Sgt. Harry Bailey admitted to VA hospital, Cheshire, N.Y. 8/12/52, STOP, No record of release or disposition, STOP."

That was all it said. Whether I'd asked for it or not, Nick had tracked my daddy down and given him to me; his way of saying the slate had been wiped clean. Nobody owed anybody else anything except strict adherence to the contract. Molly was his, he had paid for her in full with Harry Bailey. I agreed to the stipulations in the contract and he agreed that in return he would not break my legs. It had a kind of dark symmetry to it.

I called the hospital, only to learn that they did not reveal patient information over the telephone, so I purchased a train ticket that day and made the six-hour trip upstate to Cheshire, New York; a forlorn dot on the map that differed from Eula only in architecture and terrain. Nestled in a valley of the Adirondacks, it seemed as lifeless, its inhabitants wrung out and shrunk in the shadow of the mountains just as Eula's shriveled up and died in the prairie sun. It was a place like this that Molly had fled, I'd thought as I stood at the railroad station waiting for a taxicab to take me to the hospital; a place like this that I'd fled looking for Harry Bailey. And this was where he'd brought me back; not to the dazzle of New York City, but to the squalor and hopelessness of another place ransomed from the earth that God had cursed or plain forgotten; he'd brought me home.

The hospital stood on the lip of a hill, detached from the road by a swath of grass cut into the forest. It had once been a school, I was told by a longtime resident of the place who happened by while I was waiting for Harry Bailey. Once children had filled its hallways—the sons and daughters of prosperous merchants from the town, back when the canal was in its heyday, and boats and barges plied the inland waters bringing products and raw materials to the valley below. Then the railroad came, and soon after that the Great Depression and the war. No sooner had they fought off one disaster, than another came along to take its place; and before long the merchants moved away where the factories had gone and took their children with them. And when the children went off to war and came back without legs and arms and minds, the school opened its doors to them again and the town had a reason for staying on the map.

Sitting in a dimly lit corridor, I gulped clean, crisp puffs of autumn air whistling through an open window above me to mask the embedded hospital smells of stale urine and antiseptic. Not far away, a janitor swabbed the worn linoleum floor with a rag-covered push broom and a strong bleach solution, and a few feet beyond him a scarecrow figure was propped awkwardly in a wheelchair. Like a puppet whose strings had fouled, his legless torso was skewed awkwardly sideways, allowing a continuous strand of yellow mucus to drip from the base of his breathing tube into a metal vessel at his side. Further down the hall another patient, this one with all his proper limbs but eyes crusted over with salve, was drumming his fingers on the armrests of his wheelchair, keeping time to the orchestra of birds outside the window. He cocked his head at the bellow of a train whistle coming from the valley below, measuring the seconds with his tapping fingers until the exact moment when the whistle blew again and the train chugged slowly out of the station. Then he nodded off to sleep, satisfied that for just one moment he had captured time and movement and the thoughts of songbirds with his fingertips.

My being there had caused a lot of confusion at the hospital. At first the nurse at the front desk had told me there was no patient named Harry Bailey, but after re-checking her records she'd asked me to take a seat in the hall and wait. Somebody would see me soon, she told me. An hour later I was still waiting, surrounded by the halt and lame, the part of war we hadn't heard about when we'd got caught up in bond drives and newspaper collections and tin foil balls and Gold Star mothers sitting in a place of honor at the Armistice Day parade; the part that came after the band stopped playing and the last P-38s and battleships and files of marching men disappeared from the newsreels. It was life or death on the movie screen, the joy of homecoming or the mournful strains of Taps at gravesides; never the dark limbo of a hospital hallway where legless men propped like dolls oozed bile onto the linoleum and tapped the margins of their world with their fingertips.

"Mister Bailey?" The man was dressed in a tie and jacket. A nameplate on his pocket identified him as Edmund Bourke, Hospital Administrator.

"Yessir." I stood and extended my hand.

"Mister Bailey, I'm afraid we owe you an apology. It seems a terrible mistake has been made."

"My daddy's not here?"

"He is; that is to say, he was..." His voice was cracking, his eyes fixed on a point somewhere over my right shoulder. "I'm so very sorry to have to tell you that your father passed away last month."

"Passed away?" A giant fist dug into my chest and gripped my entrails.

"Due to a clerical mix-up the wrong family was notified. I can't tell you how embarrassed I am by this. I know it's no excuse, but we're severely understaffed here. Mistakes get made; I'm sorry this one had to be at your expense."

"How did he die?" I asked weakly.

"Your father was being treated for a number of stress-related problems..."

"What killed him?"

He placed a sympathetic hand on my shoulder. "The cause of death is listed as liver failure due to acute alcoholism. I'm sorry, I know that's not an easy thing to hear but it's something we at the hospital have to live with every day. Many of the men returning from the war turned to drink to wipe out the memories they brought home with them. It helped them forget, it helped them to cope. To be perfectly honest with you I can't much blame them."

"Where's he now? "

"When we received no word we buried him in the hospital cemetery. It's out back, only a short way from here. I can take you there if you want."

I followed him outside, over the rim of the hill where the land sloped gently downward to meet a shimmering expanse of water I had not known was there.

"That's Lake Champlain," he told me as we made our way to an enclosed plot halfway down the slope.

"To me it's the most beautiful spot in God's creation. This is where I want to be buried when my time comes; overlooking the lake, surrounded by the mountains." He opened the cemetery gate and led me inside where white grave markers, crosses and stars, were carefully aligned in rows. "Believe it or not I come here sometimes when things inside start to overwhelm me. There's just something about this place. I think of it as somewhere to unwind, somewhere to take stock. I know it must ring hollow to you now, but your father is in a better place, a more peaceful place. These last few years have been hard ones for him. I really believe he was ready to lay down his load."

I followed him down the rows of markers, not wanting to disagree with him even though the last thing I felt at that moment was peaceful. The thought that Harry Bailey lay somewhere beneath that unfamiliar earth, however breathtaking the water and the mountains around him might have been, did little to comfort me. It seemed that I had heard it all before, from the pulpit of the Calvary Baptist Church and Grace Ministry where life's burdens were laid down in halcyon pastures and the grime and stink of East Texas washed away in the blended voices of the choir:

> Going home, going home;
> O Lord I'm homeward bound.
> Laying down my heavy load,
> Peace at last I've found...

I'd heard it in the dinnertime preachments of the Reverend Harley Brown: *Neither death, nor life, nor angels, nor principalities, nor powers, nor things present, nor things to come, nor height, nor depth, nor any other creature shall be able to separate thee from the love of God which is Jesus Christ our Lord...*

Death, then, was a stopping-off point on your way to somewhere better, a momentary obstruction in things that straightened out quick enough when you found yourself hitched up to the Rapture. But what Administrator Edmund Bourke had not considered was that Harry Bailey was more than likely headed in another direction. He'd been a liar, a thief, an adulterer, and maybe even a murderer, depending on how strict the Almighty interpreted that crime. It was not likely there were any angel's wings waiting for him in the afterlife. Of course there was always the possibility that I'd been right all along; that God was nothing more than a blustering, posturing phony who bullied folks into doing his bidding with all sorts of threats he could never follow through on. Harry Bailey might just have gotten as far as the road would take him, and if that was the case, there were worse places he could have ended up than on a grassy slope overlooking a mountain lake.

"Your father was a patient at the hospital several times over the past few years, and during those times I got to know him rather well," Bourke reminisced. "He was a very talented man. He carved animals and birds out of wood; quite remarkable likenesses, really. I have a number of them back in my office if you'd like to see them. Maybe you'd like to take some home with you."

"Did he suffer much?"

"I don't think so. I think he just went to sleep."

"He was a good carpenter. He built us a house with his own hands, start-to-finish. Had a porch and an upstairs and everything."

"Like I said, he was a very talented man."

"You think he ever went to the Salvation Army, about the drinking, I mean?"

"I don't know. He attended AA meetings while he was here but I don't think it was a message he wanted to hear."

"What kind of animals and birds did he carve?"

"Deer, I think; and ducks. He carved wonderful ducks."

"He knew how to catch them alright. Not many knew their way around a duck blind like Harry Bailey."

We reached a marker that bore the simple inscription "S/Sgt. Harry Bailey; 1912 -1952."

"It'll be dark soon. It gets dark fast in these parts," Bourke said as he observed the sun bleeding into the crest of mountains beyond. "Maybe you'd like to spend some time alone with him to say a prayer or something."

"You think I should say a prayer?"

"That would be up to you."

"He wasn't much of a churchgoer. Matter of fact, neither am I."

"I guess everybody has his own way of saying good-bye." He turned and walked back through the rows of markers toward the gate. "I'll be in my office. Stop by on your way out and I'll give you some of his carvings."

We were alone, Harry and me; and I didn't have the vaguest notion how to say good-bye. We had never really said hello, at least not in the way most sons and fathers get to know each other over the long run, so all I had were tatters of memory torn from time, stories told in the taverns and under the hot, dusty overhangs on Main Street, stories hinted at or barely acknowledged by Mama, by Uncle Mal, by folks who wanted to love him but were afraid.

Knowing what I knew about him now it was hard to fault them; hard to say they could have tried a little harder or waited a little longer or endeavored to understand him better. Harry Bailey was what he was, and on the face of it there'd been mighty little to recommend him. Mama's family in New England must have seen that right off when they disinherited her, but she'd left with him anyway; fallen like a ton of bricks for his deep-set blue eyes, his Comanche cheekbones, his rascally ways. And there was never a day when I didn't think she'd run right back to him. Even after she'd refused to come to New York with me; even after she'd married that big-bellied, soft-handed, poorer-than-dirt excuse for a man, Harley Brown; even then I knew she would come running back because everything without him was waiting; waiting to be relieved of needing him, waiting for the spark of life to renew itself without him. Sooner or later she would have to come alive again. The wickedness in him that she loved so much and hated so much was as much a part of her as the air she breathed.

I had no prayers, only the memories. There was a copper plaque from the Veterans of Foreign Wars embedded in the ground near Harry Bailey's marker. I pulled it up and used its edge to shovel a shallow depression in the damp earth above his grave, then I took his Silver Star from my pocket, placed it inside the hole and covered it with dirt. Whether God was or wasn't; whether it was all an accident of exploding stars like Shimmelman maintained, or a glorious journey to a heavenly reward, the medal would endure. It would affirm that, for all his weaknesses, he had once put the lives of thirteen of his comrades above his own. It would testify that a sinner now rested in the company of heroes.

LeMoult

Twenty-Eight

I'd telephoned Mama as soon as I got back to the Soldiers and Sailors, and though I expected her to be upset at the news, I'd underestimated how hard she would take it. There was a gasp on the other end when I told her, followed by a long silence.

"You okay, Mama?"

"I guess so..." Her voice was fragmented, interrupted by sobs.

"He didn't suffer. Mr. Bourke at the hospital said he just went to sleep and didn't wake up. He knew Daddy—said he was a talented man."

"Will you be coming home now?"

It hadn't occurred to me that with my search completed, there was no good reason for me to stay in New York. In fact, the unwritten rules of my agreement with Nick Corsi compelled me to go; maybe not back to Eula, but someplace far enough away to guarantee him I was no longer a threat. "There are some things I've got to finish here first," I lied.

"I think I need you here, Chance."

"Why? Is everything okay there, Mama?"

"I'd just feel better knowing you were here."

"He's not hurting you, is he?"

"Just come home. Please?"

"I'll kill him if he's hurting you."

"I'm not hurt. I just need you here with me."

"I'll be back for Thanksgiving, promise."

Shimmelman agreed it was time for me to go. He told me that the Board of Directors of the YMCA had voted to shut down the Soldiers and

Sailors and sell the property to developers. Times were changing, and what had once been a vital, teeming lodging place for thousands of travelers had become a dilapidated shell, fit only for derelicts and life's losers. Now not only the building, but all of Third Avenue was slated for renewal. The elevated train tracks were coming down, and the grimy, shadowed civilization beneath them would be replaced with gleaming office buildings, boutique shops, and trendy cafes. It was time for all of us to move on, time to make way for the future.

"Where will you go?" I asked him.

"I haven't the vaguest idea. I'd kind of gotten used to this old place."

"Me too," I admitted. It was hard to fathom how I could have become so attached to the Soldiers and Sailors in just a few short months, but I had. Its trenchant smells, its careworn lobby furniture, its creaking stairs and banisters, its musty, tile-lined hallways and undependable plumbing had all burrowed into my soul and stayed. I expect it was because it had been at the center of my New York experience, and to lose it would be to diminish everything that had been about. It seemed a cruel irony to me at the time. Nothing had worked out the way it was supposed to have worked out, and in a final, wrenching twist of the knife, that vengeful old God seemed intent on obliterating the last trace of my even trying, getting back at me for abandoning him. Whether that was true, or whether everything that had happened was no more than a turn of the cards, I was finally ready to accept it. If there were any lessons to be learned by it all I would have to learn them back in west Texas where things slowed down to a manageable pace and daydreams got clipped before they ever became longing.

"What'll happen to your wall?" I asked Shimmelman. "You're not going to let them tear it down are you?"

He shrugged. "Maybe it's all for the best. Maybe the only suitable end for it is total destruction."

"But you've spent so much time on it."

"Less than a blink of the eye in celestial terms. Looking at it I often wonder whether I've accomplished anything at all. There was a time when I thought it was my life's mission; when I believed I had been singularly endowed to unravel all the great universal mysteries, but lately the wind has gone out of my sails. Possibly it has to do with the old man's dying. I've begun to think that nothing survives; not life, not literature or art, not thought processes, not even the cosmos itself. Everything seems destined to die, and once dead, collapse back into the state of nothingness whence it came."

"It'll survive if you make it survive," I objected. "Isaiah Balenkin's work survived. I finished *Womb* on the train back from Cheshire."

"And was it the greatest book you've ever read?"

"It's the only book I ever read," I admitted. "Fact is, I'm not sure what it was all about, but a lot of folks must have or it wouldn't've won that Nobel Prize."

"Not likely," Shimmelman scoffed. "I doubt whether even the Nobel Prize Committee fully understood what it meant, but they realized that to pass it by would probably open them to ridicule. That's undoubtedly the one constant in all great art; its meaning is so obscure that it fills men with awe and shame and anger for not being able to understand it. That leaves them no alternative but to honor it or destroy it."

I did not know which of those things I felt. The story of Kuryokin had a simple enough ending, but looking at it as the metaphor Shimmelman insisted it was, left me utterly confused. I'd expected that after awhile I would come to understand more of the things Shimmelman knew—things like metaphors and convolutions, and even Joe Carl's solipsisms which I'd never really understood in the first place, but now it seemed that there would be no time for that.

Somehow I knew that once the Soldiers and Sailors was demolished I would never see Shimmelman again. In all the vastness and splendor of New York we'd come together in this tiny, godforsaken speck under the El and touched each other briefly. It had been the glue that kept us from spinning apart, and I knew that after it was gone we would splinter off and go our separate ways. Perhaps that was for me the beginning of maturity; realizing the impermanence of life, understanding for the first time that it wrenched everybody out of comfort and complacency sooner or later. Everybody had to move on.

And I was ready, but before I went I knew I had to see Molly one more time, if for nothing else than to tell her about Harry Bailey and the hospital in Cheshire. Knowing she would be with The American Dance Ensemble that afternoon, I walked across town, climbed the stairs to the practice hall and waited in the corner until she finished her exercises. She seemed startled to see me there when she walked off the floor.

"I just stopped by to tell you about Harry Bailey before I left," I blurted. "He died in a Veteran's Hospital up in Cheshire, New York. Nick found him for me."

Molly pulled me back into the shadows. "You shouldn't be here. Did anybody see you come in?"

"Like who?"

"Was there a man wearing a leather overcoat outside in the hall?"

"I dunno, I guess I wasn't looking. Why?"

I could see her eyes, wide and frightened. What looked like a bruise under the left one could have been an illusion of the half-light, but at that point I wasn't taking anything for granted. "What's going on here, Molly? Are you okay?"

"Look, I'm really sorry about your father. We'll be able to talk about it sometime soon, but right now's not a good time. Your being here's not good for either of us."

I turned her toward the light and saw the purple discoloration on her cheek clearly. "Did Nick do that to you?

"You have to go, Chance. I'll call you and tell you all about it. I promise."

"I'm not going anywhere until I get an answer. Did Nick beat you up like that? Was it the guy in the hall? I'll kill the son of a bitch!"

"You're not going to kill anybody. You're going back to the Soldiers and Sailors and wait for my call. Please, for both our sakes."

"You won't call. You'll get used to it just like Mama got used to it."

"I swear I'll call, as soon as I can." She gripped my forearm with a strength I hadn't known she possessed. "Now if you care for me at all you'll let me go. I'm getting my things and I'm walking out to the hall and you're staying here. Don't go downstairs for at least ten minutes, promise me?"

I watched her leave, struggling to catch my breath. Every instinct I had told me to rush outside into the hallway and grab that leather-coated bastard and beat him to a pulp, whoever he was, whatever function Nick had assigned to him, but the tone in Molly's voice had convinced me she meant what she said. She was in trouble, and she'd be in a whole lot more trouble if I did anything reckless. For the time being I would have to trust that she would call me. The rest would come to me with time.

"He'll kill her one of these days, you know that." It was Bertie, wiping his face with a towel. "She'll never be the good little girl he wants her to be, and he's not the kind to take no for an answer."

"What's he doing to her?" I asked.

"You're not blind, are you, darling?"

"I saw the bruises. Why doesn't she just leave?"

Bertie rolled his eyes skyward. "That is just too precious for words. My God, I knew you were naive but I didn't realize you were Harold Teen in the flesh. Don't you know you can't just walk away from a man like Nick Corsi? He's invested time and money in her, and more importantly, I think he loves her in his own twisted way."

"Hitting people ain't the way to show you love them."

"It's his way. Men like him who've clawed their way up from the gutter never really feel they deserve what they've got. Every morning they wake up thinking it will all be gone, that it was all a chimera to begin with; so they're never happy just to possess things. They have to possess them absolutely. There's a gorilla taking her downstairs right now who never lets her out of his sight. That's the only way Nick can be sure she'll be there in the morning."

"I don't get it. How come he never did that before?"

"He did, it was just more subtle. Besides, there was no you before."

"There's no me now, at least not in the way everybody thinks. I'm just a kid. Molly thinks of me as a kid brother."

"It doesn't matter. Nick Corsi's not worried about competition, he's worried about losing respect. Whatever you were to Molly, it diminished his power over her, and power is the only thing that makes him a man."

"Well he didn't have to worry about that. He bought me lock, stock and barrel. I was getting ready to go back to Texas before all this."

"That would probably be the smart thing to do. You have your whole life in front of you. Why should you jeopardize it for someone who traded her freedom for her ambition?"

I could hear the catch in Bertie's voice, and I knew what he was saying was the last thing he meant. "What do you think we ought to do?" I asked him.

"We, darling?"

"You're going to help me, right?"

"Help you do what?"

"I'm not sure, but when I figure it out, you'll help, right?"

He tossed his head. "You must have me confused with some other gallant Lochinvar whose only mission in life is to save fair damsels. Let me tell you something, sweetie; I have all I can do trying to save my own ass in this city, and if I decided to risk it on somebody else you can be sure it wouldn't be some damsel. In case you hadn't noticed, damsels aren't exactly my cup of tea."

"But friends are, aren't they?"

"Christ, I hate this city."

Twenty-Nine

I spent that night sleeping in a chair by the telephone in the lobby of the Soldiers and Sailors, not really thinking I'd hear from her then, but not willing to take the chance I might miss her call. When she hadn't phoned by noon the next day I was in a frenzy, ready to dismantle the building brick-by-brick and save the city the expense of tearing it down. I almost jumped through my skin when the phone finally rang:

"Are either Mister Jerome Shimmelman or Mister Chance Bailey there please?" the male voice on the other end inquired.

"This's Chance Bailey." I tried to mask the disappointment in my voice.

"Are you acquainted with Mister Shimmelman?"

"He's right here, you want me to get him?"

"I don't think that will be necessary right now." He paused and cleared his throat. "Mister Bailey, this is Donald Carter from the Chemical Corn Exchange here in New York. We are the executors of the estate of the late Isaiah Balenkin and as such we will conduct a reading of his will at three-thirty this afternoon. Both you and Mister Shimmelman have been named as beneficiaries and I'm calling to verify that you can both be here for the reading today."

"Beneficiaries?"

"You've both been left some money from his estate," he clarified.

"I didn't know he had any money."

"Well I can assure you that's not the case."

"How much money?"

"I'm afraid I can't tell you that. Will you and Mister Shimmelman be able to come to the bank this afternoon at three-thirty?

"Three-thirty?"

"Three-thirty at the Chemical Corn Exchange, We're at Thirty-fourth street and Broadway. Ask for me, my name is Donald Carter."

Shimmelman was as shocked as I was when I told him about the call. "The old man was penniless. When I found him wandering around in Bryant Park he didn't have enough to buy himself a meal."

"Well he must've had something. The bank wouldn't have called us if he didn't."

"Extraordinary, he must have made a deposit years ago and forgotten all about it."

"That's not likely. He didn't know me years ago and I'm a beneficiary."

Shimmelman shook his head in amazement. "Then he must have contacted the bank within the last few months."

"Or weeks. He really didn't know who I was until that day Molly and I took him to the park, and even after that he had me all confused with his brother, Sergei, and a whole lot of other people from the past."

"Extraordinary."

I was reluctant to leave when Molly still hadn't phoned by three that afternoon, but the Cajun assured me he'd take a message and get a number where I could reach her if she called while I was gone.

"I didn't know your name was Jerome," I whispered to Shimmelman as we sat in a spacious waiting room outside Donald Carter's office at the Chemical Corn Exchange.

He made a face. "Nobody knows. It's a dreadful name. I was called Jerry as a child."

"Nothing wrong with Jerry. It's a nice name."

"Not when your childhood plans are to unravel the great cosmic mysteries," he snorted. "I kept thinking of untold generations of school children to come, reading about the great unified theory of existence; how everything began, Why everything happens the way it does, and where it will all end up, by Jerry! What a cruel hoax that would have been."

"It could have been by Jerome," I pointed out.

"Small consolation. As it turns out it was all academic anyway. My life's work will crumble under the wrecker's ball and I'll probably end up like the old man, wandering aimlessly through the city parks, accepting scraps of food from passing strangers."

A prim, no-nonsense secretary led us into Donald Carter's office where he sat behind a polished oak desk, thumbing through a stack of papers. He stood, shook our hands and asked us to sit down. "If it's all right with you both, we might as well get started."

Shimmelman looked around. "Aren't there going to be others?"

"You're the only beneficiaries mentioned in the will." Carter examined the papers in front of him for a moment before starting to read: "I, Isaiah Balenkin, being of sound mind, do hereby bequeath the entire sum of my worldly goods to Jerome Shimmelman and Chance Bailey, both residing at the Soldiers and Sailors YMCA in New York City, to divide equally between them."

"That's it?" Shimmelman asked when Carter looked up from the sheet.

"Pretty much, except for the dollar amounts."

"We didn't think he had anything at all. He was a virtual beggar when I found him two years ago."

"Isaiah Balenkin was far from a beggar. He deposited the entire amount of his Nobel Prize winnings with this bank in October of nineteen-thirty-six, and if I've done my math correctly, today that amount with interest comes to three hundred, forty-two thousand, six hundred, thirty-three dollars and sixty-six cents. Divided equally, that comes to one hundred seventy-one thousand, three hundred sixteen dollars and eighty-three cents apiece."

The silence in the office was overwhelming. A full minute must have passed before Shimmelman could speak. "There's no mistake?" he asked weakly.

"None. Mister Balenkin was in this office on the twentieth of this month to dot the I's and cross the T's on the final revisions. He thought a great deal of both of you. It must have been a wonderful experience having him as a friend."

"He came here by himself?"

"Oh yes, he came here often, at least once a month to check on his box, which brings us to the second part of his will."

Carter removed a metal safe deposit box from a drawer and handed it across the desk to Shimmelman. "He specifically requested that the contents of this box be bequeathed only to you."

Shimmelman opened the box and for the first time since I'd known him I saw tears in his eyes. Carefully, reverently, he lifted Isaiah Balenkin's Nobel Prize medal and held it, moving it ever so slightly in his hand, watching the light from the window glint on its golden surfaces. It was clear to me then that the medal meant more to him than all the money, more than anything else the author might have left him. More than money, more than even the medal, Isaiah Balenkin had bequeathed to Shimmelman the most precious gift a man can receive. He'd told his friend and rescuer that painting the stars was a pursuit worthy of honor, he'd confirmed that Shimmelman's life's work had not been wasted.

We walked home in silence, both of us too numb to talk. I was rich beyond anything I could have possibly dreamed; rich enough to live the rest of my life without ever having to lift a finger, rich enough to buy anything I saw in the shop windows we passed, rich enough to go back to Eula and. buy the biggest house around and sit on my front porch and kick off my boots and watch folks go by all filled with envy and admiration for me. Hell, with the money I had I could buy the whole damn town for what it was worth. I could buy the Strand movie theater and make sure they only played John Wayne movies like *The Quiet Man*, with maybe a Clark Gable war movie like *Run Silent, Run Deep* sprinkled in for variety. I could buy Stella's Restaurant and order that they serve nothing but cheeseburgers and banana cream pie. I could buy Eula's New World Hair and Nail Salon, which I would. shut down immediately; and the Eula *Clarion*, which would carry only news about Stan Musial and Ted Williams and Joe DiMaggio and Rocky Marciano, and of course the Buck Rogers comic strip.

I could saunter up the front steps of Moon's Roadside Cafe and tell that bearded, beer-bellied bouncer at the door a thing or two, and he'd step right back and let me pass because I'd have dollar bills sticking out of every pocket in my jeans. And I would buy drinks for everybody in the place, and play high-stakes poker and not even worry if I lost; and I would change a hundred for silver dollars and put one in every table crack and give that Mexican whore something to remember for the rest of her life. And I would buy the Calvary Baptist Church and Grace Ministry and get a preacher in there who didn't bore everybody to tears with stories about folks who lived thousands of years ago. And as for Harley Brown, I would fart him to death and gut him with my stag-horn knife for good measure, and nobody in the Sheriff's office would do a thing about it because I'd have bought that too.

Or I could take Molly away to Lake Champlain, across the mountain to a place she couldn't see when she was growing up on that porch of hers. She didn't need Nick Corsi now that I was rich.

"He couldn't have been to that bank every month," Shimmelman muttered as we approached the Soldiers and Sailors. "I watched the old man like a hawk. He never left his bed except to go to the bathroom."

"Somebody went there every month. Somebody had to be there to make out that will," I pointed out.

"He was an invalid, most of the time he couldn't remember his name or where he was. You said yourself he thought you were his brother. He thought you were both living back in the beginning of the century."

"Maybe that's who went to the bank then."

"Who?"

"That other Isaiah Balenkin, the one who still had all his marbles."

Shimmelman halted dead in his tracks. "Do you really think that could happen?"

"You said it could. You said the only thing that was real was what people imagined, kind of like solipsism my friend Joe Carl talked about. Maybe that's what it's all about. Maybe it's all just a dream after all."

He nodded uncertainly and continued walking up the street into a stiff October wind.

Thirty

It was not a dream, at least not the part about the money. Shimmelman and I went back to the Chemical Corn Exchange the following day to sign the paperwork (luckily I had the birth certificate Mama had sent me, otherwise I wouldn't've been able to prove I was who I was), and when I deposited my half of the money in a savings account I found that overnight I'd made an additional ninety-eight dollars and twenty-two cents, more money than I'd made working an entire summer at Purdy's Feed & Grain. It was a strange feeling, almost a guilty feeling. There I was making money for doing absolutely nothing but having money while most of the people I'd met in New York City were scratching around to get enough to eat. Shimmelman told me it was the way of the world. The rich got richer; like red giant suns they swelled with their own inner fires, while the poor got poorer; shrunken by their own gravity like white dwarf stars. To try and alter the balance would be to finagle with the natural order of things. I do not know what I thought of that theory at the time. I was still too stunned, and worried sick that I had not yet heard from Molly. Three days had passed without a phone call and I knew it was time for me to take action. I'd been working on a plan and my sudden good fortune now gave me the means to implement it.

It was Halloween, ten-thirty in the morning. The giant Radio City theater was completely dark except for the light coming from the huge arched proscenium where The Rockettes were being put through their paces by an angry, sweating Bertie. Sitting a few rows back in the darkened orchestra, the man in the leather overcoat watched the rehearsal intently, the orange flicker of his cigarette being the only indication of his whereabouts. On-stage, Bertie had, placed the dancers in two separate groups, one group forward in a box pattern, and the other spread out at stage rear, with Molly, the newest and least practiced member of the line, nearest the side curtain. The routine was entirely new, introduced by Bertie at the last minute, and it was clear from the awkwardness of the dancers and from Bertie's frustrated outbursts, that nobody was happy with the way things were going.

Suddenly the proceedings were interrupted by a noisy outburst at the back of the theater. Staggering down the aisle, the Cajun screamed obscenities at the darkness, at the dancers, at the world in general—an utterly convincing portrayal of an out-of-control drunk, honed by years of on-the-job training.

"Get that person out of here!" Bertie shrieked, and immediately two security guards rushed down the aisle and wrestled with the cursing Cajun, trying to restrain him. The whole thing took only a few seconds, but it was enough of a diversion for Bertie to hustle Molly through the side curtain, down the circular stairs backstage, and out the stage door to the street, where I waited at curbside in an idling Buick Riviera convertible I'd bought that morning. In an almost superhuman exhibition of strength and grace, Bertie scooped her up from the sidewalk and placed her in the front seat next to me, like a dancer effortlessly releasing his female partner on the stage, maintaining the illusion that she was landing on a puff of clouds.

"What' s going on!" Molly gasped as I peeled away from the curb.

"We're running away," I yelled back at her over the din of traffic.

"Where?"

"Wherever Nick Corsi and his goons can't find us."

I turned uptown, checked the rear-view mirror to make certain we weren't being followed, and picked a spot along Riverside Drive to pull over. "I'm sorry about this. I just didn't know what else to do when I didn't hear from you."

She seemed more amused than angry. "Am I being kidnapped?"

"It's the only way we could figure to get you away from him."

Molly sank back into the seat. "God, we're in for it now. You don't do something like this to Nick Corsi"

"I'm not doing anything to Nick Corsi. I'm taking you for a ride in my new car."

She looked around at the plush leather upholstery. "This is yours?"

"Bought and paid for."

"What did you do, rob a bank?"

"Well I got it from a bank, all right but I didn't have to rob it. Isaiah Balenkin left Shimmelman and me near all the money in the world, money he'd gotten for his Nobel Prize. I'm rich, Molly, just about as rich as a guy can get. I don't know how or why, but I've got more money than I'd ever be able to spend in a lifetime. I earn better'n ninety dollars a day just letting the money sit there in the bank. When the automobile dealer asked me whether I had a license to drive a car I just pulled two thousand dollars out of my pocket and that was that, no more questions asked."

"What are you doing, Chance?" Molly broke in.

"I dunno. I guess I'm just talking fast cause I'm afraid you'll be mad at me."

"I couldn't be mad at you. I'm just frightened."

"You don't have to be frightened anymore. We can take this car anyplace we want, off to that castle of yours on the Rhone River if you want. We can even hire a bunch of those running horsemen to jog alongside and plop down a carpet for you to walk on when we stop."

"He'll find us. If it takes him forever he'll track us down," she said somberly.

"He can't look everywhere. We can just keep driving until we get to a place so far away nobody would ever think of looking there."

"I came from a place like that, remember?"

"Not a place like Whitehall where nothing happens. We'll go someplace so faraway that people can only dream about it. Hell, I'll rev this car up and drive us all the way to the dark side of the moon if it'll make you happy."

She laughed. "What would make me happy right now is a hot bath and a change of clothes, I'm wringing wet from the rehearsal."

I'd deliberately left the convertible top down and I realized she must be cold. "I don't think we can go back to your place. They'll probably be there looking for us," I cautioned.

"How about the Soldiers and Sailors?"

"Same thing. Besides the plumbing's probably on the fritz again. Why don't we just keep on going until we get someplace where we can clean up and buy some new clothes and not have to worry about being spotted?"

"Like where?"

"Which way is New Rochelle?"

"That would be north."

"Then we'll go south, as far as we have to."

I followed Molly's directions south for a few miles to the tip of Manhattan, then round up north again, across the Whitestone Bridge and all the way out to the tip of Long Island, a desolate windblown stretch of sand and saw-grass called Montauk, where we found a weathered two-story clapboard hotel by the water and checked in as Mr. and Mrs. Chance Bailey.

"You two honeymooners?" the hotel clerk asked as he led us upstairs to our room, seemingly not concerned over our lack of luggage. "We used to get a lot of honeymooners here before the war, until they started building those motel places further in. Young folks today seem to want to be where the action is. Can't say I much blame them."

"But it's so beautiful out here, so peaceful and quiet," Molly said.

"It is that." He led us into our room and drew the drapes, revealing an expanse of empty beach and shimmering ocean below. "It's especially nice this time of year when all the out-of-towners are gone and the beach has a chance to get healthy again. Days are wearing down now. Indian summer'll be here in a day or two and you'll be able to lie out there in the sand and get a tan as good as in the middle of July." He handed me the key. "Hot water's iffy but it should hold out if you share. Dinner's at six; steak-and-kidney pie tonight."

I fumbled in my pocket for my wallet. "No need for that, I own the place," he said, matter-of-factly. "You two youngsters have a pleasant stay. My name's Royster. if you need anything you can call me at the desk." He shut the door behind him, leaving us alone in the room.

"Don't worry about using up all the hot water," I said, breaking a nervous silence. "Reckon I can wait a while for it to heat up again."

Molly closed the bathroom door and I heard her moving around inside - the secret noises of a woman going through her bath-time rituals, discarding garments, running hot water, the suck of her bare feet on the tile floor. I could see her naked in my mind, examining the contours of her body in the full-length mirror on the door, testing the temperature with her toe before she stepped in, easing back in the tub as the steamy water embraced the convex bulge of her belly, the smooth curve of her breasts...

There is a time, I think, in every young man's life when he is called to rise above himself, when youthful exuberance must give way to the masquerade of manhood, when he must understand that the race is not to the swift, nor the battle to the strong, nor riches to men of understanding, but time and chance just happens to them all. Plainly put, not all the scheming and plotting in the world can change destiny's course, and a man would be a fool to keep on playing when he had already won the game.

In my mind's eye, all that separated me from realizing my most cherished dream was a wooden door less than an inch thick, but it might just as well have been a universe. Like the stars in Shimmelman's painting, that fraction of an inch represented a distance so vast that I knew there was no hope of ever crossing it, and it didn't really matter. I had already won, more than I could ever have dreamed. I could step through the passageway that Molly had created in my mind, and I could hold her against me, and know that at that exact moment in time she was mine alone. Outside, an ocean I had never imagined was crashing waves on a beach that had never until that moment existed. And here in a place so hallowed it almost made me cry, the most gorgeous girl in the world was taking a bath so close to me that her steamy essence seeping under the bathroom door filled me with indescribable joy.

And I knew what Mama must have felt when she stood in the choir loft of the Calvary Baptist Church and Grace Ministry and sang the praises of the Lord, and her breast heaved with emotion, and her eyes filled with tears, and although he was a being so exalted she could only love him over an endless span of stars, he was for that glorious moment a part of her, and she was a part of him. It made no difference that the truth did not match the illusion. All that mattered was that she could go there — to a place of her own making where the air carried the scent of apples, and love was untarnished by time and tide and the pallor of reality.

LeMoult

Thirty-One

"Trixie!" She sat bolt upright in the bed. "I forgot all about her. She needs to be fed, She needs to be walked."

I stretched and uncoiled in the overstuffed armchair where I had spent the night, trying to look concerned, but about the last thing in the world on my mind right then was Molly's Yorkshire terrier. Everything was still a blur; our escape from Manhattan, the trip to Montauk, an almost sleepless night when I'd lay listening to her uneven breathing, wondering whether she was dreaming about me, or whether her restlessness was a result of the dread she felt knowing that Nick could track us down, no matter where we went.

"I'll be calling Shimmelman when we get downstairs. Is there some way he can get in?"

"The key's over the door."

"He'll take care of her for now."

"I can't just leave her there."

"We'll figure out a way of going back for her, I promise."

We'd decided we had to leave New York, at least for the time being until everything cooled down. The world was an open road map before us, there was no place too remote or too costly for us now. We could hide out on hillsides and waterfronts and in the vast prairie wilderness, travel the Nile and the Congo and probe the realm of the Hottentots where we would dance the fandango and breathe the rarefied atmosphere of mountaintops. We could lie side-by-side on the Montauk sand, watching the ocean waves deposit flotsam on the shoreline in layered tiers, and a solitary gull suspended in flight, weightless in the warm, salty currents. Royster had been right; a southern breeze had propelled the temperature to near ninety, and it was Indian summer.

"We could go up to Lake Champlain for a while," I suggested. "Nobody would think to look for us there."

Molly winced. "I came from there, remember?"

"Not the place where I was. It's beautiful there."

"Whitehall was beautiful too, that's not why I left."

"It's not far from Cheshire. I thought about visiting it on my way back just to see where you came from but the train doesn't stop there."

"It's just more of the same — same mountains, same water. It's not the scenery that's bad; it's the hopelessness of the place. It's what it does to people."

"I was going to stop in and see your folks, tell them all about how you're a Rockette and everything."

"I'm glad you didn't."

"Don't you want them to know you're successful? I'd sure want Mama to know about it if I was."

"It wouldn't matter to them. They'd want to know why I wasn't sending any money."

"Why aren't you?"

"Because that wouldn't matter either." She propped herself up on her elbows and stared out the window at the beach below. "My father was blinded in nineteen forty-two. He's spent the last ten years sitting in a wheelchair, drinking and cursing the world, and bashing anybody who came within range."

"Was he blinded in the war?"

"An industrial accident. He was a lathe operator in a furniture factory. A steel belt snapped and caught him square between the eyes and he hasn't seen a thing since. I know it's a terrible thing to happen to someone, but for him it was like a dream come true. He got to go on disability and sit around all day drinking and listening to the radio, and most of all he had a reason to hate the world. His greatest joy seemed to come from whacking my mother with his cane every time she walked by. He would have beaten me too, but I never let him get close enough."

"That's rough."

"Rougher for her. She's still going through it."

I thought of telling her about Mama and the Reverend Harley Brown but decided against it. The subject was bound to lead to her and Nick, and things were going so well I didn't want to foul her mood. "Do you think he could tap out the time?"

"Who?"

"Your father, I mean, being blind and all he'd want to have a handle on how long things took. You think he could count the seconds and minutes by tapping his fingers?"

"I don't think he cared what time it was. Why?"

"I dunno, just curious I guess."

She rolled over on her stomach and looked at me. "You're a curious boy, Chance Bailey. I think that might be one of the things I like best about you, you're restless like me."

"Shimmelman says time is a dimension, like space. He says it can twist and turn and curve right back in on itself so that things that happened hundreds of years ago could be happening right now on the other side of the curve. He believes it's possible to go from one side to another if you can find a wormhole to crawl through."

Molly eyed me skeptically. "He think you can just crawl from here to the past?"

"And the future."

"It sounds pretty crazy to me."

"Well that's because you're not mad. Shimmelman says madmen have a special knack for it."

"How about mad women?"

"I don't see why not. Aida McCracken swears she danced the fandango with the king of the Hottentots and from what they say there haven't been any Hottentots around for around a hundred years or more. The longer I stay in New York, the more stories like that I hear. There's a man they call the Wizard who says he played volleyball with somebody named Isaac Newton who lived back in the fifteenth century and he's no dope. He could a set your head to spinning with the things he knows.

You've got to say Isaiah Balenkin was pretty crazy when he was bouncing back and forth from his childhood like that. Shimmelman believes he'd found an opening where he could be here and somewhere else at the same time. He thinks that's how the old man was able to visit the Chemical Corn Exchange every month without ever leaving the Soldiers and Sailors."

"Does that make sense to you?'"

"Not really. Most of what Shimmelman says doesn't make sense to me, but that doesn't mean it's not true. He's spent his whole life thinking about things and I've only been doing it for a few months now."

"Well take a break and stop thinking." She bounded out of bed.

We drove into the town of Montauk that afternoon to buy ourselves some new clothes, and I'll have to admit shopping's a mighty different experience when you don't care how much money you spend than it is when you're counting your pennies. Molly tried on near everything she saw in every shop we visited, and by the time we were finished the trunk and back seat of the convertible were piled high with cartons and shopping bags filled with every imaginable garment a woman could want, along with a couple of leather suitcases to put it all in. For myself, I was contented to buy a few new pairs of jeans, a white knit fisherman's sweater, some shorts, T-shirts and a pair of black Dingo boots with silver hoops on the sides. All in all I spent almost six hundred dollars; a hundred at a time, peeled off my bankroll with assurance as if it was something I did every day and twice on Sundays; and the shopkeepers bowed and scraped and called us Sir and Madam and Molly would shoot me a took that said are we really doing this? And I'd peel off another bill, laughing my ass off inside. And we walked in those places together, and everybody in those places knew we were together, and I knew that if I had a million hundreds in that bankroll I'd just keep peeling them off, as long as it made her happy, as long as it kept us together.

"I made a pig of myself back there. You must think I'm awful," she said as we drove back to the hotel.

"I think you're wonderful. I think today is the best day of my whole life."

"Do you suppose there's an opening we could walk through that would make everything stand still, no past, no future, just today going on, forever and ever?"

"There might be, but then we wouldn't have any tomorrows and maybe they'll be even better."

Molly closed her eyes and gulped the warm breeze. "Maybe we can move back and forth, just like Isaiah Balenkin. We can try the future and if we don't like what we see we'll just walk through the opening and be back here again. Then we'd never have to be frightened of anything. There'll always be a warm, safe place to return to."

"You're not frightened now, are you? "

"Not now, not if I don't think."

There was a message to call Shimmelman when we got back to the hotel.

Worried that something was wrong with her dog, Molly stood anxiously by me as I dialed: "It's Chance," I said when he answered on the first ring. "Is everything okay?"

"I'm afraid not. The Cajun is dead."

I must have bolted at the news because Molly gripped my arm. "How?" I gasped, raising a hand to reassure her it was not Trixie.

"Two men drowned him in the pool."

"The Soldier's and Sailor's pool? There's no water in it."

"There is now. He finished fixing it yesterday and let it fill overnight. I told him what an absurd thing it was to do, filling a swimming pool in a place that was closing down in a few months anyway, but he wouldn't listen. That stupid, stupid man—it was as if he was driven by demons to complete the instrument of his own destruction."

"Who were these men? What did they want from him?"

"I don't know who they were. What they wanted was you and Molly."

Thirty-Two

The Cajun did not drown. Shimmelman told me the whole story when I got back later that night. I'd wanted Molly to stay in Montauk but she wouldn't, terrified of being alone so far from home, so I'd taken her to Bertie's and gone on to the Soldiers and Sailors myself, ready to face whatever they had in store for me if they found me there.

"I think one was the man he threw out of here last week," Shimmelman recounted. "The other was bigger They came in here and didn't say a word. They just walked back to where he was in the pool and started roughing him up. Well you know the Cajun; the meaner they got, the meaner he got. Next thing you know they had him upside-down, holding him by the heels, dunking him up and down in the water."

"Wasn't there anything you could do? Couldn't you have phoned the police or something?"

"By that time they were between me and the door. They both had guns." He assumed a wounded look. "I've never been a very brave man."

"He couldn't have told them anything anyway. He didn't know where we'd gone. Nobody knew."

"It didn't make any difference. It was like a sport to them. I think they took delight in seeing how long he could stay under without drowning. Every time they raised him up he'd gasp for air then curse them both to hell. The man had courage, I'll say that much for him. When the police arrived they gave him artificial respiration but it was too late. They said he must have died of a heart attack because there was hardly any water in his lungs. When I told them what happened they were less than responsive. I doubt they're planning to pursue the investigation with much vigor. The Cajun was just another drifter."

"It's all my fault. All I was thinking about was myself. For all I know they'll be coming after you next."

"Rest assured I'll not be a hero. If I have the information they want you can be certain I'll supply it. Nothing personal, mind you."

We were in Shimmelman's room, drinking a departing toast to The Cajun with the last of the Metaxa . "The probably know I'm here right now," I guessed. "More'n likely they've got this place staked out. I can leave if it'd make you feel better."

He shrugged. "I don't see that it would make any difference at this point. Whatever is going to happen will happen. There's very little any of us can do but experience it with dignity." He raised his glass. "To our departed friends wherever they may be."

I sipped the Metaxa and felt its warmth trickle into my chest, easing my anxiety. "Do you really think there's a place they go?"

Shimmelman chewed on it some. "I think there is no such thing as nothingness," he answered finally.

"Does that mean you believe in Heaven and Hell?"

"I believe the natural order of things is change. No species has ever been able to survive without it. Here on this dismal speck in space everything from microbes to mountains must be constantly reinvented, sifted and poured and stirred into the stew of creation until they become something entirely different, if you will—a part of the infinite, a world within a spanning galaxy inside a universe that forms a mote on the surface of God's eyelash."

"I thought you didn't believe in God."

"You were the one who didn't believe in God. I merely said I had no clear association with him. Those who maintain they do have simply stagnated, split off from the search and risen weightless to the top, like fat globules to be ladled off and discarded."

"Where will they go?" I asked after a thoughtful pause.

"The Cajun and Isaiah Balenkin?"

"The people who live here under the El. Where will they go when all the buildings are torn down and Third Avenue becomes shops and offices?"

He shrugged. "They'll move on, same as us."

"Do you think it'll he better without the train, without the Soldiers and Sailors?"

"I think it will he different, but who's to say it will he gone forever? Maybe someday you and I will find a wormhole in time and crawl right back here. Maybe it's already happening and we just don't know about it."

"Maybe." I drained my glass and stood to leave. "I guess I'd better say goodbye now. Who knows, I may never get back to New York after this."

Shimmelman gave me an awkward hug. "Wherever you go I know you'll do well. You have an inquisitive mind."

"I'll keep in touch and let you know."

"No you won't, but that's fine."

"Maybe I'll run into you in one of those wormholes."

It had begun to rain, a warm autumn rain that captured the flat, metallic smells of the city in vaporous clouds hovering just above the sidewalks. I drove across town without incident, parked two blocks away from Bertie's loft, and walked the rest of the way in the downpour, stopping from time to time to make certain I wasn't being followed. Shimmelman was right about one thing at least, I decided. The only thing that could he counted on was change, plain and simple. Maybe Harley Brown could live with the idea that the world had remained the same for thousands of years, but from everything I'd learned over the past few months, a body had to be fast on his feet just to keep up with the changes that transpired daily. In a few short months I'd been exposed to a world of madmen and prophets, plumbed the universe of stars and galaxies, exploding clouds of pure energy that might have been the mind of God. I'd crawled through wormholes in time to be in Vilyuisk with Kuryokin, hidden in root cellars from Cossack marauders, and. marched with Gretchko and Miskovitch against the Turkish Cavalry, carrying only a rake, a twist of twine to bind up the tatters of my courage. I'd made friends and lost them in the blink of an eye, God's eye or my eye? Would a blink of God's eyelash send universes colliding, spinning back into the stew, back to the bottom of the pot where stars got born and nothing came out the same as it went in? I was sixteen; I didn't have a clue.

"You wouldn't he going to the fourth floor, would you?" He was not much older than me, standing by the freight elevator in Bertie's building.

"Why do you want to know?" I asked suspiciously.

"Because if you are I've got a delivery for you." He pointed to a medium-size carton at his feet.

"I'm going there but I don't live there."

"But you know who does, right?"

"What if I do?"

"Then you can save me a trip. This rain's got traffic screwed up from one end of the city to the other. I'm almost an hour behind schedule as is." He eyed me hopefully.

I took the carton to the fourth floor loft and handed it to Bertie, who was waiting by the elevator door. "Thank God it's you darling, anybody else would have gotten a taste of this." He displayed a baseball bat he'd hidden behind his back.

"What's in the box?" Molly asked as she emerged from a room in the back.

"I dunno. All it says is Resident, Fourth Floor."

Bertie removed the brown paper wrapping and cut the tape flaps with his penknife. He pulled away the tissue covering inside, stiffened, and reeled back in horror. "Don't look!" he screamed at Molly

It was too late; both of us had seen the small, tufted body curled inside. There was a split-second between perception and reality; an awful stab of silence before everything sunk in and she collapsed on the floor screaming: "Nooooooo!" I knelt next to her and put my arms around her, knowing that at that moment Nick had won. Bertie folded the flaps of the carton shut and moved it away from her, but it was plain that there was nothing he or I or anyone could do to stem her grief. Without lifting a finger at Molly or at me, Nick had conveyed in the most basic of human terms that he would not he beaten; that he had climbed inside our souls, mined the depths of our resolve, and gone one awful step deeper. He was willing to destroy her to have her, willing to be hated to protect his pride, and there was nothing I could give her that would ever come close to matching that. I lifted her slowly to her feet and steered her across the wooden floor, out of sight of her murdered Yorkshire terrier, Trixie.

Thirty Three

The wind had picked up, driving horizontal gusts in our faces as we wandered the rain-swept streets of lower Manhattan. Molly carried the carton containing Trixie's body and I went along, not really understanding her need at that time but not willing to question it. I followed her because of the two of us, she seemed the least terrified, her face expressionless in the torrent of rain and wind, plodding into certain danger like the drug-reconstituted infantrymen at the Battle of the Bulge. Above us, the gray, slotted sky gave no indication of easing the onslaught.

"Maybe we should get inside until it stops raining," I suggested. "It's not helping anything getting her soaked this way."

"I have to find a place for her. I can't just leave her in an alleyway or drop her off a bridge," Molly insisted.

"Just a minute until we catch our breath..."

I darted beneath an arched brick overhang at the edge of the sidewalk where a small gold plaque identified the premises as Chapel of the Little Flower, R. C.

"It's a church. I want to go in and say a prayer for Trixie," Molly decided.

"It's a Roman church. I didn't know you were Catholic."

"I'm not but something brought us here. It just feels right."

Inside, we walked uncertainly down the center aisle of the church and sat in one of the pews. I had never been inside a Roman church before and. had no great desire to be in one now, having heard all manner of things about them back in Eula. It was said they sacrificed Christian babies to the Pope, and while I suspected that was an exaggeration, I had little reason to think there were not other blood-curdling rituals going on in there. The specter of white plaster statues looming from every niche and corner did little to ease my anxiety, and I crouched in nervous anticipation as a slightly built man wearing corduroy pants and a sweatshirt approached us. "I'm Father Troy Blaze," he introduced himself. "Can I be of help?"

"We were hoping we could just sit here for a few minutes," Molly said.

"We've just had a death," I added.

He smiled a beatific smile. "Stay as long as you like. Perhaps you'd like to come back to the rectory and chat a bit when you've finished. Sometimes it helps to talk to someone about it."

"Do you think you could say some words over Trixie's body?" Molly asked uncertainly.

"I don't see why not. Is the deceased somewhere nearby?"

Molly opened the carton flaps. "I've had her since she was a puppy, since I first came to New York."

Father Troy Blaze nodded sympathetically. "Is there any particular prayer you'd like me to say?"

"Whatever you usually say."

He lifted the carton from the pew and placed it in the aisle, then took a well-worn prayer book from his hip pocket and thumbed through it. "Her name is Trixie?"

"She's a Yorkshire terrier."

He settled on a passage: "Lord we beseech you to take the soul of your small servant, Trixie, loyal companion and friend to all since she was a puppy. Forgive her what sins a Yorkshire terrier can commit and grant both her and her loved ones the blessing of eternal life in you, through Jesus Christ Our Lord, amen." He closed the book and blessed us with a silent sign of the cross.

Billowing tears ran down Molly's cheeks. "Thank you," she said softly.

"If you'd like, I can see to it that she's buried with dignity," he offered.

"Could I spend a few minutes alone with her before you take her?"

"Take as much time as you need. I'll be in back behind the sacristy when you're ready."

I don't know why, but I followed him, down the church aisle and through an open door to a back room. "I didn't know you could do that," I said when we were alone. "I'm a Baptist and you wouldn't see a preacher saying words over a dead animal."

"Well, we're all God's creatures." He took a bottle of sacramental wine from a shelf and poured some into a paper cup. "Care for a snort?"

"Why not? I'm soaked to the skin."

"Technically, I'm not supposed to perform services for animals either, but this wouldn't be the first time I've taken an unorthodox approach to Christianity." He handed me a cup filled with wine. "I'm kind of a renegade when it comes to orthodoxy; but then, my congregants are out of the ordinary; gay men and lesbians for the most part. Around these parts I'm called the faggot priest."

"Don't you mind that?"

"Why should I? They're my people. I love them all."

I sipped the wine and found it smooth and sweet. "It's strange being here. This is my first time in a Roman church," I admitted.

"You're a Baptist?"

"Well I reckon that's what I'd be if they were choosing up sides, but I'm not even sure I believe in God."

"Me either," he shrugged.

"But you're a priest. Why would somebody want to be a priest if they didn't believe in God?"

"Because it's the most rewarding job I can think of I don't think it really matters what one believes as long as they feel they're making a contribution."

"I reckon I never thought about it that way. The way I was fetched up nobody dared question God, nobody even questioned that he was a Baptist. You just plain worshipped him and left the questions to the unchaste."

"Maybe he is a Baptist," Troy Blaze laughed. "Of course a lot of Catholics might take issue with that. My own feeling is that God is universality, that part in each of us that reaches out to help. I've never been much of a believer in a God who has such low self esteem that he demands to be worshipped all the time."

"I have a friend, Shimmelman, who thinks that everything there is, all the worlds and suns and galaxies, are just a speck on God's eyelash. He says if God had a mind to blink that'd be all there was to that."

"I'd like to meet your friend. He sounds like a stimulating individual."

"He's not Catholic either. He's a Jew."

"Christ was a Jew."

"Shimmelman thinks we can create our own universes. He creates his by painting it on the wall, but he thinks you and I find our own way to do the same thing."

"If he means that we can create our own reality I agree with him."

"He thinks reality is the hobgoblin of dolts and incompetents, that madmen have an edge in life because they're not hobble-tied by it. He says their madness is just a wormhole to another divinity."

Troy Blaze nodded. "It's a compelling idea; as good a theory as I could come up with. The church has always preached that we're touched by the divine -- that we're all a part of the mystical body of Christ, although I'll have to admit they don't always practice what they preach. My congregants would have something to say, about that."

I finished my wine and he refilled both our cups. "Do you think a dog can sin?" I asked him.

"I guess that depends on what you mean by sin. If your friend is right and we're all divinities in our own right, I doubt that the concept of sin has any validity at all."

"I wish I could believe that."

"Why?"

"Because I think there's a part of me that's wild and sinful, something in my Comanche blood maybe. Whatever it is I've caused a lot of folks trouble."

Troy Blaze thought a bit. "I'd hear your confession if you thought it would help."

"I thought only Catholics could do that."

"Like I said, I'm not much on orthodoxy."

"What am I supposed to do?"

"Why not start by telling me what's bothering you?"

I took a deep, uncertain breath. "First of all there's Joe Carl Purdy," I began. "Joe Carl was my best friend back in Texas before he went to the hospital up in Lubbock for an operation to straighten his spine. I wished him good luck and all, but deep down inside I was hoping the operation would fail because it would've made him as tall as me, and I wanted to be the tall one. Then it failed and Joe Carl died, and every day I wake up I know it was my fault.

"And there's Mama. She's married to a preacher name of Harley Brown who beats her. I don't just think he beats her, I know he does, but I made myself believe I wasn't sure because I didn't really see him doing it, just the bruises afterward. I know it was wrong not to stay there and protect her, but I had to get out. I couldn't stand the stink and the heat so I left her with him and now she's there and I'm here, and if I close my eyes and think hard about other things I can almost believe it's not really happening.

"Then there's Molly and me, we're running away from a gangster named Nick Corsi who thinks he owns her. I made a deal with him not to see her, but I went back on my word and, pardon my French, but all hell broke loose. The Cajun tried to help me get her away and Nick Corsi had two men drown him in the pool at the Soldiers and Sailors, and now he's gone and killed Trixie, and none of it would have happened if I'd lived up to my part of the bargain..."

"How old are you?" Troy Blaze broke in.

"Just sixteen, but everybody thinks I'm nineteen."

"You've taken on a lot of guilt for someone only sixteen."

"There's a lot to be guilty about."

"Have you spoken to anyone else about this?"

"I might've run it by God, but him and me being on the outs and all, I didn't figure it would do much good."

"It will now. God is listening to you now," he assured me.

225

"How do you know that?"

"It doesn't matter." Troy Blaze placed a hand on my shoulder and closed his eyes. "I absolve you of guilt, fear, soul-searching and second-guessing, in the name of the Father, and of the Son, and of the Holy Ghost. Amen."

"That's it?"

"That's it."

"Will it work?"

"That's up to you."

"What about God?"

"God helps those who help themselves." He led me out into the church where Molly was waiting.

"I think I'm ready to leave her now," she said.

"I'll see that she's well taken care of," Troy Blaze promised.

"I know you will." She kissed him impulsively on the cheek. "I don't know what we would have done if we hadn't found this place by accident. It was like a miracle."

"Sometimes I think life is just a series of accidents," he replied. "We call the bad accidents sins and the good accidents miracles. I'm happy to have been a part of a good accident for you this time."

Outside the chapel the rain fell harder than ever. We had walked all the way to a place called the Bowery in downtown Manhattan, a section of the city inhabited mostly by society's castaways, a grim, empty, love-less place where block after block of grimy tenements hugged the litter-strewn sidewalks as if they had been squeezed out of the center of the gleaming metropolis and left there to decompose. Both of us were drenched to the skin from our desultory trek, wanting only a change of clothing, and maybe a hot bath before we decided on our next move. One thing was certain: we could not go back to Molly's, Bertie's, or the Soldiers and Sailors, since our tormentors were sure to have those locations staked out. We would have to retrieve the clothes we'd left in the car, find a clean, dry hotel room where we could change, catch our breaths, and work out a strategy.

But this was the Bowery on a dark, rainy day. Rivers of brown silt gushed along the gutters, and wind-funnels swooped into the chasms, propelling soot and debris like tumbleweed along the rutted streets. The few intrepid taxicab drivers who had braved the area were in no mood to linger there. They flashed their off duty lights whether they had a fare or not, and sped past, unmoved at the sight of two rain-soaked wayfarers caught in the deluge. A block west was Third Avenue, and the entrance to the subway. After depositing two dimes in the turnstile, we traced a jumble of underground signs and. tunnels to the Uptown platform, a hollow, empty slab of wet concrete as desolate and uninviting as the street above. Molly was shivering. I wrapped my arms around her and held her close, hoping to impart my body warmth to her, but the harder I held her the more she trembled, wracked by grief and the penetrating dampness.

Suddenly the shaking stopped and I felt her stiffen in my arms. "They're behind you," she whispered, not fearfully but with resignation. "It's over, I can't run anymore."

I turned and saw them walking toward us on the platform, close enough for me to observe the man in the leather overcoat carrying a pistol at his side. The other, taller and more menacing, held a length of metal pipe in one hand, pounding it rhythmically into his other palm, matching the cadence of his steps. Molly shrank against the yellowed tile wall and instinctively I took a position in front of her. My eyes darted up and down the platform looking for another way out, but the only exit was behind them.

"It's me you want!" I shouted into the abyss, and my hollow voice bounced off tile and concrete and hundred-year-old steel stanchions like echoes of faraway artillery fire. "You can have me. Just leave her alone!"

My bravado only seemed to amuse them. The larger man increased his tempo, slapping the pipe into his palm with shorter, harder bursts, tapping time with his steel truncheon like a blind man with a metronome ticking in his head. Beneath me the platform seemed to heave as they approached, the sensation seeped from my legs, my daydreams of gallantry and valor evaporated in spasms of fear and doubt.

"Mister Corsi would like it if you came home now." The man in the leather coat declared, looking past me at Molly. The taller man stopped his tapping and stood expectantly, poised to attack if I made a move.

"She's not going anywhere with you," I heard the echo of my voice saying.

"This ain't about you kid; now why don't you just step aside and let the lady come with us? We don't want anybody getting hurt here."

"You'll have to come through me to get to her." The words spilled out without conviction.

"He's right. This isn't about you." Molly's hand gentled me aside from behind. "It's about me and Nick. It's about things you just don't understand."

"I understand he's trying to kill you! I don't need to understand any more than that!"

"Yes you do, maybe some day you will." She began walking toward them.

I grabbed her arm and pulled her back. "Don't do this, Molly."

"I'll do what I want to do." She yanked away from me. "If I want to go back to Nick that's where I'll go. What makes you think you have the right to keep me here?"

"But you don't want to go," I protested.

"How the hell do you know what I want?"

The man with the pipe had begun his rhythmic slapping again, matching the distant rumble of a train approaching in the tunnel.

Molly turned toward me, contorted with anger. "Listen to me; it was fun while it lasted but you're in way over your head now. It's time to go home to Mama and play with kids your own age. I've got a life to lead here."

"What about all the stuff we planned? What about the palace on the Rhone, those running horsemen? What about the dark side of the moon? That was more than just talk."

"Grow up!" she screamed. "Go back to west-wherever-you-come-from and marry some cheerleader and raise a passel of pink-cheeked kids and have a good life, but leave me the fuck alone! I'm not what you think I am, I never was. I danced naked in front of men, remember? I let them see my tits!" She tore away her blouse and stood with her taut breasts heaving in the half-light, dimpled from the cold, lined with tiny blue veins. "I spread my legs for them. Get it?"

"I think what the lady is trying to tell you is, get lost," the man in the leather coat elaborated. "You're outa your league here."

I stood, trembling, determined not to cry as she walked out of my life, bleeding inside with every step she took down the platform toward the exit with her custodians flanking her on either side, not even bothering to turn and glance and tell me with her eyes that there had been a moment when she'd meant it all; when words and whispers were promises to keep.

Then, in the instant it takes to rearrange thought, she bolted. She was halfway down the platform, running as fast as her dancer's legs could carry her before both men took off after her and I took off after them, the noise of our footfalls lost surrealistically in the clamor of the approaching train. As fast as she was, they were faster, closing the distance between them with every stride until they were almost upon her. I reached the tall one first and tackled him from behind, driving us both to the ground with a sickening crunch.

Ahead, the man in the leather coat got to Molly just before she reached the stairs. A pale rectangle of light at the stairway exit framed them, pinched and slowed by the curvature of time. As he grabbed for her, Molly executed a flawless *fouetté*, a far better spin than any I'd seen her do in ballet class. The toe of her outstretched left foot caught him just below the chin and sent him careening backward, but at the moment of contact Molly broke stride just enough to lose her balance. The train roared into the station just as she slipped from the platform onto the tracks below, a blur of metal, light and sound that never even slowed down as it passed over her, and when I raised my head it was gone and all that was left was the eerie echo of its passage, *take-it-to-me, take-it-to-me, take-it-to-me.*

Thirty-Four

Bertie maintained that it was impossible for someone to execute a full *fouetté* on a dead run, but after I demonstrated the move to him in the hospital waiting room he had to admit Molly had done it; a feat of strength, precision. and grace he said he'd never witnessed first-hand in all his years as a dancer. It was the first of two miracles that day, we both agreed; the second being that Molly had survived being run over by the train. She was critically injured. Both her legs were broken badly, several ribs were fractured, and there were yet untold internal injuries that might prove fatal, but somehow she had managed to roll to the middle of the tracks and avoid being cut in two by the wheels. Only time would tell, the doctors said. If she lived, it was impossible to say whether she would ever walk. One thing was certain; she would never dance again.

She was lucky to be alive; we both were. If the two goons in the subway hadn't panicked and run, they could have finished us both off right there. Bertie said they probably should have. Nick wasn't going to be happy to learn they'd damaged his investment, probably beyond repair. Outside of a fractured collar bone I'd gotten in my fall on the platform, I was still around to rub his nose in it and that was bound to infuriate him even more. Bertie speculated that if they'd been dumb enough to give him the news, he'd already fitted them both with concrete coffins and sent them to the bottom of the East River. Nick Corsi wasn't the sort of guy who tolerated screw-ups.

Molly was unconscious when they let me in to see her; covered with a clear plastic oxygen tent, surrounded by pumps and drips and gadgets with hoses that drained and nourished her. I stood by her bed and watched her fitful breathing, feeling more helpless than I had ever felt, realizing that even if she recovered she would wake to find that her dreams of being a ballerina, of dancing in the Radio City Music Hall Christmas show, were now unattainable. She would be a cripple in New York; consigned like so many other marginal souls to the dark, windswept comers of the city; places like the Soldiers and Sailors, The Exchange Buffet, McGovern's Saloon with its imbedded smells and attitudes where she would grow old and toothless on her stool, cackling about past triumphs, about being Miss America, and dancing the fandango with the king of the Hottentots; another life, another reality a million, million light years away from the fantasy of fame and glamour she'd constructed for Mona Chalfonte.

I knew then that I could never let that happen, that I would love and protect her no matter what. She would be my life, my sweet ruin. I would take her far enough away to quell her memories, far enough for her to build new dreams in a proscenium of mountains, water and sky. It was something worth believing in, something to live for. Watching his mother suffer the agony of *il viaggiare di dolore*, Nick Corsi had said that a man without belief was nothing more than a shell, and though I hated him I knew he was right. Some things transcended reason and logic and hurt and anger and humiliation. They were so intrinsic that they defined us to ourselves, they rearranged our star stuff and gave us substance. Standing there at Molly's bedside I knew my shell had fallen away and I had finally found my purpose, the only belief that made any sense to me. I blew her a soft, tender kiss through the oxygen tent and departed for the Soldiers and Sailors. I knew what I had to do.

The pool was two and one-half inches shy of twenty-five yards long. The Cajun had painstakingly measured it before he'd begun his repairs; six lanes for swimming, each thirty-nine inches wide and demarcated by white lines painted on the bottom that seemed to curve as the deeper water refracted the light. Twenty-six inches deep at the shallow end and almost eight feet at the deep end; rimmed by two hundred and forty cylindrical white tiles, most of which were pitted or cracked and had to be replaced (where he'd gotten them we hadn't dared ask), its transcendent glory was the molded concrete gargoyle adorning the far end, rising from the emerald water with sightless eyes of brimstone, teeth like a panther, a coiled tongue like a rattler ready to strike. The Cajun had replaced the pipes and valves, and patched the worn concrete where water seeped through, allowing the stream to gush full-bore from the gargoyle's mouth.

I tested the water with my toe, and eased down into the shallow end until I was crouching on the bottom with water up to my shoulders, knife-edged, and pricking the fringes of my consciousness, accentuating the pain in my collarbone. I let myself go limp and sank beneath the water-line, resting underwater for a moment before allowing my natural buoyancy to lift me, I re-emerged on the surface, fifteen or twenty feet from where I had started, and began swimming; arm-over-arm, my elbow cocked at a right angle to the water at the top of the stroke... fingers slightly parted, brushing the hip on the downstroke; smooth and easy, rising and dipping to the white line on the bottom, keeping an eye out for debris, discarded mining equipment shimmering through the mineral-green currents, empty milk cans you could get stuck in and drown and when they found your body you'd be fish-bell white, strangled on S-cargoes with your tongue gagging out the size of a medicine ball. The gargoyle fountain kept the water boiling just below the surface and the bottom fell away like a zephyr. I turned on my back. Water spewing from its mouth surrounded me, blinded me. The pain in my neck and shoulders was excruciating.

Indian pride, Indian high on loco weed

Coughing and choking from the lodge fires; the smoke-houses where braves with painted faces danced the dead into the afterlife, danced the sun and the stars back into alignment so the dead could travel the ribbon of light between them, so their pinto ponies could follow them to the pastures of the great beyond where the spirits of Elk and Buffalo dwelt, where Rabbit and Squirrel gathered worlds for the winter, Puma bellowed thunder from the mountains, and Coyote chewed pieces from the moon.

Lances decorated with beads and feathers and bison scalps with horns marked their deeds, their bravery was embedded in the earth near their burial mounds. Old men smoked and talked about them in the fire-light.

Where it is warm. The thunder of artillery cannot relieve the awful cold: bodies stiff in my arms like cordwood, stacked on flatbed trucks and hauled away behind the lines. My feet are black and swollen but I know I have to stay erect; to drop in the snow is to freeze. Three men like me can form a standing tripod, wrap our arms around each other's shoulders and drop our heads and sleep like that for a minute or two until an order comes down from Battalion or a shell rips us to shreds. The earth is frozen hard, nowhere to dig and burrow down and curl together in an embrace of death and still they come, tanks and half-tracks and Uhlans on horses dripping froth from their yellow mouths, breathing fire from their nostrils.

Arm over arm, fingers slightly parted to reduce friction underwater.

My odyssey had taken me here, back to the place of my cowardice, my humiliation. I'd crossed the Ukraine and sought out citizens I had wronged and made amends to them for past transgressions, but they looked at me with empty eyes, victims all of the famine and the Great October Revolution. I could hear the artillery in the distance, puff-puff-puff; weightless like dandelion tufts, a shallow pumping in my ear. Tomorrow I'd be back at the front where the German soldiers were. I'd get a weapon and find the precise spot where the blades of grass were bent and the air held a scent, and the totems told of their crossing, squaws and braves and horses dragging travois. They would not suspect, burrowed as they were from the prairie cold, and when we descended on them with bonnets of bison hides and war paint and fearsome war cries and they would hide beneath their beds and. pray for deliverance, but we would show them no mercy. Blood was our heritage, Harry Bailey's and mine.

I could float on my back from time to time and watch the reflections from the water dance above me on the ceiling. Spears of white, bellying out to earthbound kine, a blur to me now.

I ate a rat, a blur to me now, tasting a little like chicken I think, but a bit tougher, its tiny body ribbed with tendons burned black from cooking. Gretchko, Miskovitch and I sat on the steppes and bragged about our courage in the face of the Turkish cavalrymen, and drank a whole bottle of vodka between us. Then as foolish old men will, we talked of conquest and compared the size of our penises. And we peed together off the end of the embankment, and the twisting streams of our urine met and disintegrated in a fine mist. And the flat gray sky echoed with our laughter, and the smoke from our campfire carried it away.

They gave me Blue Eighty-eight, sodium amytol to cloud my brain and take me back. Somebody played a phonograph record of battle sounds, mortar shells whistling in, lighting the night sky. I wanted to reach up and grab one and haul it down and bury it underneath my poncho where it could melt my guts and stop me from shaking apart. God damn, a flask of red-eye would've tasted good right then; put it up to my lips and feel it hot inside like an awakening morning glory in my chest, and take a Mexican woman out behind the bandstand and dance the fandango with her until she breathed her hot breath into me and thawed out my frozen limbs. And I'd bring her to the bedroom and lie on top of her and make her forget about New England and how much she hated this place. She thought I didn't know how she sneaked upstairs and opened her steamer trunk and unfolded her memories fragrant on her cheeks. All I could do was hold her then, stroke her where it hurt. All I could do.

0 say can you see

mud-caked empty huts

the mistral's come and gone

Brought the grime along

and took the folks away

from that place

where artists limned their simple ways

in simple strokes...

Amen, Brother. Wrap yourself in the spirit of the Lord and He shall comfort you, and provide you warmth. You can bury your head between her milky breasts and feel her heaving beneath you, Hallelujah. Bite her nipples then, Hallelujah, and hear her moan. Amen, Brother. Great is the way of the Lord God Jehovah; blessed is his deliverance.

Floating on my back I could propel myself by kicking a few feet at a time. Not nearly as fast, but it eased the pain in my neck and shoulders.

The Germans crossed exactly where I had set up my ambush; laughing and joking, unaware of the terrible fate that awaited them. Except for their jackboots and spiked helmets they were boys like me (older than me for having tasted so much of war, which should have turned me to pity, but my mission was clear, to atone for my disgrace in the face of their tanks and artillery). I had the element of surprise on my side. My weapon was a broken tree branch, pitifully inadequate but it would have to do. Noiselessly I hunkered in the tall grass the way the Indians do at powwows, but war was on my mind. My face was painted white and black and ocher, the time for talking had come and gone. They came abreast of me, six of them, and when I leapt from the bushes brandishing my weapon, singing, *Long live the glorious Red Revolution, eeeeei-eeeeeei-o*, they seemed more startled than afraid. For a fraction of a second we stood unmoving, each of us sizing up the other, then one of the German infantrymen raised his rifle and sighted on me across the barrel, and wet his thumb and checked the windage like he was zeroing in on a quail, and that explosion, that lightning flash from his muzzle was the last thing I ever saw in this lifetime. Amen.

Amen, Brother, for the righteous man will be delivered from this vale of tears, and will pass over into the rapture, and so the scriptures will be fulfilled.

And I took her picture into battle and kept it in the warmest part of me, inside my undershirt where it would have gotten soiled if I'd been able to sweat, but the cold and fear were numbing and the picture stayed intact so I could. reach inside and pull it out now and again and look at her sweet face—a soft, sepia side view taken years before by a Boston photographer, her legs drawn up in front of her, looking for all the world like a movie star with her shimmering hair pulled back above her forehead and her eyes set off in the distance. All the men had pictures; squad-to-corps, thirty thousand or more of them had pictures; wives, girlfriends; some even had pictures of saints and martyrs inside their clothing, pictures of the past, pictures of the future. When they died the corpsmen placed their dog-tags between their teeth and slammed their jaws shut with their rifle butts, and if there was time they'd go through their clothing and find the pictures there, and if they could pry them loose they'd sometimes take them for themselves; a different past, a different future, a filter to warmth, and wholeness, sanity and survival.

I'd finished thirty laps of the pool, or was it thirty-one? Thirty laps made the math easier—thirty laps at twenty-five yards per lap made seven hundred-fifty yards, less two and one-half inches per lap. Maybe if I'd gone to high school over in Breese Falls I'd've been able to work the calculations better. Seven hundred fifty yards was near half-a-mile, even with the inches taken off; half-a-mile unfolding, a lifetime or two spit out by that sightless, gargoyle. Let him get under my skin, I did, that Devil incarnate vomiting water down at the end of the pool. A few more laps, a few more strokes, arm-over-arm, fingers parted on the downstroke, brushing the hip with my thumb. I could slide right through him, move to the left and move to the right and burrow like a toad right under his nose, keep him thinking all the time. Sooner or later one of us would have to come up for air, and it wouldn't be me. I knew what I had to do and I had what it took to do it. It was Harry Bailey's boy he was dealing with now.

LeMoult

Thirty-Five

Shimmelman's pistol, a .38 caliber revolver, was in the drawer of his nightstand, right where the Cajun said it would be; a well-cared-for gun, oiled and wiped clean of dust, primed and prepared for the night he would take it and press the muzzle to the roof of his mouth and pull the trigger. The gun was a snub-nose, perfect for concealment; the kind of gun Cagney and Bogart and Raft would use when they were wrapping up the loose ends of the movie, bringing everything to its natural conclusion before the credits rolled across the screen and the house lights lit and the audience filed up the aisle and went home. Somewhere at the end of it there had to be room for revenge. They had to know the bad guys got what was coming to them, that good won out after all.

Shimmelman dozed at the front desk as I passed him in the lobby and went outside to the car. I pulled away from the curb, made sweeping U-turn under the El and headed uptown. A line of police barricades halted me at Forty-second street where another parade had just concluded. It was Armistice Day this time; files of uniform-clad veterans from both World wars were breaking up and going home after marching up Fifth Avenue, the blare of horns and cadence of drums socked away in their memories. High school drum majorettes in letter sweaters and short white skirts carried batons limply at their sides. Floats covered with flowers, crinkly crepe paper, and banners heralding their affiliation lumbered away to be disassembled somewhere: U.S. Army First Cavalry, Nieuport-Verdun, Never Forget… Ninth Marine Division, Okinawa—Iwo Jima. To our fallen comrades… I searched for a banner from the 101st Airborne Division at Bastogne, Belgium, but couldn't see one.

Maybe there was someone in that departing crowd who'd served with Harry Bailey, I thought. Maybe out there behind the horns and drums and high-stepping majorettes there was somebody he'd shared a foxhole with in the frozen earth; somebody he'd embraced for warmth at night, propped against in standing sleep, or dragged half-dead from the battle-field to safety. Maybe they were alive because of him. Maybe a part of them rested with him up in Cheshire, overlooking the lake and mountains he'd preserved for them with his bravery. Halted as I was by this com-memoration of the dead, it seemed strange that I was on my way to kill, but I did not doubt it was what he would have done. Life preserved and life taken, it was all part of that grim, enduring symmetry that made liv-ing with pain and injustice seem a tolerable thing.

The sky deepened from streaky gray to black on my drive to New Rochelle, and by the time I'd reached the entrance to Nick Corsi's private peninsula, a misty yellow moon was rising just above the tree line. I parked the car alongside the highway and made my way inland on foot, gauging direction and distances in the dense woods from the sounds of traffic behind me and the flicker of light coming from the house ahead. The gatehouse was to my left. I could see the guard inside through the trees, reading something, smoking a cigarette as I crept past him, shield-ed by foliage and darkness. When I was safely away I stood and made my way to the main compound. It was a time for me to bring all my stealth and cunning to bear, I knew; everything I'd learned about tracking from Daddy and Uncle Mal. Anything could give me away, a start, a cough, even my own heavy breathing. I had to walk like the Indians walked: toe-heel, toe-heel, so as not to rustle a leaf or snap a twig, invisible as a milk snake, sharp-eyed as an owl.

I crouched at the edge of the woods, calculating the distance between me and the house; A hundred feet or more of open space, a clear grazing field of fire for the gunman out there with his shotgun slung loosely across his shoulder. I could not see him but I knew he was there, lost in the night, a solitary deity with firepower and the will to use it. It was all about instinct, judging the exact moment when his unseen eye would blink, when his silhouette would turn against the blackness for that frac-tion of time it would take me to cover the open ground. I could hear time tapping in my head, the wooosh of blood pumping through my ears. I clutched the revolver tucked in my waistband, took a deep breath, and sprinted across the open field, expecting at any moment to hear the report of the shotgun and feel the impact of a hundred lead pellets tearing me in two.

I reached the house and huddled against it, breathing heavily and trying to plot my next move. Nick's study was in the front, I remembered, the side facing the water where he could sit at night and watch the canopy of stars over the water through a picture window. If he was there he would almost certainly see me coming from that direction, lit by the spotlights he'd rigged along the shoreline. Even with the moonlight at my back, I was less of a target where I was. All I had to do was find an open window or door, something that would give me access to the inside where I could creep up on him and hold him captive for our final confrontation. I would take my time. Before he died he would know exactly who was killing him, and why. I would not kill him in haste, in panic or in rage. I would lay it out, plain and simple the way a good old country boy would like to do, Then I'd level that .38 snub-nose revolver at a spot between his eyes, and. hopefully he'd beg and whinny some, but even if he didn't I would wait and give him time to think about what he'd done and what was about to be done to him. *Jealousy is the rage of man; therefore he will not spare another in the day of vengeance. He will avenge her straightaway as an ox goeth to the slaughter he will avenge her. So sayeth the Lord.*

I tried several windows before I was finally able to pry one open and wiggle clumsily through. Amazed that I had made it inside the house without tripping an alarm, I focused my eyes to the darkness and saw that I was in a butler's pantry of sorts, lined with cabinets and sinks and the unwashed dishes of what must have been that evening's meal. I could hear voices in the adjoining kitchen, the clatter of metal pots and pans. At the other end of the pantry a wooden door opened onto an unoccupied dining room, and further out to a hallway that I knew led to Nick's study. The hall was faintly lit, most of the illumination coming from the dim blue carbon bulbs that highlighted the individual paintings on the walls. The only other light came from beneath a door at the end, tracking soft white, bleeding into the plush oriental carpet. I stood with my feet in the light for what seemed an eternity, nervously fingering the pistol's handgrip, smelling the dark, oiled mahogany, summoning my courage, until I felt the crystal door handle turning in my grip and the door swinging open.

"Who's that?" Nick squinted across the room from the desk where he sat, writing in a large, leather-bound book.

"Chance Bailey. You remember me."

I saw him flinch and I drew my revolver. "I wouldn't do that if I was you. I learned to shoot before I learned to walk. Out where I come from a man's not a man 'less be can shoot the eye out of a crow from a hundred yards away."

"How did you get in here?"

"Well it wasn't real hard, but that don't matter much now. What matters is why I'm here, and what I'm gonna do."

Nick eyed the gun in my hand. "And what's that?"

"I'm gonna blow you to kingdom come, same as your hoodlums did to the Cajun, same as you tried to do to Molly and me. Do you know where she is right now? Do you know what they did to her?"

"I never meant for that to happen, but I don't expect you to believe that."

"It really don't matter what I believe now, does it? Molly's never going to dance again - maybe she won't ever walk again. And you did it. Maybe you didn't push her under that train but you might just as well have."

"The men who did that to her have been dealt with. Even if you don't believe how bad I feel about this, you can believe that I'll spend the rest of my life making up to her for it. She'll have the best care money can buy for as long as she needs it; private doctors and nurses round the clock, anything she needs to get better. I was signing a blank check to the hospital when you came in, no amount, whatever it takes." He raised the book in front of him and pointed to the check.

"Your money won't do it for you this time, Nick. There's only one way you can pay for what you did to Molly, and that's with your scummy, worthless life." I raised the pistol and sighted along the barrel.

"You know you'll never leave here alive. As soon as you pull the trigger this room will be swarming with my bodyguards."

"I'll worry about that when it happens." Sweat dripped down my forehead into my eyes. I wiped them with my free hand and steadied the revolver.

"Killing a crow and killing a man are two different things," Nick noted. "That barrel's doing a helluva lot of shaking for somebody who learned how to shoot before he learned how to walk."

"You're cracking pretty wise for a dead man."

"Go on, if you've got the guts." He leaned back in the chair and folded his arms. "Personally, I don't think you can do it. I didn't get where I am without knowing something about people, and I think I know something about you. I think you got guts, but not the kind of guts it takes to pull the trigger on an unarmed man."

"It don't take guts to shoot an unarmed man."

"But you're about to do this gutless thing? I'm disappointed in you, kid. I woulda thought you had more character than that."

He caught me momentarily. "You're pretty slick but you ain't talking your way out of this one," I shot back after a pause. "The Cajun was unarmed, Molly was unarmed, and that didn't stop you."

"But you're not me. You never killed a man before, did you?"

"What's that got to do with it?"

He shrugged. "Nothing, I guess, if you don't mind surprises. It's not like you think it's gonna be."

"Killing you'll be pure pleasure."

"No it won't. It won't even be satisfying. Your brain just shuts down, it's like you're fixin a toilet or patching a roof; dog work. You walk away thinking shit, what's the big, fucking deal?"

"Why are you telling me this?"

"I dunno, I guess because I like you. I don't want to see you do anything stupid. Look at it this way; you kill me you've got maybe five seconds before my guys come in here and put a cap in your brain. Now we're both dead, and Molly's got nobody to pay her bills, no way to make a living, and nobody to take care of her. Weigh that against five seconds of satisfaction, which I already said you won't get, and what do you come up with? I don't know about you, but if I held that hand at the poker table I'd fold it."

He leaned forward on the desk, deliberately keeping his hands in my view. "But why should you take my advice? When I was your age I never listened to anybody. I did what I had to do and learned from my mistakes, so go ahead, put one in my eye." He pointed to the right one with his forefinger. "This one, country boy. Let's make all those crow-shooters back in West Asshole Texas proud."

My finger curled around the trigger.

"Of course you've got another choice," Nick went on. "You can tuck that piece back in your drawers and walk away from here. I'll see to it that nobody bothers you ever again; Molly will be taken care of, and everybody goes on living their lives like nothing ever happened."

"You really think I'd be dumb enough to take your word for that?"

"I think you'd have to be pretty dumb not to. I've got no beef with you. In a way I actually respect you. You fought good like that marlin I caught down in Cuba; and just like him, I'll let you go, no bad feelings, no regrets, no questions asked. I'll even give you carfare."

"Molly too." I insisted.

"Molly's mine."

"Then I guess I've got no choice after all." I pointed the pistol at his right eye and cocked the hammer.

"Make it a good one," he said without changing expression.

"I ain't about to miss."

"I ain't about to grovel," he shot back.

I swallowed hard, wanting to squeeze the trigger but frozen.

"There's a button underneath my desk," Nick said calmly. "I'm going to push it now; that'll bring my men coming on the run, but don't panic. They won't do anything unless I tell them to."

"Go for that button and you're a dead man."

He reached beneath his desk and the revolver went limp in my hand. Outside, a siren wailed, and the clamor of running footsteps filled the hallway.

Thirty-Six

There were six men, all armed. One pinned my arms to my sides from behind while another took the revolver from my hand. The others surrounded me, pistols at the ready, as Nick stood and walked around the desk. "You can let him go now," he instructed. "Bobby, you stay. The rest of you take off."

The man holding me stepped away while the others obediently cleared the room. Nick emptied the bullets from Shimmelman's gun, examined it briefly and gave it back to me. "It wouldn't've worked anyway. The firing pin's been filed down. It's a good thing for you that you didn't pull the trigger."

I stared at the revolver. "He was going to kill himself with it."

"Who?"

"It doesn't matter."

"I guess not." He selected a bottle of Amaretto from a cabinet by the door, poured two glassfuls and handed one to me. "*Salut.*"

"What now?" I asked him.

He sipped his drink. "That depends on you. Like I said, you're free to go, but I need some guarantee you're out of my hair once and for all."

"What kind of guarantee?"

"Your word will do."

"What's to stop me from giving it to you, and going back on it soon as I get out of here?"

"Nothing except your own honor."

"Who the hell are you to talk about honor?" I exploded. "Where's the honor in drowning a person just for fun? Molly's a cripple because of

245

your honor!"

Nick moved back behind the desk and motioned for me to sit in a chair opposite him. He drained his glass, placed his hands palms-down on the green felt surface and thought a bit before answering. "I never lied to you," he said finally. "I told you I'd do what I had to do to protect my investment and that's what I did. Whether you agree with it or not, it's what I had to do; whether you think it's right or wrong's got nothing to do with it. It's a matter of principle."

"Where's the principle in murdering a little pet dog?" I challenged. "Out in Texas we kill animals all the time, all kinds of animals, Deer, live-stock, birds. We gut 'em and dress 'em and hang their bodies out to dry, sometimes we just kill 'em for sports but in all my life I never saw any-body kill a little pet dog, not ever. That's about the ugliest thing I ever saw a human being do."

"It's not supposed to be pretty, it's supposed to make a point."

"Well it made a point, all right. It showed Molly what kind of a per-son you really are. Do you think she could ever love you after that?"

"That's not important."

"It's not important? Why would you go to all this trouble in the first place if it wasn't important? Why would you even want her back if it wasn't important? You love her, don't you?"

"That's not important either. What's important in this room is you and me, our word to each other. In Italian it's called *equipaggiare*, man-hood, being a man. That's an interesting word, *equipaggiare*. Like a lot of Italian words it sounds a lot like what it means. *Equipaggiare*, like equip-ment, see how it goes? It means you have the equipment it takes to be a man - you have the balls to do whatever you have to do to prove you won't be trifled with. That's what you and me are here, *uomo a uomo*, man-to-man, looking for strength."

"Don't take much strength to kill a Yorkshire terrier," I noted.

"Could you do it?"

"Reckon I couldn't."

"But you'll kill a deer, you'll kill a pig and gut him to feed your stomach. What about your manhood, what feeds that? He grasped himself between the legs. "Manhood isn't just here. It's here and here." He pressed his closed fist against his heart and head.

"If you give me your word in this room, and then go out and break that word, you don't deserve to be called a man."

"I don't think I could tell you I'd never see Molly again and mean it."

"Better you tell me that now than try to deceive me."

"So what happens now?"

He shook his head. "I dunno, kid. You thought you had a chance to kill me and you didn't; that's got to count for something. But on the other hand you've backed me against a wall. I kept my word to you from the beginning. I offered you a job, I offered you money, I even found your old man for you. Now there's nothing more I can do. You've got _corragio_, I'll give you that. I wish I could let you go like I did that marlin, but you've run me clear out of choices here."

"There's still one choice left."

"What's that?"

"You're a gambler. We could play cards for her—one hand of poker, winner take all."

Nick shook his head in amazement. "You got more balls than I gave you credit for, kid. Just how would that work? I already have Molly, I already have your life. What else do you have to put on the table?"

I reached into the hip pocket of my jeans, removed my Chemical Corn Exchange bankbook, and threw it on the desk. "Near as I can tell there's something like a hundred sixty seven thousand dollars in there. I can't say for sure—they add another ninety bucks or so interest every day."

Nick's eyes went wide as he read the total. "Where'd you get money like this?"

"Like you said, it's not important. What's important in this room is you and me, man-to-man."

"Let me get this straight, We play poker, one hand. If you win, you get Molly. If I win I get all the money in this account and you're out of Molly's life forever?"

"Sounds about right to me."

Nick tossed the bankbook across the room to his waiting henchman. "Go see if this checks out, Bobby."

"The bank's closed this time of night," I reminded him.

"Don't worry about that, I've got my sources. And bring us back a fresh deck of cards," he yelled after him.

"I suppose your sources could figure a way to get you that money without playing cards for it," I speculated when we were alone.

"You still don't get it, do you? It's not about money, it's about winning and losing."

"Who's to say you'll pay up even if you lose?"

He shook his head reprovingly. "I already told you there's two things I don't fuck around with, God and gambling debts. If we play, the game will be final. I secure my bet with my word, and you secure your bet with your life."

"Seems a little lopsided to me."

"House rules," he shrugged.

Bobby returned with the bankbook and the cards. "The dough's there, Boss, everything it says and more."

Nick waved him to the back of the study with a toss of his hand. "You're sure you want to do this?" he asked, handing me the bankbook. "There's still time to pull out."

"And what, get killed?"

'That'd be up to you."

"I think I'll take my chances with the cards."

The deck was fresh, sealed and covered with cellophane. I tore the wrapping away from the box, broke the seal and removed the cards inside. "Back home we break for deal, loser gets to call the game," I said, removing the jokers from the top and bottom and positioning the deck in the center of the desk.

"Texas cuts," Nick concurred with a small grin.

I cut a nine of diamonds, right in the middle.

"Jack of spades", Nick announced as he turned it over. "My deal, your call."

"All I know is five card draw."

"Then five card draw it is." He shuffled the deck expertly, slid it across the desk for me to cut again, and tapped it even on the green felt blotter when I was finished. "One hand, winner takes all." He began to deal.

Out by the Yellow Spur, which is an abandoned lead mine about a mile outside of Eula, Joe Carl and I would hide among the rotting beams playing Buck Rogers, or we'd laze outside in the arroyos worn by the tram cars, smoking cigarettes and watching the sky turn cartwheels above us. In the spring, blooming stalks of wild cannas, Indian paint brush and bluebonnets flourished, and it was there that I'd spent a whole afternoon once, watching a hummingbird. suspended. above the acacia, sucking nectar from the tender blossoms. Uncle Mal claimed that a humming-bird's wings beat faster than the human eye could see, but if you focused your gaze on a spot just to the right or just to the left of where they were, time slowed down, like the frames of a movie running on a slower speed, and you could count their individual wing-beats out of the corner of your eye. He did not explain to me why this was so, and I doubt that he knew the reason himself. It was just one of those things a body learned living close to nature, the way Indians could track a bear by the smell of tree bark, or Harry Bailey could stake out an elk by the texture of the grass. I do not know whether it was instinct or experience that caused me to focus on a spot just to the left of Nick Corsi's hand, but whatever it was, time slowed down enough for me to see his fingers dealing from the bottom of the deck out of the corner of my eye.

"What the hell is that for?" Nick demanded as my hand shot forward and snatched the card he'd dealt me in mid-air.

"Look at your dealing hand."

"I'll be dipped in shit!" He removed his hand from the bottom of the deck self-consciously. "Now where the hell did you learn to do that?"

"Down in Mexicali where the hoochy-kootchys grow. Bottom deal-ing's a regular art down there. Man's got to be quick as a snake just to stay in the game."

"Well you're quick, I'll give you that."

"I ain't bragging but I can catch a wild hare by his ears."

He leaned back from the desk. "So now what?"

"I caught you cheating. Where I come from that means I won the game."

I could feel Bobby closing in from the rear. "Do you want me to take care of him now?" I heard his voice ask Nick.

"No. Let him go." he replied wearily.

"Does this mean you won't bother Molly and me any more?"

"I gave my word, didn't I?"

I stood uncertainly and backed away from the desk. "I'd say see ya, but truth told, I hope I never do."

"Sure you don't want to play one more hand; double or nothing for that bank roll of yours?" he asked.

"One thing I learned down there in Mexicali; you stop playing when you've already won the game."

Thirty-Seven

And so I won Molly in a card game, or so it seemed for a while. She remained in the hospital's Intensive Care Unit until her condition was upgraded from critical to stable, during which time I was not allowed to visit her, other than to wave encouragingly through the glass partition of the ward, or simply watch while she slept, buoyed by her even, untroubled breathing, relieved that she was finally out of the woods. She had undergone three separate operations; one to mend her fractured ribs and stem the damage they had caused to her internal organs, and two more to repair her legs. She would be able to walk, the doctors concluded after the final operation, possibly without aid; but the idea of her ever dancing professionally again was out of the question.

"It won't be so bad," I tried to comfort her after the final operation. "I'll bet ninety-nine percent of the dancers in the country wish they'd gotten as far as you did. You were a Rockette. That's something they can only dream about."

"What do you mean were a Rockette?" She'd bristle. "I am a Rockette, and I intend to stay one, at least until I dance in the Christmas show."

"Christmas is next month. You'll probably still be in the hospital," I pointed out.

"So it won't be this Christmas. I can wait another year,"

"Don't you think it'd be better not to set your hopes too high? We've got a real good life ahead of us without that. We've got money, we've got freedom, there's a whole world out there we haven't seen."

"Bertie says you won me in a poker game."

"After a fashion, I reckon."

"So what does that make me, a prize?"

"I just didn't want to see you get hurt."

"I know. What you did took a lot of courage, and I don't mean to be ungrateful. It's just that maybe I had other plans for my life while you and Nick were gambling away my future."

"What kind of plans?"

She sagged back into the pillow. "Being a dancer is all I ever wanted. It's the reason I came to New York in the beginning and what's kept me going ever since. This hasn't changed any of that. All it means is I'll have just have to work harder and longer to get there. I have to believe that, Chance. If I stop believing that there's nothing left for me to believe in."

"You can believe in me."

She reached up and touched my cheek. "I know that. You're a sweet, wonderful boy, and if throwing in the towel and settling down was what I wanted to do right now, it would be with you, hands-down. But this is my dream. I can't stop wanting it. Not yet. It'd help to know you wanted it for me too."

"I'll be there every step of the way. You know I'll always be there for you."

"I'm going to make it, you'll see."

"I believe you will," I concurred, and at that moment, as impossible as it all seemed, I meant it.

I visited Molly each day for as long as the hospital would allow until it was time for me to fly home for Thanksgiving. Uncle Mal picked me up at the airport in Lubbock and we drove south to Eula in his Ford pick-up, following the rim of the Cap Rock on Route 87 through cattle ranches and farmland, hay-bales and dry cornstalks shivering in the wind, rock-hard cotton fields stretching as far as the eye could see. Even in cold, desolate winter I felt it tugging at me as we drove southward; drawing me to its sweat and stink and loneliness like a bad habit I wanted to break but couldn't. Harsh and gray and unyielding, the landscape seemed almost comforting. There were no choices there, no strained ambiguities, no wormholes to madness or doubts about fantasy and reality. The reality was the hardpan, the wind that blew ceaselessly across the plain, cold and clear and unimaginably liberating.

"How's Mama?" I asked him after we'd driven wordlessly for a spell.

"She'll be better now that you're home," he replied.

"Is that preacher hurting her?"

"I reckon that's something you'll have to find out for yourself."

We drove a few more miles in silence. "I found fortune in New York, Uncle Mal," I said finally. "I want to pay off your note at the bank so you can have the farm free and clear."

He chewed on it some. "Appreciate it. You fixing to come home and do some farming?"

"I don't think so. There's someone back in New York who's got a tough row to hoe and I want to see her through it."

"Reckon that's the proper thing to do."

"I visited Daddy's grave up in Cheshire, New York and learned all about how he'd been a hero. Got a Silver Star for gallantry above and beyond the call of duty for saving thirteen men in Bastogne, Belgium.

"Sounds like Harry. He was always doing something confoundedly dumb, and confoundedly brave."

"He would've come back to us after the war but he had a stress disorder that obliged him to stay in New York."

He spit a chaw of Red Man out the truck window.

Mama was waiting when we drove up. I could smell the aromas of cooking inside the house as we hugged on the front porch: Turkey and stuffing roasting in the pan, oranges and sweet potatoes and cranberries and pearl onions and pie hot from the oven cooling on the kitchen windowsill.

"How are you, Mama?" I asked.

"Fine, now that you're here."

"Where's Harley Brown?"

"He's at the church, readying things for this evening's service."

She looked tired, but otherwise unharmed. "Is he hitting you, mama?"

"I'm fine." She ushered me inside. "It's Thanksgiving and I'm grateful to the Lord for all he's given me, the good and the bad."

"You don't have to take the bad, not anymore. I'm here now and I can take care of you, so you can tell that preacher to take a hike for himself."

"Are you staying then?"

"I can't say that. There's business in New York I have to see to, but I'll promise you this; no matter where I am, or where you are, I'll take care of you. Nobody will ever hurt you again. I'll vow that to your Lord."

"He's your Lord too."

"If it'll help get that evil, pus-mongering bully of a preacher out of this house, I'll testify for him here and now. One thing I learned in New York City is it don't make much sense to lock yourself into one way of thinking or another. There's just too many minds working at the same time for any one of them to hold sway for very long."

She hugged me again and I felt her tears warm on my cheek. "We ought to clear his things out of here before be gets back," I suggested.

"What's going to happen to him then?"

"He'll find himself another widow, I reckon."

"I'll never be able to show my face in church again."

I stood back from her. "Go outside and take a look around, Mama. This whole place is a church. Every day you're alive out here you're worshipping."

We rifled through chests and cupboards for his things, put them all in cardboard crates and set them out front by the road where he was sure to see them when he drove up. Mama continued the meal preparations, naturally distracted by events but seeming happier than I'd seen her in some time. Her ear caught the sound of Harley Brown's Nash coming up the road long before mine and I followed her to the window to witness his arrival.

"What's going on?" he fumed as he stormed through the front door. "Who put my things out there in the yard?"

I stood before him, blocking his way. "I put them there, and now I'm telling you to leave with them. You've had your last meal in this house."

"Is that so, Addie?" he asked over my shoulder. " Are you a part of this? Have you fallen victim to this boy's blandishments?"

Mama remained resolutely silent.

"I'm telling you again, real nice. It's time for you to go," I repeated.

"I see Satan's work in this." His voice was trembling. "The boy has brought the evil and iniquity of New York City into this house and we must pray to have it purged from us..."

"One more time. I don't have a lot of patience for this."

"Pray with me, Addie. Oh Lord, pray with me now that we might be delivered from the scourge of the tormentor..."

"If you don't leave I reckon I'm going to have to throw you out."

"Woe unto them that draw iniquity with cords of vanity, Woe unto them that call evil good, and good evil. Woe is me for I dwell in the midst of people of unclean lips; for mine eyes have seen the King, the Lord of hosts..."

"This is your last chance, Reverend."

"For the Lord Jehovah is my strength and my song, and also my salvation. And I will punish the world for their evil, and the wicked for their iniquity; and I will cause the arrogance of the proud to cease, and I will lay low the haughtiness of the terrible..."

The blow came from somewhere down around my knees, arcing upward, with every ounce of strength I could put into it, and landing flush on the point of Harley Brown's nose. The force of it sent him reeling backward through the door, out onto the porch and down the front steps to the yard below.

"Sorry Reverend, but I'm the only one gonna be doing any laying low around here!"

He sat on the ground, trying to staunch the flow of blood coming from his nose with his fingers. Mama grabbed a towel from the kitchen and brought it to him.

"What are you doing, Addie?" he blubbered as she stood above him on the lawn. " It's Thanksgiving day."

"And I've got a lot to be thankful for, Harley. The Lord's been good to me this day." She took the bloody towel from him and came back into the house.

LeMoult

Thirty Eight

It was three months before Molly could walk by herself, and almost another three before she felt strong enough to dance. Like a beginner she started at the barre, straining to withstand the agony as she stretched dormant muscles, worked stiffened tendons to make them supple, loosened calcified joints that were held together with wire and pins. Away from the barre, the dance floor was as treacherous for her as an unfamiliar sea.. Center practice was a few halting turns and kicks, a pained arabesque, an excruciating pirouette, an entrechat that sent her sprawling to the practice floor in a sobbing, birdlike mound. Bertie was with her for every failure, comforting her, urging her, stretching her boundaries, pressing her beyond the limits of her endurance, never letting her quit. By the summer of nineteen fifty-three, she'd begun to practice with the American Dance Ensemble, and the following fall she confounded all the experts by appearing in a production of *Giselle*. The role was less than demanding, her dancing flawed, but Bertie said that in all the years he had been a choreographer, he had never witnessed a more courageous performance.

By Thanksgiving she was rehearsing with the Rockettes for the Christmas show. Bertie had choreographed a production in which she was to play the central role, one that took full advantage of her strengths and concealed her disabilities. I flew Mama in from Texas for the performance, put her up at the Plaza Hotel, and had her taken to Radio City Music Hall in a chauffeured limousine on Christmas Day. We sat fourth row center in the orchestra, close enough to see the individual notes on the pit musicians' sheet music. Prior to the opening curtain, everyone was given a program of events, and I read mine with a mixture of awe and undiluted pride:

Gift of the Magi

A Christmas Dance Celebration

by the World Famous

Radio City Rockettes

Starring in her First Feature Performance

MONA CHALFONTE

The house lights dimmed and music from the pipe organ filled the cavern of the Music Hall. And the great proscenium came alive with spots and arc lights and costumes and dancers... *five-six-seven-eight, turn-turn-kick-turn, kick-kick-kick-kick. Lift those flabby thighs you wasted bunch of sows. What do you think this is?close-order drill for chrissake— Five-six-seven-eight, five-six-seven-eight, turn-turn-kick-turn...*

And Mona Chalfonte danced center-stage in a skintight costume of pale blue organza, and if she hurt it never showed. I was close enough to see her radiant smile, that look of triumph that only she had known would come, and I found myself exulting with her even though I knew at that moment I could never have her. She had hitched a ride to the dark side of the moon where there were gardens with flowers and tall ferns, and waterfalls that fell in crystal, pools, and dreams came true if you believed enough. If only you believed enough.

Turn-turn-kick-turn, turn-turn-kick-kick, take-it-to-me, take-it-to-me, take-it-to-me. Move that gorgeous ass, sweetheart. There are a thousand more who'd give their left tit to be standing where you are right now. Turn-turn-kick-turn, take-it-to-me, take it to me, take-it-to-me, take-it-to-me...

She collapsed in the dressing room after the performance, before I ever had a chance to tell her how wonderful she had been. The doctors said it was an embolism, a blood clot from her injuries that had attached itself somewhere inside of her, broken loose in the exertion of her performance, and traveled through her bloodstream to her brain. It had been painless, they said, like going to sleep. We held her funeral at the Chapel of the Little Flower in the Bowery, and Father Troy Blaze, the faggot priest, gave the eulogy:

"Mona Chalfonte came to me in a time of need, and I hope I was able to help her. Those who loved her say that she had a driving, indomitable will, and that perhaps it was what ended her life, but I prefer to think that she chose to be a participant in the miracle of life, that she cherished God's gifts to her and would not waste them.

"Most of us are wasteful people. We waste time and energy and friendships, we waste love. I told Mona that I sometimes believed life was just a series of accidents; that we called the bad accidents sins and the good accidents miracles. That seemed to comfort her, and it comforts me now. Mona Chalfonte made a miracle of her life, a wonderful miracle she shared with those who loved her most. Nothing was wasted, and in giving everything, she left us with the miracle of her memory. It lives with us now. She still dances in our minds."

She was buried in a. small cemetery behind the chapel, next to Trixie, her Yorkshire terrier. Bertie and I shook hands and said good-bye and promised to keep in touch but I know neither of us believed it. The earth had taken a few turns for better or for worse while we'd been in it, a solipsism we'd shared with Molly as the glue that held it all together. Now that world was bound to change and somehow it seemed all right. Somehow everything seemed all right, as elegant and symmetrical as one of Bertie's choreographed ballets. There was no guilt, nothing left undone. I'd done all I could do. All I could do.

So I went back to west Texas, not because I yearned for it but because it was in my blood. I did not go back to Eula. Even I was not dumb enough to romanticize that festering dustbowl of a place. I bought a ranch out by the Guadeloupe Mountains and called it the Running Horsemen; six thousand acres of wild prairie and table-top mesas, and coulees with wildflowers abounding, and enough grass to feed a thousand head of cattle and a hundred horses, which I had, and a lake called Tahamika which legend says was once a stopping-off place for Coronado and his army on their march to conquer the southwest. Cattle drives and stage lines stopped there too, for the clear, green alkali water and the sheer beauty of the place. Walk a few hundred feet in any direction and you could still see their wheel ruts, timeless channels dug into the earth; and if you listened hard enough you could hear their voices in the rustling of the grass.

The mountain is called Round Top, a sacred mountain to the Comanche and Kiowa who once lived there. The story is told of young braves destined to become shamans who ritually climbed the mountain alone when the sun hung lowest in the sky and the herds of bison began moving south. They built crude huts of sticks and stones and antelope hides, cut their hair and hung it on the ridgepoles, and hunkered down for the winter. Snow came in blinding blizzards, temperatures on the mountaintop dropped below zero. Those who stayed stripped off their clothes and knelt facing the wind until their eyes were frozen in their sockets and their folded arms froze to their chests; and it was then that they had visions. Then they communicated with the spirits. And when they came down from the sacred mountain they had great power in the tribe, and they were called *Kkukumanuu kwiipu*, "men of smoke," and they could conjure potions and cure illnesses, and see the past and the future, and dance the world back into balance through the power of the dead.

I have never climbed the mountain. What I want to remember of the past is fixed indelibly in Shimmelman's stars. There are days when the sky is so clear and the air is so pure that I can see it all exploding, a billion, billion light years into space, curved back on itself so I can reach out and pull it through that wormhole in my mind, and for a moment I can be mad, and only the crows and the searching wind will know.

Epilogue

The Soldiers and Sailors YMCA was demolished along with the Third Avenue El in 1954.

In 1965, Nick Corsi was shot to death while eating at Colanani's Restaurant in lower Manhattan.

Bertie left the Rockettes in 1958 to travel throughout the world with The American Dance Ensemble. He established the Mona Chalfonte Scholarship of Dance for inner-city youth and, in 1974, was honored by a Presidential commission for outstanding humanitarian achievement. He died of AIDS in 1989.

Jerome Shimmelman vanished shortly after the Soldiers and Sailors was destroyed. His painting of the stars was discovered in the debris by antiquities scavengers and brought to the attention of municipal officials. Restored, it now hangs in the Metropolitan Museum of Art.

Addie Bailey died peacefully in her sleep, sitting in a lawn chair by the lake where Chance had placed her.

Chance Bailey married Audrey Lou Hawley and fathered two sons he named Bertie and Jerome. He still ranches in West Texas.